REAL ALPHAS MATE

THE ALPHA-HOLE DUET

C.R. JANE

MILA YOUNG

Contents

Dedication

For all wolf shifter loving readers who are addicted to possessive alphas, warriors who are like big cinnamon rolls on the inside, and the psychos who'll reward you with your enemy's finger if it means getting you to smile...

Welcome to book 2 in the Alpha-Hole duet

Lots of love,

C.R. & Mila

THE ALPHA-HOLE DUET
FROM C.R. JANE AND MILA YOUNG

Real Alphas Bite
Real Alphas Mate

A complete duet

Born Without A Heart
Faouzia

I Will Be There For You
Bella Goldwin

Anybody Else
Faouzia

Power
Isak Danielson

Back From The Dead
Besomorph

War of Hearts
Ruelle

Sorry
Halsey

Ghost of You
5 Seconds of Summer

Moonlight
XXXTentacion

Love You To Death
Chord Overstreet

Next To You
Little Big Town

Infinity
Jaymes Young

Listen to the Spotify Playlist Here

Real Alphas Mate

Syn is the girl no one wanted...

And now, they'll light the world on fire to claim her

Syn never believed in fairy tales until she met the three men who stole her from her fated mate. They may be a dark fairy tale, but every touch, every kiss, every whisper seals their bond. She now calls them her alphas...her future.

But when her past returns with vengeance, she must defeat the monster determined to break her again.

Before the dust settles, lives will be lost. And she must find a way back to her three mates.

Even if it means sacrificing everything...

Hendrix

He was acting strange today.

Well—my father was acting stranger than usual. Which I hadn't thought was possible.

All day I'd caught him just staring at me. At the breakfast table, while I was eating my Fruit Loops, he'd hovered in the doorway of the kitchen...watching me with a feverish glare.

"Dad?" I'd asked hesitantly, but he'd just shook his head and stalked away, only to return a few minutes later to keep watching me.

I'd moved into the living room, trying to work on school work, and there he'd been again.

River, Caspian, and I were outside now, riding our bikes. I'd just glanced back towards the house and he'd been standing at the window...staring at us. I could feel his gaze boring into the side of my head.

"River," I whispered, not wanting Caspian, our youngest brother, to overhear and start to worry. "Have you noticed anything weird with Dad, today?"

River snorted, shaking his head and looking back at the

house. His bike swerved when he saw our father still standing in the window.

"I heard him talking to himself in his room all night," River muttered as he narrowly missed crashing into a bush.

I frowned, dread flickering through me as I tried to glance at my dad surreptitiously so he wouldn't know that I was watching. "Let's go play in the back of the house," I suggested, and my two brothers quickly followed behind me, like they could feel the menace in the air as well.

The dark curtains that my father had installed at the beginning of the year were blissfully still as we played in the backyard, but I couldn't get rid of the sensation that he was still somewhere nearby...watching.

The sky began to darken, fading to dark blue as we finally made our way into the house. My body was laced with tension as we walked through the back door. It was unlike our father to let us play outside all day. He hated when we wasted our time with "foolishness."

What had made today so different?

We quickly washed up in the bathroom and then hustled to the dining room for dinner. I had barely stepped foot in the room when I came to a screeching halt, River smacking into the back of me and almost knocking me to the ground from the sudden stop.

It was six o'clock. The lights should be on, the candles should be lit, and the fine dining should be set out. The table should be loaded with food and there should be servants bustling in and out of the room.

Just like every night at this time.

Except, it seemed, for tonight.

The table was completely empty, the lights dark, no sign of my father or any of the servants. I hurried over to the door that led to the kitchen and swung it open, muttering a soft curse when I saw that the kitchen was empty, those lights off as well.

Where were all the servants?

"Let's just go up to my room," I told my brothers, who were both looking...frightened. I grabbed a loaf of bread and some peanut butter from the pantry and then began to shepherd my brothers out into the hallway so we could head up the back stairs to my room.

"Going somewhere?" my father asked coolly from the base of the stairs, as if he'd been watching us this whole time. He never used the back stairs; he'd told us very sternly, many times, that they were for the servants. So for him to be here, waiting for us...

He glanced down at the bread and peanut butter I was carrying. "The servants have been dismissed," he said, reaching out and grabbing the food from my hands.

"Dismissed for the night?" I was confused. The servants were never given any time off. Not even holidays.

"Permanently," he replied nonchalantly, as if he hadn't just dropped a huge bomb on us.

Caspian sniffled behind me. He was still little, and his nanny, Becky, was his favorite person in the world. For him to have let her go without letting Caspian say goodbye...

Asshole wasn't a strong enough word to describe my father.

"Grab your shoes. We're leaving," he continued.

I shifted warily in place. My father was a creature of habit. Breakfast, lunch, and dinner all at the same time every day. He took his coffee in the same way. He hung his clothes the same way.

He was not the type of male to suddenly decide to go for a drive at the drop of a hat.

"We have our lessons first thing in the morning," I insisted, knowing I was risking a fist to the face by pushing back at him. "We should probably go to bed soon."

A scary smile spread across his face, and he was glaring at

me, but it was like he wasn't actually seeing me...it was like he was looking right through me.

"Go get your shoes on," he ordered again in an icy voice that sent chills down my spine.

"Come on, Hendrix," River whispered, grabbing my arm and leading me down the hall to where our shoes were stacked neatly by the garage door. "Let's not make him mad."

I peered over my shoulder as we walked and saw my dad staring at the wall in front of him, moving his lips feverishly, but with no sound coming out.

A shiver shot through my spine, everything inside me screaming to grab my brothers and run away.

But I knew that wouldn't help us. We'd already tried that before, and we'd been picked up by the cops hours later a mile from shore, our stories of abuse falling on deaf ears thanks to the extra padding my father made sure was in all of their pockets.

Not for the first time, I cursed my mom for leaving us with him and taking off. I could see her clearly in my head. Her warm smile, the sound of her laugh. The way her hugs had felt. The cadence of her voice as she'd read us our favorite books. That woman seemed very much at odds with what had happened.

What kind of mother leaves her sons with a monster to save herself?

I pushed the thought away, knowing it wouldn't help for me to mourn someone who evidently had never existed.

We got our shoes on, and then we waited impatiently for our father to appear.

"I'm hungry," sniffed Caspian. The shadows under his eyes hinted at being exhausted too. Playing outside all day was definitely a lot for a little kid. If his nanny was here, she'd be hustling him to bed right now, after making sure he ate all of his vegetables for dinner.

A wave of despair hit me. How was I going to take care of my brothers without help? How was I going to keep them safe from him? I already took most of the beatings for myself. My shoulders slumped, and I battled the urge to cry.

I couldn't let my brothers see that. I couldn't let *him* see that.

My father appeared at the end of the hall, a large, shapeless, black bag in his hand that provided no clue about what was inside.

The alarm bells inside me were at DEFCON 1 now, my wolf flickering around inside of me, desperate to get out—if only I was old enough.

If only Caspian and River were older as well. My father was huge. An alpha whose aura was seemingly a million times more powerful than any other alpha I'd met.

He was terrifying and barely had to lift a finger to beat us when we disappointed him.

"Please, Father. Can I have something to eat?" Caspian cried, his lower lip trembling. Panic laced through River's features as he pinched the back of Caspian's arm, both of us desperate for him to be quiet.

I expected a blow to the head, a hand around the throat, a kick to the ribs...something. But it was as if my father hadn't heard him. He brushed past us into the garage without a word.

River's wide gaze shot me a terrified look, and he pulled Caspian closer to him.

"I promise we'll get you food right after this, bud," I murmured, hoping I was telling the truth.

Where the hell was he taking us?

He was already in his truck when we shuffled into the garage. The garage door was closed, but the truck was going, its fumes beginning to fill the whole space. He was just staring ahead, his lips moving silently again.

The picture of a crazy person, really...

Suddenly, his head turned, his eyes staring daggers at us as he watched us with a gaze full of...suspicion?

I hustled my brothers towards the truck and made sure they were buckled in the backseat before I hopped in the front. My father would never deign to make sure they were safe in the car.

He backed out of the garage quickly, the move sending me shooting forward, the seatbelt locking against my chest in a harsh vice.

I shot a glance into the backseat and saw that Caspian was silently crying, his little hands shaking as he held onto the side of his car seat. River's hand shot out and he patted his knee soothingly.

"Demons. Everywhere!" my father suddenly muttered in a panicked voice as he lurched off the brake and began to drive like a bat out of hell.

"Have to get rid of the demons," he muttered, before humming a strange tune I'd never heard before.

"Father?" I questioned hesitantly, bracing myself for the backhand. He'd broken my nose several times while I was in this seat.

But he ignored me, his eyes flickering around our surroundings wildly, like he was expecting someone...or something to pop out of the woods around us at any moment.

"Demons!" he shouted loudly again.

Caspian's silent tears had turned into loud, scared sobs in the backseat, and I shot River a look to try and get him to quiet before Dad did something I couldn't stop.

"Let's just go back to the house," I started soothingly.

Smack!

The hit I'd been bracing for earlier came out of nowhere, sending a blood spray all over the dashboard and glass in front of me as my nose broke.

I growled and threw myself harshly back into my seat, my

hands coming up to my nose as my eyes watered and pain exploded across my face.

"Filthy, wicked demons. In my own home! They are everywhere. Filthy. Wicked. Demons." His chant didn't let up and he didn't spare any of us a glance as we continued to race down the road.

My mind was racing, trying to figure out a way out of this.

But I was coming up blank. The throbbing, agonising pain pulsing through my brain wasn't helping me have any clear thoughts either.

We turned left down a dirt road, barely slowing down at all as the tires spun in the loose dirt.

"Almost done. Almost free. Filthy. Wicked. Demons," he chanted.

I couldn't take it.

"Stop the fucking car—"

Smack!

Another hit to the same place and the world began to spin, fragments of bone splattering through my skull, sparks filling my vision.

I howled, faintly aware that River was screaming something from the backseat, and Caspian's cries had grown louder.

And through it all was that same, terrifying chant.

"Almost done. Almost free. Filthy. Wicked. Demons."

I writhed in my seat as we continued to drive, losing consciousness at times and then coming back to the same terrifying hellscape.

I was so delirious with pain that it took me a second to realize when the truck actually stopped. Capillaries in my eyes had burst from the impact, and it felt like there was blood trickling from my eyeballs.

"Just get it done. Just get it done," my father whispered next to me. I heard him get out of the truck and then River saying something to me, but it was as if everything was underwater. My head was pounding so bad, I couldn't move it. I didn't think this was something my shifter healing powers could fix. He'd really done it this time.

Was I going to die?

My door opened just then, and I fell to the side, my seatbelt catching me before I could tumble out of the truck.

"Demon!" my father seethed by my ear, and then I felt a pinprick in my throat.

What was that?

The pain in my face immediately faded, but it was replaced by a tingling sensation all over my skin. Blood was pouring into my mouth from my nose, and I tried to move my hand to wipe some away...

But I couldn't move anything. I couldn't even lift a finger.

My father's chant had changed into humming, that same tune he'd been spouting this morning. He stepped out of my vision and I heard the door behind me open on River's side.

I tried to yell something, to warn my brothers that they were about to be drugged, but all I could manage was a gurgle. Even my tongue was numb from whatever he'd shot me with.

Is he going to kill us?

The thought shot through my head as I heard River yell something and the sound of struggling behind me.

There'd been many times that he'd stared at me like he hated me, and some of my beatings had been so bad I'd actually wanted to die...but nothing had ever happened like this.

And where the fuck were we?

The struggling had stopped, and there were just garbled moans coming from River now.

But Caspian...my sweet little brother, was shrieking in fright. I could hear him trying to get out of his car seat, but I knew he wouldn't be able to.

"Hendrix!" he was screaming as the truck door opened on

his side. I couldn't see what was happening since I couldn't move my neck, but the sound of it was horrifying.

And then...there was just silence.

I tried to scream for Caspian again, desperate to know he was still alive, even though I knew the effort would be fruitless.

But all I could hear were River's grunts behind me.

There was the sound of crunching footsteps, and then he was standing next to me again, reaching over me to undo my seatbelt. I immediately slumped over and he caught me right before I fell, dragging me easily out of the truck and onto the soil-covered ground.

My cheek was pressed against the dirt as he grabbed one of my arms and dragged me along the ground, tiny rocks embedding themselves into my skin. Thank goodness for the drug, I supposed. I could feel the pressure of the sharp edges digging into me, but the pain that should have been there as my skin was scratched off was non-existent.

We finally stopped, and I felt something cold and wet against my outstretched hand when he dropped it. The ground beneath me was also cold and wet. Sand maybe?

Something tickled my extended hand again. Water. I was near the water. It was small waves licking against my skin.

There was the sound of something being dragged across the ground towards me, and a few seconds later, River's form appeared next to me. His eyes were wide and devastated as we stared at each other. I couldn't give him any comfort. I had none to give.

I let out a bleating moan since it was the only thing I was capable of and listened as my father dragged Caspian towards us as well.

Of course he couldn't just pick us up even though he was strong enough to hold all three of us at once. No, we had to go through the indignity of being dragged to our demise.

Caspian was plopped in between River and me.

"Demons!" my father abruptly screamed into the night air. "I will now free myself from the curse that has stained my house since the moment of their birth. I will be free!"

He stepped over our heads and then he grabbed all three of our still outstretched arms and began to haul us deeper into the water. Deeper and deeper until my body was floating and water was pouring into my open mouth.

I guess I hadn't really thought much about my future. I had always just been dreaming of the day when I'd be free and able to get my brothers and me out of my father's household.

But now here I was, at the end. I guess I was going to be free after all, just in a different way than I'd dreamed about.

I felt my father let go of my hand and then I was drifting, drowning...dying as I sunk below the cold depths.

The underwater world around me had drifted to a pinprick of blue, and I was at the end when suddenly, sparks started to light up my veins. The sparks moved through my body until they got to my heart.

I was on fire. All traces of the cold and the numbness... gone. I tried to move my leg, and I was able to kick out. Bubbles blasted from my mouth as I moved towards the surface, bursting above the water and gasping in huge gulps of air. My whole body was tingly and full of light. I moved to dive back down to try and grab my brothers, but they both popped up a second later, taking in heaving breaths of air.

I could see my father walking towards the truck in the distance. Suddenly, white-hot rage carved my insides up, combining with the strange sparks remaking me.

"I feel weird," gasped Caspian. I was temporarily yanked from my anger and back to the situation where my little brother was trying to tread water. He'd only learned to swim in the spring. I swam over to him and arrived there right as River did, and then we worked together to head towards the beach.

The tingles were still all over my body, gathering in intensity and distracting me as I tried to get us to safety.

Except...it didn't feel like trying. It wasn't hard actually, not how it should have been since we'd just been drugged and almost died. I knew from my lessons that my body should have continued to shut down.

So what was happening to me?

We somehow made it to the shore as we heard the truck starting. I fell back against the sound, my body shaking...and not from the cold.

"Hendrix," River cried out sharply, and I glanced over to see that the same thing was happening to him.

Abruptly, white-hot pain flashed through me, and I screamed in agony. Pain like I'd never experienced before laced every cell in my body.

I prayed for death like I'd never prayed for it before. My brothers' screams mingled with mine in the air, and I wondered why we'd been spared a watery death only to experience this. What god had we angered before we were born?

Just when my mind was about to crack from the pain, it completely disappeared. Besides the sweat dotting my brow and my breath coming out in gasps, my body felt fine. Better than fine. I felt energized and strong. Like I could run forever if I needed to. Like I could lift anything. I'd never felt this way.

I scrambled to my feet, gasping in relief when I saw that my brothers' features had both calmed as well.

I opened my mouth to ask if they were alright, and then I heard *his* voice.

"Demon, you will die!" my father cried out hysterically. I looked up and saw that he had a rifle in his hand and his whole body was trembling, his eyes rolling around crazily in his head. Froth was bubbling out of the side of his mouth.

His finger moved on the trigger...and it was as if time

froze. Something dark unfurled inside of me, and an inhuman growl burst from my mouth as I lunged forward.

Everything flickered in and out after that. There was the metallic taste of blood. The taste of flesh. Hysterical screams in the air. The sound of my brothers yelling.

When I came to, I was on my knees in front of a pile of flesh.

My father had been ripped into pieces. So many pieces that the only thing telling me it was him was the scraps of fabric in the same color that littered the ground and floated in the breeze around me.

"Hendrix," River murmured, coming up beside me and staring at me in awe.

I didn't need him to tell me what had happened.

I could feel it inside of me...waiting.

Something had happened in that water. Something had been born inside my core.

A monster.

CHAPTER 1

Now

SYN

I had the weird sensation I was back in my parents' home, waking in the middle of the night to the sound of shouting. To the crackle of flames, to smoke choking me, to my father trying to kill my brother and me.

Panic crawled over me. I shoved myself to a sitting position, frantically looking around, my heart racing.

Instead, darkness yawned back at me.

A bedroom engulfed by night. No flames.

And still, those vivid memories suffocated me.

It was when I twisted to get out of bed that a sharp twinge cut across the front of my neck.

"Ouch." I lifted my hand to the ache, when something heavy pulled against my wrist. The clang of chains sounded, and I blinked through the night at the shackle that was around my arm and attached to a metal ring on the wall. I cried out as instinct kicked in, and I shuffled out of bed and began tugging against the metal fetter. "No. No. No!"

My heart beat with rage, and I desperately hauled at the restraints, while my neck screamed with pain.

Everything that had already happened came forward, along with the memory of me being taken against my will.

A growl vibrated through me, my wolf awake and shoving forward. I wouldn't be anyone's slave. Never again. I knew this dark world too well, I'd grown up with hatred and inflicted pain. I knew it well enough to understand that if I remained here, wherever that was, I'd end up used and tortured. And most likely dead.

I desperately pulled at the restraint, my wrist burning with the metal rubbing my skin raw. Tears rolled down my cheeks as I pictured being attacked on the beach with River outside his mansion.

How quickly the men pounced on us in the night, how we barely had a chance to respond. I felt turned inside out at the reality I'd been taken prisoner again. This was arguably the second time I'd been kidnapped from a place I lived, and I fucking hated it.

Anger thundered in my veins as I opened my floodgates and called to my wolf, unleashing her because I stood no chance to escape without her. "Please help me, Moon Goddess," I whispered to the night.

The freedom my wolf awakened within me spread over my body, filling every inch of me with a feeling of pure exhilaration. I felt my wolf sliding against my insides, her fur soft and welcoming. She groaned, rushing out of me without needing to be asked twice.

But just as she pushed against me, a terrifying pain sliced across my throat. I whimpered, falling back against the wall as I clasped my neck. There were bandages over the wound where the attackers back on the beach had stabbed me. The wound felt slightly damp to the touch, and the tips of my fingers came back tainted with blood.

The pain kept me prisoner, and I waited a few moments for the ache to stop, swallowing softly to chase away the panic.

Try again, try again, I kept repeating in my mind.

With a deep inhale, I called to her, needing my wolf. And she responded just as quickly...we were one, connected, and as such, the heavy boom of my heart filled her too.

A flash of pain flared almost instantly as she pushed for freedom. Stars pulsed behind my vision, and instead of a wolf, I cried out from a horrible pain across my neck, feeling like someone jabbed shards of glass into my flesh.

She whimpered, retreating deep back inside me. My tears came for her as well, for how much my neck stung. I pressed my hand to the wound and slumped down to the floor, my back to the wall.

I closed my eyes. My heartbeat thumped in my ears, and nothing I did eased the hurt burning across my throat. Whatever my captors did to patch me up, I'd somehow ruined it because I sensed the trickle of blood rolling down the front of my neck and over my collarbone.

All around me, darkness seemed to be reaching out to me, attempting to drag me away into hell. To keep me hostage in this madness.

Every inch of me pulsed. I clutched my neck harder, wondering if this was how I'd finally meet my maker? Alone in the dark, bleeding to death.

I fought the pain, but I needed to be bandaged again, that was clear, so I awkwardly removed my tee, thankful I still wore a bra underneath. I fashioned a bandage out of the fabric and clumsily fastened it around my neck to apply pressure and hopefully stop the bleeding.

Hendrix flashed in my mind, and his last words to me after he forced me into an orgasm came to mind. *I'll always own you, little wolf.*

I wasn't sure I wanted him to come for me, but as I sat on

the cold floor still chained up, my stomach clenching at how much trouble I'd ended up in *again*, maybe he wouldn't be such a bad person to rescue me.

I had no idea how long I sat there, but when an explosive shouting match broke out somewhere in the house, I almost jumped out of my skin.

Raspy, barbaric voices, all male, boomed into an argument. A thunderous bang echoed against the walls that shook my room. Their voices escalated, but they were too blurred, too furious to make out the words.

I was on my feet before I knew it, crossing the room. The chain on my wrist permitted the distance to the door, as long as I kept my arm stretched out behind me. Curiosity got the better of me, and I had to know who took me. I wasn't anything if not relentless in finding a way to survive, and that meant getting to know my enemy.

Placing my ear to the door still had the voices sounding muffled, but the shouting escalated, and by the thumping into walls, I was convinced the whole house would come down. What the hell were they doing out there? Wrestling?

Cautiously, I pushed down on the handle, and to my surprise, it opened. With my heart in my throat, I pried it open just enough for me to peer through and not give myself away. I'd snuck around enough in my life to be good enough at making no sounds.

I stared out past a dark hallway and into an aristocratic-looking living room with leather couches that had been turned over, a coffee table smashed to pieces, the chandelier swinging wildly in the dimly lit room.

A flash of someone being thrown backward and landing on the floor came instantly, followed by another blur of a person flinging themselves at the man lying down. They clashed, the battle bloody. Other voices came from somewhere in the house, cheering them on to fight.

Growls shattered the air, their battle ferocious, blood splattering from each strike.

The overhead fixture swung back and forth, the light bouncing off their torn clothes, their bloody wounds, their claws, their terrifying speed.

One man had short, trimmed hair, and the other had dark and shaggy hair around his face like it had been left to grow wild.

My stomach tensed as the smell of wolf fur, of pungent blood, of electricity in the air constricted around my throat. And with it came a familiarity. A scent I knew too well...it wrapped around me like the chain binding my wrist.

And instantly, I knew exactly who I watched straddle the poor guy on the floor and deliver one deadly punch after another into his face.

Brayden.

I crumbled on the inside, shattered like shards of glass all over again. I trembled, and I fought the urge to cry out that he'd found me. That the monster who'd rejected me, hurt me, promised me a life of misery...once again had me in his clutches.

I wasn't his. *Please, Moon Goddess*, I couldn't be his. Even if he hadn't rejected me, I had rejected him a million times over since that time.

Hatred flared within me, ignited with the terror of what he'd do to me to pay for leaving him. Sure, his father gave me away, but idiots like him never saw reason. They only saw excuses to hurt.

I couldn't move but watched, failing miserably to catch my breath. The swinging light distorted the scene, and the longer I stared at Brayden, the longer he resembled the real monster he was.

I still couldn't believe he'd tracked me down and had the balls to come after me. But why should I expect anything else?

The asshole rejected me as his mate, then kept me as his personal slave. As someone to torment because no matter what I did, my wolf still felt a connection to his. And I despised that side of myself, hated that any part of me would desire a monster.

The fight continued, the hooting from onlookers deafening. But only when a bigger man stepped up and wrenched Brayden off the unconscious man, did he stop.

"What the fuck?" Brayden swung around, spitting blood.

The newcomer was taller than him, broader, older. He didn't strike Brayden but stood his ground, his expression twisted into hatred. "Fucking enough. Killing Adam won't change the fact that bringing her here wasn't part of the plan."

"Fuck you," Brayden snapped, shoulders curling forward. "We did what you wanted. Your pack got revenge against the Khan pack, and you took your fill of Hendrix's gun stock. So, I got back what the asshole stole from me. Seems fair to me. Now, get the hell out of my face or next time, you'll be on the ground instead of your friend there."

He twisted and spat on the dead man's body, then marched past the tall man, knocking his shoulder into his. "Move!"

"My father will skin you alive for not killing the Khan brothers and instead risking our mission by bringing that whore into our home."

"Fuck off. I'll deal with the Khan brothers," he growled thunderously.

I let out a slight gasp and regretted it instantly.

Brayden swung his attention my way.

Our gazes clashed.

Panic strangled me, and I shut the door instantly, then scrambled backward in the room. I fought the need to scream and cry out, and instead put that energy into wrenching against my restraints and scanning the room for anything to use as a weapon against Brayden.

Heavy footfalls grew louder on the other side of the door, and I crouched down with my back to the wall near the bed. I hugged my knees to my chest, hating how scared he made me. How I wished nothing more than to make him hurt.

The door suddenly swung open.

My breaths turned shallow, caught like a deer in headlights.

Darkness filled the doorway, the faint light behind him giving no features away.

Unease choked me, and I gasped for air as my spine curled forward.

"Bitch," he growled, striding around the end of the bed and standing there, staring down at me.

Moonlight from outside cast a silvery hue over his contorted face. "Get up," he commanded.

I swallowed hard and reluctantly obeyed because I knew him too well. He was going to hurt me no matter what I did, but the length and intensity worsened depending on how I responded. Today, he looked ready to murder me.

He'd been a vapid, spoiled asshole before. But in my absence, he seemed to have changed. My fated mate was now the devil with death in his eyes. Death for me.

His dark gaze lowered to the rapid rising and falling swell of my breasts. I stood there with no top and a bra, my top tied around my stinging neck, and I shivered at his lecherous glare over my chest. But just as quick, it turned to disgust. The familiar urge sparked to curl in on myself, to drag something around me to hide the burn marks on my body.

Despite his presence, somehow I steadied my quivering.

"You thought you were free of me," he muttered while unbuckling his belt.

My heartbeat rushed, my blood pumping hard. I knew

what was coming... I'd been here before. A dark place I wouldn't wish upon anyone. And for a short time, I actually believed I'd escaped him.

"Brayden, I had no choice. Your father—"

His backhand came fast, and I hit the wall. I tasted blood on the back of my throat, half my face burning like he'd set it alight, while the cut on my injury screamed with sharpness.

I looked over to him, knowing exactly what this pathetic alpha was. What all the petty males like him who beat their women were.

A disease on society. They knew nothing else, just destruction to make up for how fucking destroyed they were on the inside. How utterly pitiful he'd become.

"I hate you," I murmured, wiping the blood from my mouth. "Nothing you do to me will change that you're a disgusting excuse for an alpha who hurts those weaker than him. Kill me, I don't care. I will always hate you."

His lips peeled back over perfect white teeth, closing the distance between us in one long stride. He snatched me by my hair, wrenching the fistful to the side.

I cried out, slamming my fist into his arm. Then he hauled me into his face. This close, I saw the splatters of blood across his cheek and chin from where he'd butchered the other man.

"Emersyn," he began, and I gritted my teeth, detesting when he used my real name. On his lips, it sounded like an insult, like a curse. "I will not bless you with death. You think I'm that kind? You'll pay for that asshole, Hendrix, laying a hand on me. You'll pay for my father giving you away. You'll also pay for humiliating me by being with the Khan brothers." He tightened his hand on my hair, my scalp on fire, tears already building in my eyes from the pain. It stung so badly that I dug my fingernails into his arm, drawing blood.

He never released me.

Never even flinched.

"I saw the way you stared at him, the way you giggled like a fucking whore with River. How many times did you spread your legs for those pricks? Did they fill your cunt with their cum?"

He shook me, and I whimpered.

"Tell me," he bellowed in my face, but a half cry fell from my lips.

"Fuck, you're pathetic." He shoved me backward, releasing my hair.

I stumbled over my own feet and slammed into the wall. "Asshole," I spat back just as a flare sparked in the middle of my chest with my wolf. She shoved forward, furious, murderous. And I wouldn't hold her back, no matter how much it hurt.

My wolf rushed forward just as two things happened at once. One, the excruciating pain in my neck had me shuddering, the pain unbearable. Two, Brayden's belt whipped across my thighs, stinging like acid.

I screeched, my knees buckling under me.

I hit the ground, crying out, my world blurring in and out.

"You seem to have forgotten your place to speak to me that way. I own you." His strikes came again, this time the leathery whip biting right into the flesh across my side, curling around my back.

My cries muffled with more screams as I tried to drag myself away from him, trying to frantically fit under the bed.

"I will do anything I want to you, and you, bitch, will beg for more." Powerful hands grabbed one ankle and yanked me back out from under the bed.

Digging my fingernails into the floorboards, I left nothing but scratches on the worn wood. I twisted around and looked up to face the monster.

"Brayden, please," I pleaded, trembling wildly.

But looking down at me was a man with only hatred in his

eyes. He shouted at me, his belt coming down on me, again and again. His roar filled the night, while my cries fell on deaf ears.

My world collapsed around me, and I had no idea how long I endured his beating because with all the pain came an unrelenting darkness. And tonight, I welcomed it.

I begged it to steal me away because I wasn't sure I could ever live like this again.

"Where the fuck is Syn?" I shouted, standing in the doorway to her bedroom in the middle of the night. Her bed was untouched, while the curtains billowed wildly from the open French doors leading onto the balcony.

"Hendrix," one of my men called out from down the hallway behind me, running toward me frantically. Panic was scribbled over his face. What now? "River, he's down by the beach. He's been shot."

"What! By who?" My insides tensed, anxiety and anger warring over the fact that my brother was hurt. I pivoted and raced down the corridor, pushing past the man. "Syn," I growled. "Is she with him?"

"No," was all he said, and I charged down the stairs like thunder, seeing nothing but red.

I launched myself out the front door, running like madness across the front yard and through the gates that were flanked open. My legs pumped, my boots smacking the ground.

We hadn't had a direct attack on our island in years. No intruders in just as long.

My feet sunk into the sand as I swung my attention to the three guards huddled by the shore, crouching forward.

River. My gut tensed. I shoved them aside and found my brother lying on the ground, groaning. His bloody hands were clenched to his gut where more blood poured out of him.

Who the fuck would do this?

"River," my voice croaked as I dropped to my knees near my brother just as a guard arrived with bandages. He started to clean him up there on the sand with the lapping of waves up and down the shore.

I helped wipe the wound to see how bad the damage was. Just a small hole, but it was impossible to tell if it hit anything major. It'd have to come out though, that's for sure.

River stared at me with panic in his eyes.

"You'll be alright," I reassured him, then turned to the guard. "Bullet has to come out, then he needs stitching. Go wake up Liam. He needs to fix him up now."

Liam was our sous chef and handy with butterfly stitches, but this bullet wound would need real stitches once we could get our doctor here from the mainland. River would heal soon enough, but we had to give his body a helping hand.

I turned my attention to my brother, his trembling hands pressing against the wound. "Hang in there, River," I urged, ignoring my rolling stomach at seeing him this way. My chest tightened.

All I'd had for so long in this world were my brothers. For them, I'd destroy the universe to keep them safe. As much as they pissed me off, they were my family. Flashes of our upbringing pulsed in my mind. The times Father hurt them, when I did everything to take the beatings instead of my younger brothers. Even now, I'd take River's position in a heartbeat.

He blinked up at me, his gaze hazed over. Blood streaked across his cheek and brow, but his face was losing color fast.

"Who attacked you?" I asked.

His parched lips opened, and on a hushed breath, he said, "They took Syn." His eyes fluttered upward and he broke into a wince, his body tensing as more blood gushed out past the bandage and through our fingers.

Any human with this wound would have spelled their death. Thank God River was a wolf shifter. A damn powerful one at that. He'd survive. He had to.

"Hold on." I grasped onto his arm. "Don't you fucking let a bullet injury take you down. You hear me?"

Defiance flared behind his gaze. "I believe I've told you before," he hissed between clenched teeth. "I'm only going down one way. In battle." His attempt to smile morphed into a grimace as he fought the pain.

Fury burned through my veins, and I held onto his arm while my three guards lifted him off the ground and into their arms. "Take him inside now," I roared. Then I turned to Mateo, my most loyal guard. "Scour the beach, searching every inch for any clues. I want those who did this hanging from a noose by dawn."

The other guards hurriedly carried River back into the mansion, and I stayed close on their heels. My mind ran amok on what the fuck happened here. Who would dare to do something like this?

I sniffed the air, and a flare of saltiness tore through my nostrils. With it came the metallic smell of River's blood, the heaviness of wolf perspiration from my guards. Beneath all that, the sweet nectar that drove me to obsession flooded my mind with images of Syn.

She'd definitely been out here on the beach with River when they got attacked.

The breeze had carried away the scent belonging to the attackers though, and I cursed under my breath.

Anger hummed in my bones, ready to ignite into flames, and I clenched my hands into fists. I was going to fucking murder them.

Syn's gorgeous face spun in my mind. I hadn't protected her. I had to get my little wolf back.

And the ones responsible for taking her were all going to die.

The motion of the guards carrying River drew my attention, and I swung toward them when a glint in the sand caught my eye.

I bent down to pick up a leather wristband embedded with an obsidian stone. I frowned, twisting it around between my fingers for any kind of symbol or name on it, but I found nothing.

Instead, I pressed it to my nose and sucked in a deep inhale. The thing about these leather bands was that the underside absorbed perspiration and the wearer's scent.

My nostrils flared with a masculine smell, a perspiring staleness, and with a hint of wet dog fur. It triggered fury within me instantly.

I recognized the smell. "Fucking bastard," I roared in the night. "I'm going to slaughter Brayden."

He took her. That spineless weasel came back for my girl. I paced up and down the shore, sucking in the hard air, my chest pumping for oxygen. I trembled, my monster shoving forward for release.

The more I inhaled his smell, the more I squeezed the leather band in my fist, the more I knew exactly what I had to do.

Fury ripped through me, making me sprint after my brother River. I'd save him, and then I'd let my beast out to go hunting.

I tracked River down on the dining table, lying on his back. Caspian was there, holding down his shoulders as Liam poured vodka directly from a bottle onto River's wound.

River growled through gritted teeth, thrashing, sending the whole table skidding across the room. I lunged toward them, grabbing hold of River's legs, pinning him down.

"This is going to hurt," Liam groaned, his hair messy as he'd literally been dragged from his bed. Using large stainless-steel tweezers, he went in to retrieve the bullet.

River hissed, and I pushed harder to hold him down.

"A bit of pain now, brother, for no infection later," Caspian muttered reassuringly. Then he glanced at me with a quizzical stare.

But it was Liam who grabbed my attention. "Bullet hasn't shattered. That's good news." He eventually plucked out the thing from inside River's stomach, and a rush of blood followed.

Frantically, he worked on stopping the blood, pushing a towel down against the wound. "Hold this down tight," he ordered one of the guards.

"What the fuck happened here? Who shot him?" Caspian asked, staring at River, then at me, clearly drawn into this blindly.

I relayed everything I knew, which was very little. Except for the leather wristband I found and who it belonged to.

"Brayden," Caspian growled. "He's so dead." His face twisted into something hideous, something terrifying.

River hadn't completely calmed down, and when I stared down at his thrashing body, I saw his eyes were fluttering. Was he going into shock? His hands gripped the edges of the table. Liam was stitching him up, threading the needle through his flesh, his wound tidy considering the amount of blood.

"We've had a break-in," Caspian told me abruptly. "Someone's gotten into our storage at the back of the island. Two guards were killed, and the majority of our arms stock was stolen."

"What the fuck is going on?" I roared. We'd had arms stolen from us a couple of weeks ago by some of our men—who were now six feet under. I'd thought that problem was fixed.

He nodded. "I assume it's the same assholes who shot River and took Syn?"

Coincidence? It left me deep in thought just as River cried out beneath my hold, and I focused on him for now. "You'll get through this," I reassured him once more, but on the inside I was livid. My heart was a ticking time bomb and I was about to go off.

I was planning a million ways I was going to torture Brayden. For him to sneak into my island, steal my merch, then attack us? He had a death wish. He had no idea what was coming for him.

"What's the plan?" Caspian's voice boomed in the room, drawing me out of my thoughts, and I lifted my gaze, my heart punching against my chest at the fury swallowing me.

"You and I are going to pay Brayden a visit. We're getting Syn back, then I'm skinning the bastard alive." And anyone who stood in my way would die.

By the time Caspian and I arrived at the Madfur pack home in the Hallow sector, I was heaving for breath, seething. Heat infiltrated everything and sweat dripped down my back from this backwater desert town. Why the fuck anyone chose to live out in the middle of nowhere where it was bitingly hot and so far away from the sea baffled me.

My wolf lingered just below the surface, his fur brushing against my insides, desperate for release. He'd grown just as addicted to Syn as the rest of us. He'd connected with her wolf—I felt it deep in my soul.

Morning light spilled over the arid landscape as we rushed from the car. Behind us, several guards followed, fanning out. They were already sweating from the heat, one of them licking his dried lips.

The Howler Bar was so far from everything else that there were few people around. Especially at this ungodly hour of the morning. So, there were no busybodies to notify the soon-to-be-dead alpha of our arrival.

I kicked open heavy, metal doors into the bar, and they swung open with a great crack from where I'd snapped the lock.

Caspian charged in first, moving like a demon.

The place was empty, and it reeked of stale beer and wet dog fur. Caspian had jumped up and over the counter, breaking everything he could get his hands on. I lunged for the back door and threw myself up the stairs. I charged into the first room I found, slapping a hand to the door.

It swung open abruptly into an office.

And my sights fell on Anton, the Alpha of the Madfur pack and Brayden's father. Right now, the old prick had a blonde bent over his desk and he was fucking her, grunting like a damn donkey.

His eyes flew open wide as he swung his attention toward me, pulling his cock out of the poor girl who looked half relieved at my arrival. She had to be at least half his age.

"What the fuck?" he growled, until he did a double-take and saw who'd just stepped into his room. "Alpha?" He practically choked on my name.

"Get the hell out of here, now," I commanded the blonde, stepping into the room.

She shoved her dress down from around her waist, grabbed her underwear from the floor, and darted towards the door. Her cheeks were on fire, and I was convinced I heard her whisper *thank you* silently as she passed.

"I see where Brayden gets being an asshole from."

Anton rapidly tucked his limp dick away and zipped up his pants, before turning to me. "If I knew you were visiting, I would have been better prepared." He licked his lips nervously.

An explosion of shouts echoed from downstairs, but Caspian was capable of looking after himself.

"Brayden," I stated. "Where is he?"

Anton blinked at me, the scent of his perspiration filling the room. When he didn't answer, I took a step forward.

He recoiled. Smart decision. Well, except for the fact that he'd run out of options.

Anger and adrenaline kept my head clear and focused. "I won't ask again," I growled.

"Whatever he's done, we can come up with an agreement. You are a man of reason," he went on, and his gravelly voice only agitated me further.

"There's no coming back from what Brayden did. And deep down, you must know this by my presence alone. I let him go the first time, which was my mistake."

I moved with swiftness, snatching Anton by the throat and slamming him into the drywall that cracked around him from how hard I'd shoved him.

There was a rumble in his throat—his wolf, no doubt.

"Where is Brayden?" I asked in slow motion, my fingers squeezing around his throat. Sure, it was counterproductive to cut off his windpipe, but I didn't want him to think I wasn't serious.

Anton was a disgrace. As evidenced by the fact he'd raised a pathetic excuse of a son like Brayden, or permitted someone as innocent as Syn to be mistreated under his roof...not to mention the cuffs he'd had placed on Syn so she couldn't shift.

He clawed at my hand, his face paling. Writhing against me, I let him go and the prick fell to the floor, his knees buckling out from under him.

Clutching his neck, he craned his head back to meet my gaze. Impatience was killing me right now. "He's not here. He's been gone for about a week with his friends and a few followers."

His face quirked behind his fearful mask. Of course the bastard wasn't telling me the full truth. I could see it in his eyes. He would do anything to protect his son. Fair enough. I would do anything to protect my family, and that included Syn.

I snatched him by his white hair and crouched down in front of him. "You're pissing me off. Where the fuck did he go?"

"Please, whatever he did, he's the only son I have."

"I don't give a fuck," I yelled in his face, and I shook myself. "See what you made me do? Made me almost lose my shit."

Staring at this man's round face, I was reminded of Brayden, those beady eyes, and that androgynous look many women would find attractive. He was pushing me, acting like a petulant child instead of the alpha who should have fought back by now.

When I got back only a whimper, I growled and pulled out the blade from my belt.

He cut me a deadly stare and ripped free from my grasp, his back smacking into the wall.

"I've had enough," I snarled and snatched him by the ear so quickly he never saw my blade-wielding hand come down to slice it right off.

He screamed, blood gushing out, covering his ear.

"I'm going to slowly cut bits off you until you talk. So what's next? Your useless dick?"

Blood drained from his face as red dripped down the inside of his arm where he clasped his now missing ear.

"D-Dorse Island," he spat. "That's what I heard him mention to a friend."

I blinked at him for any twitching signs that he lied. Even his scent was pure fear. Moving closer, I gave him a few hard smacks across the side of his face with an open palm. "There, that wasn't so hard now, was it? And just to be clear, if I don't find him there, I will be coming back for you." I grinned.

I would kill him no matter what for all he'd done to Syn, but if I needed more information about his son, he would be more useful alive for now.

He grimaced while I swallowed hard.

"Good, we have an understanding." I turned to get the fuck out of there, my thoughts spinning on what I knew of Dorse Island. Not much, considering there were hundreds of islands occupied by fuck knew who, but I'd find out more once I got back home. Then we'd go hunting to rescue my little wolf.

"He really is a good boy," Anton whimpered behind me.

Something about him trying to justify what Brayden did only made me more furious. It eliminated my self control. I suddenly saw only fire.

I whipped around with all the fury of my wolf behind me and marched up to the old asshole.

He backed away, but nothing would stop me. I snatched a handful of his shirt around his throat and drew him up to me so we were face to face, so there was no misunderstanding.

"Your son forgot the order of the world. Worms like him shouldn't ever decide to play with monsters." Before I allowed him to respond, I gripped my blade and drove it up under his ribs, shoving it deep, aiming for the heart. Whether I did or didn't hit it wasn't a problem when he started gurgling blood.

"If it gives you any joy, your beloved son will be joining

you soon in the pits of Hell." I dumped his body and he hit the floorboards hard, clutching his bloody chest.

Images of River bleeding to death on the shore had me clenching my teeth. I held no pity for this fucker. I must have been out of my head by thinking I'd let him live for now. I didn't need him or anyone else to warn Brayden that we were coming for him.

Wiping my blade on his pants, I tucked it away and stormed out of there, not bothering to look back at the dying man.

The main bar was littered with half a dozen men while Caspian was sitting on the bar with blood-splattered hands, guzzling back a beer.

"Find him?" he asked, hopping down.

"He's not here, but I know exactly where the prick is. We're going hunting tonight."

"And this place?" he asked, finishing off his drink before tossing the glass to the floor, where it smashed into dozens of shards.

"Get the women and children out. Then burn it down. I want it all gone," I growled.

Chapter 3

Syn

The woman who was tending the deep lashes on my back was humming as she worked. She was dressed in a sparkly, short black dress with bangles all over her arms, her hair in an elaborate updo, like she was going to some kind of nightclub and not fixing my wounds. She'd already tended to my leg while I'd been passed out from blood loss. I wasn't sure what kind of witch she was, but my leg was barely twinging. I still felt incredibly weak though, like a gust of wind could topple me over.

She was dipping cloth into some kind of sweet-smelling liquid and then carefully placing the wet cloths into my wounds.

There was almost instantaneous relief each time a cloth was placed on my wound, and between my shifter healing and whatever magical stuff she was using...the wounds on my back were healing fast.

The injuries inside me, the mental ones from what had happened...it might take forever to get rid of those.

I came to, laying on my side, a sob bursting from my lips as the full spectrum of pain from the wounds across my back came into focus. I didn't want him to hear my cries, but I hurt so fucking bad, it was impossible to keep them all in.

Brayden had dropped the whip and was sitting in a chair, scrolling through his phone.

Fucking bastard.

Suddenly he glanced up, his eyes locking with mine. And I began to tremble because that glare in his eye...I knew it.

The lashes were going to be nothing compared to what was about to happen. I moved to shift and he lunged towards me, grabbing my leg and cracking it to the side, stopping my shift immediately as my powers went to work, trying to heal my leg before I died.

Brayden laughed darkly and then kneeled in between my legs, pushing them aside and making me scream as the bone he'd just broken shifted in my leg as he stretched me.

He made quick work of the bra and underwear I'd been in, and then I was laying there bare, a puddle of blood spreading out underneath me.

"Still so beautiful," he murmured as his fingers stroked up my inner thighs. "Especially when I can't see your scars."

I clenched my eyes closed as he made it to the top of my thighs, bracing myself for what was about to happen...

Tears fell down my face as the memory stretched and pulsed in my mind. At least he'd been interrupted before he could actually rape me.

A small mercy. Although it was just delaying the inevitable. As soon as he got the chance, we'd be there again.

She placed the last strip on my back and then stood up and walked into the bathroom attached to the room. A moment later, she appeared with what looked like two small scraps of fabric in her hands.

The witch must have seen the fierceness in my eye because she stopped and raised an eyebrow. "I wouldn't try anything if I were you. I assure you, you won't succeed."

My shoulders fell, even as I scowled at her. I knew she was right. My wolf growled inside of me, obviously wanting the chance, and I tried to reassure her.

First opportunity I got, where it wasn't a suicide mission, I would let her out.

Apparently satisfied I wasn't going to pounce, she resumed walking toward me and tossed the fabric at my chest. "Get dressed," she ordered.

I lifted the fabric, my eyes widening when I saw how freaking tiny it was. "Are these my underthings?" I asked in a gravelly voice, my vocal cords worn thin from my screaming earlier.

She sniffed, as if she was offended I'd dared to talk to her.

"Those are your clothes for this evening's festivities. Now get them on. I still have to do something with your hair," she snapped, gesturing with disgust at my head.

I stumbled to my feet, cringing as my burn scars and the remnants of my lash wounds stretched.

I picked up the clothes and then shifted awkwardly when she didn't move.

"Can you at least turn around while I change?" I murmured through gritted teeth.

The witch smiled but made a big deal of turning around. "Again, I would remind you it's not a good idea to try something."

I didn't bother answering her. Gingerly, I slipped on the two pieces of fabric, biting my lip in annoyance at how naked I still was. The top basically just covered my nipples, showcasing the top and bottom of my boob like the world's smallest bikini top. The bottoms were fashioned like a thong, covering my front, but showcasing my entire ass.

Fuck. I could only imagine what I was going to be doing in this getup.

"Are you done?" she snapped. "You're not allowed to be late."

"I'm done," I answered sullenly as she turned around and stared at me appraisingly.

She walked in a circle around me, and I closed my eyes as embarrassment and shame rolled through my chest. I'm sure my scars looked amazing in this.

Not.

The witch clicked her tongue in disappointment when she made it to my back. "This won't work at all."

Something hot skittered across my back, and I yelped.

"Perfect. A temporary glamour for the night so everyone doesn't have to be assaulted by your scars."

I didn't thank her. Obviously.

"Get in the bathroom," she sneered, her hands sparking. I hustled to the bathroom as fast as my injuries allowed me...just in case she got it in her head to turn me into a frog or something.

I couldn't help but gasp when I saw how smooth my skin looked in the mirror. I reached back to touch it, and flinched when I felt the familiar ridges of my scars.

It was indeed a glamour.

My hair was suddenly yanked to the side and the witch attacked it with a brush. She must have been trying to scalp me based on how hard she was pulling. She grabbed some pins from a drawer and pressed them into my head. Alright, strike the hair removal...she was actually trying to turn me into a human pin cushion.

My eyes were watering as she worked, somehow transforming the bloody bird's nest I'd been rocking into a sleek updo similar to hers. Magic that could remove blood seemed really useful for a villain. I'd been drenched, and now there wasn't a drop on me.

"Last but not least," she announced after she'd disappeared into a small closet off the bathroom. In her hands was a collar attached to a gold-colored chain. My eyes widened as I took a step backward.

She smiled at me malevolently. "Please. Make my day and struggle."

"What the fuck is wrong with you?" I snapped, unable to hold it in.

Her evil grin widened. She blinked and then I was screaming as the full effect of the lashes on my back came roaring back. I collapsed to the floor and she let me suffer for what felt like forever...until suddenly, the pain was gone.

Her laugh assaulted my eardrums and then the collar hit the tile floor next to me with a loud clunk. "Put this on and get your ass off the floor. We've got five minutes."

I grabbed the collar right as the door burst open and a man I hadn't seen before appeared in the doorway.

"Is she ready?" he growled, his eyes greedily devouring every inch of my skin.

"Almost," the witch simpered sweetly, her voice completely different from how she'd just been screeching at me.

Evil cow.

She grabbed the collar out of my hands and quickly and efficiently snapped it around my neck...she was obviously practiced.

The witch handed the chain connected to the collar to the asshole in front of me, and his lecherous grin only grew, especially when he yanked me forward for the fun of it, and I had a nip slip. Her laughter filled the air as he grabbed my boob roughly, flicking my nipple before pulling the fabric back up to cover me.

My wolf roared inside of me, and a second later she lunged forward, my mouth lengthening into a snout with razor-sharp teeth. And I tore that fucker's throat out.

The witch cursed behind me, and then I was writhing in pain, my wolf retracting back inside me...but somehow, it didn't seem to hurt quite as bad.

I was drooling when the pain stopped, wondering if any part of my mind was going to be intact after this.

The man was still lying on the ground, blood all over his front.

And he was definitely dead.

I guess there was a limit to the witch's ability to heal wounds.

My neck was snapped forward when the witch yanked my chain sharply. "You're going to pay for that, you little bitch."

There was a shout from outside the room, and she closed her eyes and took a deep breath. "Later," she murmured, her voice thick with promise.

She kicked the body as she passed, pulling me towards the door and then out into the hallway.

A few turns later and we were going through a door into a luxurious backyard filled to the brim with debauchery of every kind.

There was an enormous pool, loaded down with a crowd of mostly nude swimmers. I cringed, thinking about having to touch that water. There was basically an orgy happening in there, and I needed bleach for my eyeballs.

Loud music was pumping through speakers all over the large open space. Bars and kegs were spread all over the place, as were tables of food. Despite what I was seeing all around me, hot shame still flooded my veins as I was dragged by the witch through the party crowd towards where Brayden was seated with a group of other menacing men. There were girls and guys draped around them. One girl was massaging his shoulders while another was kneeling in front of him, her head bobbing up and down as she...

I swallowed the vomit trying to come up, sweat trickling

down my back that had nothing to do with the humidity in the air.

I could still feel his fingers on me and in me, my pulse drumming loudly in my ears—

"Get your shit together," the witch snapped, most likely smelling the stench of my panic.

For once I was grateful for her bitchiness; she'd somehow successfully snapped me out of a panic attack.

"Here you are," she said, nodding to Brayden as we got within a few feet of where his group was seated. Brayden kept his eyes locked with mine as he moaned loudly and came down the poor girl's throat.

I didn't miss the frown of annoyance from the men seated next to him. Not that what they were doing with the followers around them was any different. They were all disgusting.

My wolf growled inside me, wanting a repeat performance of what she'd done earlier.

Not now, I warned sternly, knowing we'd be torn to bits around this crowd.

The witch handed Brayden the chain and he yanked me forward, wrapping it around his hand as I tried to keep my chin held high.

Once he got me next to him, he licked up my face. I shivered in disgust, locking eyes with the witch who was still right outside of the group, longing and hatred warring in her eyes. I made my own promise to her then: I would make her pay for what she'd done today.

Later.

Brayden yanked my chain again when he saw I wasn't paying attention to him. The girl still at his feet glared at me as he dragged a finger across the top of my breasts.

"Feed me," he ordered, his head nodding towards the table loaded with food. The men chuckled around us.

Assholes.

For a second, I allowed myself to imagine Hendrix's monster charging through the crowd, his claws slicing through them all. I imagined how easily he could tear through Brayden's skin.

"Emersyn," Brayden snarled, his voice thick with annoyance and warning. I snapped back to the shit show around me and grabbed some grapes, knowing this would be another moment I'd never forget. My hand trembled...with anger...as I took the grape and moved it to his opened mouth.

His tongue licked at my fingers, and I couldn't hold in my shiver of disgust. He yanked the chain forward and then licked the side of my face to punish me.

My fingers were a much better sacrifice than my face, I decided. When he let me go, I fed him grapes, trying my best to hold in my fury every time his tongue grazed my skin. His eyes were staring aptly at my face, just waiting for me to mess up.

It struck me then, how I had almost forgotten the feeling of sorrow I'd carried around me when Brayden had been in my life every day. I'd forgotten the pit in my stomach of knowing the moon goddess had thought so little of me that this was what I'd been given for my soulmate.

Now that I was in his presence again, it was all back.

With one exception.

I'd used to long for him. I'd pretended like it didn't exist, because it felt so pathetic. But it had been there. Even with how much I hated him, I'd still carried a pathetic hope in the deep recesses of my heart that he would change and I could be complete.

That was gone now. The tendril of feeling had been wiped away. I didn't know what exactly had done it—or who had done it—as terrible as it was to be in this situation.

At least I felt like I'd been cut free from the burden I'd been carrying since the moment I'd realized I belonged to him.

One of the males that had been seated with the group stood up, and the raucous party almost immediately came to a halt. Everyone gave him their rapt attention, and the music quietened. He was obviously an alpha, his body twice the size of almost everyone around him. He had curly auburn hair that should have given him a friendly appearance were it not for the darkness of his eyes. I didn't think I'd ever seen anyone with eyes that black. It was unnerving to just be staring at them, let alone experience their glare.

"In two days, all of our hard work will finally come to fruition. The Khan pack will pay for the servitude they've forced on us all these years. Their guns are ours, and soon... their heads will be ours."

The crowd roared in delight, and his answering blood-thirsty smile made my blood chill.

Looking at the size of the group at this gathering, it would be quite the attack, even with all the soldiers that Hendrix and his brothers kept on their island.

Crates were dragged in by men who hadn't been among the partiers. They threw them in a pile and then lifted the lids, showcasing a multitude of weapons.

"We all know that the Khan guns are the best in the business. Can you imagine that cunt Hendrix's face when he sees his own weapons pointed at him?" he crowed.

Brayden was laughing uproariously next to me, the idiot. Hendrix had told me how Brayden cowered and begged like a worm the night they'd made their "deal."

Brayden's muscles were vanity muscles, designed to look good but not actually be of use. If this attack did happen, he would do well to stay as far away from Hendrix, River, and Caspian as he could.

Because the end result of an interaction with them wouldn't be pretty.

I was certain that Brayden would not have the luxury of being spared this time.

Everyone suddenly had a cup in their hands, and they all raised them in unison with the male who must have been their leader. "Down with Khan," they screamed before guzzling their drinks.

Worry spiked through me, thinking of the attack. What were they doing right now? Had River survived? Were they searching for me?

Did they even care?

I was used to being disappointed by the male species. Hendrix had certainly disappointed me in a way I wasn't sure I could forgive.

But that weak, stupid part of me was hoping they were out there, hunting for me. That some part of them was desperate to have me back.

Brayden yanked on my chain again, motioning for the cup on the table that he'd just held in his hands for the little war chant everyone had been a part of.

I gritted my teeth, thinking of the million ways I wished I could kill him at the moment.

That was the great thing about that hope being gone. I never could have ended him before.

Now, as I pressed the cup against his lips and tilted it back for him to get a drink...I could think of a million ways to kill him, each worse than the last.

My wolf growled in agreement with my bloody thoughts.

After I'd given him his drink, he pulled me onto his lap.

I almost started laughing. Because I realized I was totally having a Princess Leia moment. I was dressed like she'd been in the movie when she'd been chained to Jabba the Hutt or whatever that gross slug monster guy had been called.

Honestly, I thought Leia had the better gig. A slug monster would be way better than having to perch on your asshole fated mate's lap, a hard erection poking your ass as he murmured all the disgusting things he wanted to do to you.

The party was growing wilder. The crowd was a writhing, drunk group that probably couldn't even feel their butts at the moment, they were so intoxicated.

Brayden was growing handsier the more he drank, and every cell in my skin was crawling. It was all I could do not to throw up on the bastard.

I tried to think of a way out of this, but with the collar cutting into my skin, and with the fact that the rest of the leaders sitting around us did not appear very intoxicated, I just couldn't think of how to manage it. There was also the matter of the witch. She lurked near the leaders, throwing longing glances at them. She was probably way more powerful than they were, and yet there she was, desperate for any scrap they could give her.

I'd learned her name was Astoria. Or at least, that's what some of them had called to her. I wondered what had happened to her that she'd become this pathetic, evil creature. What had taken her sense of self-respect?

I would have felt sorry for her, if not for everything she'd done to me earlier. I liked to think that no matter how low I got in life, I'd never take it out on another woman.

I was distracted by my thoughts, and I shouldn't have been. I flinched when he kissed my neck, and the next second, his fist struck my cheek and I flew off his lap, my collar yanking on my neck as I fell to the ground.

I laid there for a second, my breaths coming out in gasps, and my body shuddering in pain. My wolf howled inside of me, mourning the fact that we were chained.

Furious tears were gathered in my eyes as I pushed myself off the ground, my cheek throbbing in pain.

All my senses left me. All I could feel in that moment was

a thick rage that burnt my tongue as I stared at the disgusting being in front of me.

"Fuck you," I snarled, enjoying the shock in his eyes at my curse. "You're pathetic, Brayden. And worse...you're forgettable." I smiled at the embarrassment and fury building on his features. The men seated around us had all quieted, and I could feel their eyes watching me. A voice in my head was screaming at me to shut my mouth before I went so far that I couldn't come back...but I was done. I leaned forward, a mocking smile on my lips. "You're right. I did fuck the Alphas of the Khan pack...and I enjoyed every minute of it. It was amazing to experience sex that actually felt good. It was refreshing that I didn't have to lay there and fake it. My orgasms were all real. They have more power in their pinkies than you have in your whole body...not to mention the size of their dicks."

Brayden's face was a mottled, almost purple color. He was frozen listening to the words he'd never imagined his poor, pathetic little mate was capable of.

Since I'd gone that far, I couldn't help but go one step further.

"You're going to die, Brayden. And it's going to be soon. I hope it's by my hands, but I'm good with anyone killing you —" I continued...my voice fading off as the sensation of being watched by someone very familiar stroked against my skin.

I was just imagining—I turned and locked gazes with vibrant green eyes that I hadn't been sure I'd ever see again.

They'd come for me.

"Looks like we have company," Caspian murmured under his breath just loud enough for Hendrix and me to hear.

I raised my head and looked out toward the other end of the beach of Dorse Island where yachts glided in and out of the harbor dropping off guests.

"They're holding a fucking party. Hip hip hooray, this is one function they won't forget for a long time," I growled, the bandaged wound suddenly pinching across my middle. I gritted my teeth, riding the pain. At least it wasn't as bad as last night after I'd been left to die on the shore.

Memories I wanted to forget lashed my mind, mostly blurred by the excruciating torment of being shot in the gut. I couldn't stop them from bulldozing over me.

Inky black water. It splashed up my knees, its icy touch like claws digging into my flesh. Night engulfed me. Where the fuck am I?

"River!"

I swore I heard my name in the wind when a huge wave crashed into me. It came fast and unexpected, wiping me out. I lost my footing and fell into its grasp, my head plunged underwater as I scrambled to fight the tide that tried to wrench me out to sea.

Panic gripped me. It swallowed me as I was thrown back to my childhood. To when Father tried to drown us, to kill us. Terror clutched my chest, and I beat my arms and legs, needing to escape. To get away.

"Demon, you will die!" my father cried out hysterically.

Daddy no! Please no! I screamed in my head.

I frantically tried to find purchase in the sand shifting beneath my feet. I swallowed the salty water, leaving me to choke. My head swam with confusion, unable to discern between the present and the past. I kept waiting to see Hendrix and Caspian in the water. For my brother to finish our father. To turn into his monster.

But none of that came. Only the water that kept dragging me under and under.

Pushing myself forward, I crawled against the pull of the water, completely drenched, coughing, but the tide was relentless. My muscles ached while disorientation had the world tilting on its axis.

Someone was suddenly at my side, tugging on my arm to help me get out of the water. I glanced up at the most beautiful face. The moon behind her made her appear almost angelic and glowing. For those few seconds, I let myself believe it might be an angel coming to collect my pitiful soul from having drowned.

She shifted, and I saw her face clearly.

"Syn?" I finally said, gasping for air, my head spinning as I tried to make sense of what happened. Trying to recall how I got out of my room because it had been a long time since I walked in my sleep. "I was asleep. I almost drowned myself," I sputtered the words along with water.

She helped me up, and I wrapped my arms around this gorgeous girl with magenta hair that glowed in the moonlight *and caught in the breeze. My savior, she peered up at me, smiling, but worry flared behind those gorgeous eyes.*

She went on to tell me she'd seen me from her window and came to me.

I blinked, staring around at the mansion and walls, noting there were no signs of our guards. "How did no one stop me?" I murmured, mostly to myself as I stumbled on my feet, moving away from the water.

But something felt off. The hairs on my nape lifted. Where were the guards?

"Something's not right," I said, holding Syn close to my side, scanning the mansion as we moved closer toward it. "We need to get—"

The familiar sound of a gun being cocked came too quickly from behind us for me to react.

The shadows around us suddenly took a life of their own. They moved with a blur. Syn was snatched from me, her cry throttling me.

I whipped around just as something sharp and hard whacked into my gut. Something so fast and painful that it threw me off my feet. I grunted, clutching my stomach, feeling the warmth of blood pouring out of me. And the last thing I recalled was hearing Syn's cries in the night as darkness inhaled me.

"River." Caspian shoved a hand into my shoulder, wrenching me out of my thoughts. "Are you going to pass out?"

I blinked at him at first. "What?"

"You've got that glazed-over look in your eyes. If you can't do this, then go back to the boat."

My shoulders reared back. "Fuck that. Get out of my way," I growled and shoved past him. I wasn't 100% fixed just yet, but my wolf side healed fast. And nothing in this fucked up planet would make me miss out on delivering justice to the assholes who shot me and stole Syn.

My chest burned up at the thought, but with it came something else...guilt. It cut through me that under my watch, I didn't protect Syn enough. I let her get captured. And that shit was destroying me.

I grew up watching my prick of a father beat us up, especially Hendrix. And at the time, as terrified as I'd been, I made myself a promise: I'd never let anyone I cared for get hurt. But I'd fucked up with Syn, hadn't I?

They ambushed us on the beach, and regret was slowly killing me.

I should have done more. Should have torn them apart. Fuck. I clenched my hands, fury hammering in my chest.

Hendrix suddenly signaled for us to follow him amid the myriad of palm trees covering the island. With a wave of his hand to his three dozen guards at our rear, he sent them round the back of the mansion. The dozen guards vanished into the shadows.

"Let's move," I uttered, wanting this as much as I needed oxygen. I had to get Syn, had to make them pay.

Night concealed us, and considering the number of attendees, our infiltration would be easier than we anticipated.

We'd left our boat just off shore, the skipper taking it far enough to not raise suspicions. The plan was set in motion, and this little shindig would only help us conceal ourselves among the sheep.

"Maybe we're not so underdressed," Caspian commented, his attempt at a joke falling flat. We were all in black for a reason, and it just happened that it matched the guests.

"We're not going inside to mingle with them," I snarled, still agitated as hell to know that Syn was in there somewhere, god-knows-what was happening to her, and we were still out here.

"Chill the fuck out," Caspian hissed. "Don't lose your shit. We work better as a team. Remember that."

"Tell that to Hendrix," I said, lifting my chin toward our oldest brother who thundered ahead of us as if he was on a mission by himself.

He was fuming and focused, not seeming to have heard a word. The Alpha lingered on the brink of releasing his beast. Tonight would end in a bloodbath, and each of us was ready for the rampage.

I fucking welcomed it, my sights set on destroying anyone standing in my way to get Syn.

We moved with speed through the night, dodging palm trees, coming up on the mansion. A lavish piece of shit owned by a pack I knew little about. Another gang running their activities from these island headquarters. Regardless, they were going to be dead soon enough. And maybe we'd claim this as our vacation home.

Music permeated the air the closer we got, voices humming in the distance. Much to our benefit, the local pack's guards were congregated around the dock, welcoming visitors.

Darting through the shadows and around palm trees, we came to the edge of open, manicured grounds.

Perfectly styled lawn, several fountains of naked maidens holding jars of flowing water, blinking lights on strings overhead, and benches everywhere. Beyond that rose an enormous mansion, four stories high, and it screamed opulence. Here I thought we were the only ones with a castle for a home, but I'd been wrong.

"Who exactly are the cocksuckers living here?" Caspian whispered over his shoulder.

Hendrix watched everything with the prediction of the predator he was, barely paying us attention. We remained hidden in the shadows, watching every guard, every camera, every damn thing.

I kept staring at the windows glowing with light from inside. *Where are you, Syn? Which room?*

Lucky for us, most of the cameras I noted were all pointed toward the front of the house, to where all the visitors arrived.

The longer we waited, the longer anger rolled over me, echoing inside me. My skin pricked, and overhead the sky growled. A storm was coming.

Hendrix jerked his attention toward us and pointed to the rear of the house where he must have seen an opportunity to enter the mansion. "Over there," he finally said, pointing to a waiter emerging with a silver tray filled with flutes, most likely with Dom Perignon. Something we'd serve our guests if in the mood to impress.

"We need to hurry. Stay close," he whispered over his shoulder. Then he made a mad rush across the lawn toward the back of the property.

Caspian and I lunged right after him. Keeping our heads low, we moved on silent steps and sprinted. My heart jacked in my chest that we'd be caught, and while I had no problems starting to slay these fuckers early, I preferred to find Syn first.

It was funny how when she first arrived at my home, I wanted nothing to do with her. I kept telling myself that she still meant nothing to me. But I'd never been good at lying to myself.

As much as I hated to admit it, she did something to me...I thought about her constantly, her candied smell never left my nostrils, and even in my sleep, I heard her voice. When I closed my eyes and thought of her, I felt the softness of her skin on mine.

For a long time, I believed I was too brutally broken to deserve anything more than women you fucked and walked away from. But maybe I never had the courage to admit to myself that I deserved more. That even monsters need love.

And Syn was definitely the kind of girl I could become obsessed with, who I couldn't live without. She was proof that even when you'd lived an existence that felt like hell, angels still existed for savage assholes like me.

Hendrix ripped open the door, dragging my attention, and he ushered us inside. Caspian took the lead, taking out the guard who had his back to us. He snapped his neck, and I caught the guy as he fell over, then I dragged him into an empty storage room I found. Dumping his body in there, I shut the door carefully and caught up to my brothers.

We moved fast after that, sticking to shadows, to hallways, darting left and right to avoid being seen. The mansion was sumptuous in decorating tastes. Only the most extravagant tapestries were on the walls, diamond chandeliers hung from the ceilings, and door frames, and banisters were all gold in this part of the house which all revolved around the central entertaining hallway that led into a massive ballroom.

The three of us were tucked into a small broom closet, peering out down the hall to where people were mingling and drinking. From my vantage location, there was a tall blonde in the middle of the hallway, naked, and her body painted completely gold as she sat on a small stool and played a soft tune on a harp. With the music coming out from the ballroom and outside through the open doors, her attempt fell on deaf ears.

Who the fuck were these wankers?

I turned to my brothers. "Okay, I can't see Syn out there. What's our plan?"

"We take out as many of the guards as possible without anyone noticing. Then I'll notify our men and we all go in for the attack. Let's not give ourselves away just yet."

"Deal."

Caspian was cracking his knuckles. "I'm ready to spill blood."

Before we knew it, we'd emerged from the room and made good on our plan. I gripped the blade I'd brought with me and jumped the first guard standing at the end of the hall. Well, he turned and saw me approaching. Eyes bulging, he knew we weren't guests, so I charged him and collided so hard, I drove his head into the wall. Maybe with a bit too much gumption, considering I heard the crack of his skull, and then he dropped like a sack.

"Well, you're no fun," I whispered, grabbing his ankles and hauling him into a side room where Caspian held the door open for me. It was a reading room by the looks of it, complete with a study, meaning anyone could come in and find him tonight.

"Quickly stash him here," Caspian said, pulling back the curtains. I rolled my eyes at him, but did as he suggested. I just wanted to get to Syn.

I dumped the body and kicked his legs until they were tucked up behind the curtain enough to be concealed at first glance.

Caspian was by the desk, spinning an envelope opener in each hand, rolling them over his fingers, before hurling them at the painting on the wall of an old white-haired fart on a yacht.

Give my brother a piece of paper, and he'd fashion it into a deadly weapon to carve out your heart.

"Stop fooling around," I said, then darted back out just as Hendrix sliced a man's throat right in front of our door.

"Fuck," I hissed and retreated for him to drag his victim inside the study, while I slid back out, desperate to find Syn. To know where the fuck Brayden had put her. The problem was, the more I looked where the crowds were at the entry to the mansion, the more I was certain she'd be over with the guests and not somewhere alone.

And I couldn't exactly stroll up there dressed like a ninja.

Nope, that wouldn't work. So another plan formed in my mind. I backpedaled into the shadows, spotting a guard in his navy, tailored suit uniform with silver stripes across his shoulders several feet away. He didn't notice me.

The ass was on his phone, and then suddenly he darted deeper into the house, away from the party. And I was on his heels.

Swallowing hard, the hairs on my arms rose that I'd be spotted since the guy was turning left and right down various corridors. It was only when he entered a room and shut the door quickly behind him, that I took my chance.

I charged in there after him. Sure, not my brightest move, but I'd had enough of playing nice.

It just so happened that I burst in on the guy as he pulled open the front of his pants and snapped a photo of his junk.

"Fuck, man, is that necessary?" I blurted.

He startled so much at my abrupt entrance into the bedroom, that he fumbled with the phone and dropped it.

And that was when I attacked, having no time to spare. I slammed into him and he hit the ground hard. I straddled his chest, my knees pinning his arms down. I pressed the tip of my blade just over his eye and stared down at him.

Terror blanched his face as he breathed heavily, his body trembling.

"Listen here, dickhead. Either you can remove your clothes and give them to me, or I'm scooping your brain out through your nose with my blade. And trust me, it's gonna get messy."

He whimpered, and apparently that was all I needed to do–threaten him. He nodded desperately, and in less than a minute, he'd stripped and dumped his guard suit on the end of the bed.

"Now be a good boy and tell me where Brayden and the pink-haired girl are in this shithole," I growled, collecting the rope used to tie up the curtains and lassoing the guy up to the four-poster bed in the room. Of course, he fought me, but I snatched his arm and snapped it in half over my knee to teach him a lesson.

His cries irritated me. "Shut the fuck up. And answer my question. Where's the girl?"

"S-she's in the courtyard with Brayden." He sniffled like a damn baby, crying louder.

In his boxers, he was spread out like a starfish. I yanked his sock off his foot and stuffed it into his mouth to shut him up.

Then I rushed over to get changed just as the door burst open to another guard. I'd just stripped off my own clothes when the newcomer decided to interrupt me. I sighed, pissed at his interruption.

"Really? You had to come in now?"

He glared at me, then at the guy I assumed was his boyfriend on the bed to explain why he'd found us so easily. With a growl, the bastard came at me so fast I couldn't respond quick enough. He tackled me around the middle and slammed me up against the wall.

Breath expelled, I grunted as he knocked the wind out of me. "Fuck, you're a big bastard, aren't you," I groaned in his face.

"What the fuck are you doin up here? You're not a guest," he droned in my face.

I snarled, shaking with agitation that he was wasting my time when I had Syn to find. Darkness shrouded my thoughts, and I went wild. I head-butted him right in the face, giving me just enough leverage to shove my hands against his chest.

The idiot with a bald head stumbled backward, his upper

lip curling up over lengthening canines. The scent of wolf fur flooded the room, and I figured I'd take him down with ease, whatever form he took.

"Bud, get the hell over here, you pussy," he snarled at the guy tied up in bed.

His friend started to thrash, transforming into his wolf form, his binds loosening...and, well, they forced my hand. I lifted my gaze, narrowing my eyes at the fucker who'd just pushed me too far. Savagery and purpose pulsed in my veins, along with the hunger to spill blood intensifying.

I ripped open the floodgates, calling to my wolf.

He gushed out in a heartbeat, moving with speed, tearing out of me, my skin splitting, bones cracking. I fell to the floor on all four paws, my silvery fur covering me. I unleashed a growl, lowering my head, ears pasted to my skull as I eyed both my enemies closing in on me, both in animal form. Both dark as the night.

Anger hit me like the crack of a whip.

Syn was all I saw in my eyes, and these two stood in my way.

My growl deepened, turning feral, and I charged for them both. This wasn't my first rodeo, and it sure as fuck wouldn't be my last.

We clashed, and rage consumed me, the room filled with growls of ferociousness.

Fur and fangs. Blood and wounds. I didn't stop and only saw fury. The walls trembled as I threw one after the other aside like rag dolls, and there was no stopping. Not when I'd come so far.

Just the flash of torment filled me, images of Syn being tortured. Thoughts of Brayden laying a hand on her. I screamed on the inside at the depraved images painted in my mind. And I lost it, my form pulsing with fury.

No one would survive tonight if my girl was hurt.

It was only when my feet slipped and I hit the ground, my face smacking into something wet, something slimy, that I shook my head and really opened my eyes to my surroundings.

Blood.

It covered everything. The walls. It ran across the floor, and some even got on the ceiling.

The two wolves were nothing but pieces scattered around the place.

Well, look at me. I'd tried my hand at interior decorating.

Licking the blood from my lips, I retracted my wolf, my body knitting back together. Fur vanished, bones forming back into their human form, and in moments I stood naked, covered in blood.

"Okay, this is a challenge then." So I improvised. I walked over to the bed and grabbed the covers untouched by the splatter and started wiping myself clean. By the time I finished, I felt slightly sticky. I collected the guard's clothes and my boots that somehow managed to sit by the window unscathed by the massacre, and headed out the door.

The hallway was dead empty, and I breathed easy as I rushed to the next few rooms until I found the bathroom. There I locked myself inside and did the world's fastest clean. Looking in the mirror, blood covered my face, but I had to get it off me to avoid giving away the strong pungent scent when I arrived at the party.

So much for a quick plan to just get a guard's outfit. As long as no one went into the other room until the party was over, we'd be fine though.

Clean and blood free, I stepped out of the bathroom as a new man in the guard's clothing, giving a fresh meaning to a wolf in sheep's clothing.

Running a hand through my partially wet hair, drying it off my face, I strolled quickly toward the party.

A guard came my way, and I gave him a curt nod. He

didn't even pay me attention. Good. I hurried faster now. Just then, someone grabbed my arm out of the shadows, an arm locked around my throat.

My heart slammed into my chest.

Hendrix. I smelled his wolf instantly.

"Fuck, Hendrix," I choked. "It's me, you bastard, let go."

He sniffed and released me. I whipped around, a quizzical expression on his face. "River! Shit! What did you do? You smell like a blood massacre."

I shrugged sheepishly. "It's all good. Are we getting Syn or what? She's in the main courtyard. Let our men know we're going in to attack now. You and Caspian stay close." No idea where Caspian was, but he'd find us once the sounds of war kicked off.

Hendrix gave me a pointed stare, obviously struggling with me taking charge. But last time I looked, I was in the guard's clothing, so I made the first move.

"Are you sure you've got this?" he asked. "You observe, get as close to her as possible until we arrive, then you take her and the rest of us will distract them."

"I got this," I snapped, well aware that Hendrix was emotionally invested and might buckle once he saw Syn. Fuck, I might too, with how much despair had been gnawing at me since she'd been gone. But I'd hold it together. I had to. "Just unleash your monster and destroy them," I reassured him, knowing he ached for her as much as Caspian and I did. "Now let's do this."

I drew quickly away from Hendrix and threw myself back into the hallway. Hastily, I ran my hand through my hair, straightened my jacket which fit me a bit too tightly, and marched with confidence toward the gathering crowd.

Luxurious guests, each one a criminal for the numerous packs around these islands. Most of them would probably know Hendrix in a heartbeat, but I was the brother who avoided these gatherings like the plague, so they wouldn't recognize my face. Not that I recognized anyone I was passing. They didn't need to know us to understand that my brothers and I were feared and hated. That most would do anything to steal our power and accumulated wealth. So who gave a shit who they were...end of the day, they were my enemy.

I pushed into the noisy group of guests, following the wave of chatter out the open doors of the ballroom and into a courtyard with a pool where various hedonistic activities were taking place. I scanned the place frantically, searching for her. And it didn't take long before her bright purplish hair stood out amid the crowd.

Something warm wrapped around my heart at the sight of her, to find she was alive, to lay eyes on the most beautiful creature I'd ever seen.

For those few moments, I was locked in place, the floor holding me prisoner. She wore practically nothing–just the tiniest bikini–the pieces of cloth leaving nothing to the imagination. My wolf trembled under my skin the moment I lifted my attention to the metal collar around her neck. The chain was fastened to her and the other end wrapped around Brayden's hand.

A growl rolled over my throat, and I stepped forward, fury punching me in the chest.

Brayden tugged on the chain with a snorting laugh, forcing her to stumble toward him. She snatched a handful of grapes from a bowl on the table and then pushed them one by one into his open mouth. The asshole licked her fingers, then yanked her closer and licked the side of her face.

Fuck. His death was not going to be quick.

Her scornful pinch of her lips showed her disgust, as did the way she moved to stand as far from him as possible.

Fucking pig.

The bastard reached over and slapped her ass, coaxing

laughter from the six men sitting at their table. Syn shoved his hand away, her shoulders bunching up, ready to attack him.

My heart leapt with how much I fucking wanted her in that moment. To see her fight back did something to my heart, and I needed more.

The other men nearby laughed, while Brayden snatched her hand, forcing her by his side. I couldn't hear their heated conversation, but they all seemed to be laughing at her.

Brayden seemed to eventually release her, and she moved to stand away from him, but his death glare promised her pain. Oh, he had no idea that I was going to rip off his dick and make him eat it.

That was when I spotted another woman standing at the other end of their table in a short, black dress, arms covered in golden bangles, her hair pulled off her face. She might appear young, but something about her felt old. She watched over Syn strangely. Everyone stepped around the woman as if knowing she represented danger.

Regardless, I wanted them all dead. They were going to fucking die tonight.

Brayden suddenly tugged on Syn to stand closer to him once more. She caught herself and tossed daggers with her glare. The other woman kept watching Syn carefully. My skin crawled.

Her fighting spirit kept her alive, I was certain of it, and when we got out of this, I was going to teach her myself how to fight. How to destroy an asshole like Brayden in a few simple moves. No one would ever lay a hand on her again.

I stumbled forward of my own accord once more, drawn to Syn, furious to let anyone lay a hand on her that way. To see her being embarrassed publicly murdered me on the inside.

A storm brewed through my chest as I continued to watch the bastard and Syn. I curled my hands into fists, and I couldn't wait. Not another fucking second to free her. To rip his head off his shoulders.

One of the men from her table stood up, and the room fell silent. "In two days all of our hard work will finally come to fruition. The Khan pack will pay for the servitude they've forced on us all these years. Their guns are ours, and soon... their heads will be ours."

The crowd cheered, while my blood boiled. Fucking cock-suckers.

Then I watched as they dragged crates into the room to add to the others in the room and ripped open the lids to reveal the weapons they stole from us.

Watching these assholes all raising their cups and cheering, "Down with Khan," only made me more furious.

I held back from going into full war mode just yet and kept hanging out in the shadows of the courtyard, listening to conversations, and keeping an eye on my girl until the right moment.

Suddenly, my gaze clashed with her vibrant green eyes.

Her mouth fell open at seeing me, recognizing me immediately. For those few seconds, I held onto that image with all her beauty. The rest of the party faded away, and it was just us two, alone, finally brought together. She seemed to glow, and I knew that I stared at a woman who'd been fighting her whole life. What the dicks around her didn't know was that they would never burn her down when she shone so bright. I was going to remind the fucking world how precious she was.

She mouthed my name, followed by *help*. A flicker of hope danced on her face, her posture straightening.

I nodded quickly, not wanting to give away too much, but I hoped she understood we were there for her.

Voices behind me talked about drugs and arms exchange, about an army of expendable soldiers. All things that perked my ears. Such intelligence impacted our business, but I stood no chance at tearing my gaze from Syn or focusing on anything but her.

Causally, I strolled through the courtyard, pretending to replicate a guard on duty, though I always kept sight of Syn from the corner of my eye.

Someone abruptly grabbed my arm, and I turned to one of the men from Brayden's table. A younger man with dusty blond curls and an ugly grimace. "We don't pay you to enjoy the party, you fucker. Go collect the beer kegs from the boats and take them down to the kitchens."

I stared into his face, holding his stare, contemplating how good it'd feel to break his face with my fist. My spine stiffened when I realized he still had his stick fingers on my arm. I braced myself with a deep inhale to hold my shit together, but I also had no intention of leaving Syn out of my sight.

She watched me. I sensed her the whole time. Even when Brayden hauled her by the chain to sit on his lap as he groped her in front of others, she kept glancing at me. She kept shoving against Brayden, and I loved seeing her fighting the bastard.

I'm not going anywhere, baby.

"Did you hear me, or are you stupid?" the man barked in my face.

I swallowed hard, and just as I reluctantly said, "Sure," Hendrix charged the party. Ten feet tall, black fur all over his body, he'd unleashed his monster. Sharp spikes ran down his back, his black fur glinting beneath the lights. Claws extended, he threw himself at the nearest table, his eyes red at the blood he'd spilled from the throat of the old fart he'd just slashed open.

Oh, fun. The real party was starting.

It all happened so fast, and the moment he unleashed an ungodly roar, exposing his serrated shark-like teeth, the whole room turned into chaos.

Caspian was on his heels, hurling blades at everyone and anyone, with a gun in his other hand peppering the crowd, taking them out so fast you'd miss it if you blinked.

My heart thundered with adrenaline for Syn.

I turned toward her, the man who seconds ago was in my face racing back in her direction. I lunged, snatched him by the scruff of his neck, and yanked him back. Snatching the sides of his head, I twisted it so hard, so aggressively, that the cruel snap of his spine announced his finality.

That was when the strange woman in the black dress charged for my brothers. I already felt the sizzle of power running up my arms. She was a fucking witch.

Just as she hurled her hands out, sparks dancing on her fingertips, a silvery glint caught my attention. An envelope opener spun through the air with lightning speed, coming from Caspian's direction.

Thwack.

It struck the witch, right in the eye, piercing deeply, and I didn't need to be a doctor to know she wasn't going to be getting up any time soon. She convulsed, her knees dropping, and she fell hard, her body shuddering, her cries ignored. Those around her ran over her in their panic.

Hell yeah.

Caspian punched the air in his own victory dance, then flung himself toward three guards. Hendrix was leaving a trail of blood behind him, torn bodies, and terrifying screeches from those trying to escape him.

Gunshots rang in the air, and I ducked as I tossed the man in front of me aside.

I sprinted toward Syn while most of the guards charged for my brothers. Our backup guards poured into the area too, and like planned...the night turned into a bloodbath.

But nothing mattered unless we saved Syn. I threw myself toward her as she frantically pulled against the chain Brayden held. He was attempting to escape back through the ballroom while a group of guards flanked him on either side. "Protect me," he yelled at them like the sullen shithead he was.

"Stop fighting me, you bitch," he snarled, hatred in his eyes for Syn. Then he slapped her hard across her face. In an instant, Syn flew at him, her small fist knocking right into his nose. My girl was fierce and I fucking loved it. He shoved her backward, raising a hand to her when a guard grabbed his arm to drag him away. Syn stumbled behind them no matter how much she dug her heels in and yanked against him.

Fire torched my insides.

She kept looking at me frantically, tears running down her cheek, then stared out at Hendrix and Caspian who carved a path of death and destruction through the crowd. Others screamed and tried to escape back through the ballroom as well thanks to the large fence with spikes that surrounded the courtyard.

"Syn," I called out, rushing up behind them.

I grabbed her wrist, whispering, "I've got you. I'm here for you." Then I tore at the metal fetter around her neck, unlatching it, freeing her. Syn's skin was red from where it rubbed her, and a growl ripped from my throat at the marks.

"Get the fuck away from her," Brayden snarled, but I was so fucking furious that I hurled the metal collar in my hand right at his fucking face with all the force behind me. It whacked him dead center in the face, blood gushing from his already broken nose, not to mention the huge scratch across the face.

He recoiled, crying out like a child, clasping his bloody face.

"You sonofabitch," I cried out. "I'm going to chop you up and feed you to the sharks. And even then, that's not enough punishment to make up for what you've done."

"She's not yours. She never will be," he snarled, blood rolling down his nose.

"River." My angel tugged at my arm. "You came for me."

I turned to her, my heart bleeding for her... knowing that deep in my soul, I'd give her anything she wanted. My emotions were not things I often shared or even permitted myself luxury in exploring. But now, they ran rampant.

"We'll get out of here in just a minute. But first, Brayden is going to suffer as are the others in this place." I grabbed her arm, holding her close just as a furious Caspian arrived, hurling himself at Brayden's guards.

Blood. Death...anarchy surrounded us. I welcomed it, but I also needed to get Syn somewhere safe.

A sudden boom exploded around us. It was earth-shattering, my ears ringing. It came so fast, so hungry, that it ripped the ballroom in half.

Walls shaking, floors cracking open, and everyone thrown in every direction. The front wall of the ballroom fell away. Plumes of smoke billowed around us, chunks of the ceiling falling down.

Fuck, had someone bombed the mansion? The smell of something burning filled my nostrils, the smell stinging my eyes.

Syn's terror-filled scream covered me in shivers, and in a flash, she was ripped from my grasp. I frantically called out after her, panic tearing me in two.

She vanished behind the wall of grey dust. Everyone was screaming, running madly in every direction, and I no longer heard her. But I threw myself in the direction I saw her vanish, blindly rushing into anyone in my way.

"Syn. Syn!" I bellowed, my heart thumping against my ribcage.

Out of desperation, I never stopped. I had her in my grasp... *Moon Goddess, don't take her from us now. Not again.*

Darkness slid into my thoughts that I'd find her dead or stolen again by her asshole fated mate.

The world spun around me as a real sense of horror collided into me.

I kept running, never stopping, not caring that I tripped over bodies, falling over myself. Nothing would stop me. And the whole time, I kept frantically screaming for her. "SYN!"

Chapter 5

There was smoke everywhere. It clouded the night air, sticking to my lungs, and my skin. My eyes burned as the ashes fell all around me. My lungs were tight, my breath coming out in gasps as I struggled to suck in oxygen. Pain was ricocheting across my body. There was a ringing in my ears and everything seemed to be spinning as I grappled to sit up off the ground.

"River," I tried to gasp, since he had been the one closest to me right before the blast, the first blast. I briefly remembered there being a second one before I'd passed out.

Nothing but a croak came out as I called out his name.

A deep, wracking cough burst out of me, and I collapsed back to the ground as I struggled to get ahold of myself.

After what seemed like hours of torture, my coughing finally stopped and I was able to sit back up and examine my surroundings.

And when my eyes cleared, and the world stopped spinning...a scream got caught in my throat.

The extravagant mansion and the lush jungle was gone.

In its place was scorched ruin.

My mind was having trouble comprehending what I was seeing. I remembered my guys—the guys, appearing out of nowhere and ripping people apart...and then the explosion.

"Hendrix," I tried to scream as panic swarmed in my stomach. "River! Caspian!"

Where were they?

I stumbled to my feet, ash puffing up from the ground as I moved. I was faintly aware of warm liquid dripping down my face–blood, I assumed, based on the fact that a drum seemed to be beating in my brain–but I couldn't find it in myself to care how badly I was hurt.

I had to find them.

I kicked something on the ground that began to roll away from me. It took me a second to realize that it was a charred skull. A scream belted out of me, the sound tearing at my tender throat. When I really paid attention to what was around me, I quickly realized that I could see lumps of burnt carcasses...everywhere. Flames licked at some of the clothes of the still bodies, and I could make out features on some of the faces.

But others I couldn't.

Were some of those bodies...them?

A sharp sob burst from my lips as I scanned the bodies, shuffling towards them hysterically as I searched for anything I recognized. But some of the bodies were too badly burned for me to make anything out.

"Heeelp me," a voice croaked from somewhere nearby, scaring the crap out of me.

I limped a few steps and realized that it was the witch, Astoria. She was lying on the ground, half of her stuck under a large tree trunk that had fallen to the ground, what looked like a letter opener stuck in one eye while her other one stared at the world around her in shock and disbelief that this was her fate. Her arm was charred and bloody. I didn't think there would be any magic that could bring that back.

Her unhurt grey eye met mine, and there was no sign of the hate it had carried before; there was only desperation.

My wolf was demanding that I leave her there, and I did take a step away.

"Ple-ase..." she croaked out, and I froze. I was desperate to search for the guys, but I was pretty sure this would haunt me if I didn't try and help her.

I darted towards the trunk and pushed on it as hard as I could, her gasps of pain heavy in my ears. The tree didn't move. Frowning, I bent down to see if parts of the branches were stuck in the ground or something.

Fuck.

Nothing was stuck in the ground. A branch was stuck in *her*. Going right through her stomach.

"I don't know what to do," I told her softly, and she whimpered, tears falling down her face, creating streaks through the ash that covered her skin.

"Ple-ase," she rasped again. "Ju-st...take it out."

She was dead either way. It was obvious. The least I could do was free her from the tree—I was just hoping it didn't take any entrails out of her.

I pushed again, but the problem was that now that her magic was gone, my pain that had been hidden before was growing. The blast had only made it worse. Every push was agonizing.

Grabbing a rock, I began to saw at the base of the branch since my pushing wasn't going well with it connected. My muscles burned, sweat dripping down my face as I worked. After what seemed like forever, the branch snapped, and I was able to heave the tree away.

"This is going to hurt," I warned, yanking on the branch and pulling it out. The squelching sound when I did wasn't a good sign. You didn't have to be a doctor to know that. Even with how bad it must have hurt, her scream was feeble.

Blood was streaming out of her midsection. I put my hands there, trying to slow the flow, but it just kept going. She moved the hand that wasn't burnt over mine.

She didn't speak. But she didn't need to. Her words were written in her gaze. Any rage I'd felt against her before disappeared as I watched the light fade from her face. In her last moments, she'd been so fucking...relieved. Relieved to say goodbye to what she'd become.

It was awful.

I was shaky when I stood up from her still body, the dizziness in my head getting worse.

My steps were shaky as I continued my search. They had to be here. They were magical, right? That whole almost drowning in the lake thing had to have given them the power to withstand the blast.

It had to.

Palm trees had fallen everywhere from the blast, and I had to carefully make my way across fallen pieces as I frantically searched for them. All the while, my ears rang and my head spun.

The air around me had been eerily quiet—not even the birds were chirping—so when I heard a loud whirring sound, my senses went on red alert.

The sound grew louder and I began to walk towards it, thinking I could hide in the tree line if it was something dangerous.

As I got close to the shore and peered onto the beach, I saw that the sound had been from motor boats. Ten of them. Armed men in uniforms I recognized from the government were pouring out of the boats...guns drawn.

I hid behind the tree, my pulse hammering in my throat. Squeezing my eyes closed, I tried to think of what I should do.

I'd never been given a reason specifically to distrust the government—besides the whole Reject Island thing. They usually left the packs alone and allowed them to rule over themselves, but what would they be doing here?

All of a sudden, voices were right behind me, and I bolted forward, deciding on the fly that I didn't want them to discover me. I needed to find my men. And I didn't think the government was going to be very helpful with that. Despite the power that Hendrix, River, and Caspian held, I didn't think they would be crying if the most powerful warlords in the country were suddenly dead and out of their hair.

"There! Stop!" a voice cried as I took off into the trees. Footsteps thundered after me. With my injuries, I wasn't fast, and a second later I was tackled to the jungle floor, my bones pounding from the impact.

The soldier yanked my arms behind me, and I hissed in pain as my burn scars and the wounds on my back stretched. "Stop struggling. We're here to help," he ordered soothingly, but it didn't do much for me since he was currently on top of me...restraining me.

"Hendrix," I screamed, every cell in my body desperate for him to appear with a roar from behind the trees.

But he didn't come.

The soldier wrenched me to my feet and began to march me towards the shore. I couldn't help but struggle. With a heavy sigh, he picked me up and threw me over his shoulder, ignoring my fists beating into his back and my screams fading into the air.

As soon as we got near the boats, he set me down, and I immediately tried to take off. With an exasperated sigh, he grabbed me by the waist and then used some rope from one of the boats to tie my feet and hands together so I couldn't run.

I sat there on the cool sand, watching as the soldiers went in and out of the lush jungle, pulling bodies to the shore with them. Every new body was a terrifying experience thinking that it could be them.

But it never was.

Finally, once darkness had completely fallen, they all congregated back to the boats and started piling the bodies in. The soldier who'd dragged me to the beach picked me up and set me in one of the boats.

"Wait! Where are we going? My pack isn't here. That can't be all the bodies. "

He looked at me with a mix of exasperation and pity. "The rest of the bodies are just body parts. It would take resources we don't have to bag them all up and try to identify them. This wasn't supposed to be this kind of mission. We heard there were stolen weapons on the island, and we were sent to retrieve them. We weren't expecting this…"

I was stuck on the words "body parts". "You didn't find any survivors?" I whispered in an aching voice.

He pressed a hand to my head that I guessed was supposed to be comforting if not for the fact I was still tied up.

"I'm sorry. There's no one alive." He cocked his head. "Who was your pack?"

Tears flooded my vision until everything around me was distorted and dark. "It doesn't matter now," I whispered as my world once again fell apart.

Chapter 6

Five Months Later

Syn

The wind whipped around me as I headed to my next class, matching the permanent frenzy left in my brain after that fateful night.

The soldiers had taken me to the mainland. I'd sat huddled in the front of the boat, wrapped in a coarse blanket I'd been given, staring into the nothingness as the ocean spray licked at my skin.

They'd taken me to Fervian City. And I'd fallen apart on the shoreline the moment we'd landed, screaming and crying because just hearing the name of the city reminded me of Hendrix. I'd been taken to one of the government shelters for the night, and then a government-sanctioned therapist had arrived the next morning.

"Tell me about your pack," she said sympathetically as I sat in the overstuffed armchair across from her.

"Why does it matter? They're gone," I whispered.

"I've heard rumors that you were taken from your original pack by the Khan pack."

My eyes snapped to hers. She was doing her best to look sympathetic, but I could see the hardness in her gaze. This was just a job to her. She didn't care.

"I wasn't taken. I was sold to them," I murmured, even while I knew it was a little bit of both as I thought about that first meeting with Hendrix in the middle of the night in my room.

"Your alpha in the Hallow Sector was murdered. Did you hear about that?"

I wasn't surprised. He'd been asking for it. Especially with everything his son had ended up being involved in. His biggest mistake had been his desperation to protect Brayden at all costs.

"I didn't," I finally answered, belatedly realizing how long it had taken me to answer.

"You don't have to protect them anymore, you know. They're gone now. They can't hurt you."

I didn't know why my first instinct was to protect them and say they wouldn't hurt me, because obviously, the past showed that they had. "Can you tell me where their compound is? They've stolen a lot of things from a lot of people."

"I don't know," I answered coldly.

Her lips pursed in frustration. "You're suffering from what's called Stockholm Syndrome, Emersyn. I know you feel like they're important to you. But they aren't. They were bad men. The worst kind. The world is better off without them."

I was numb, her words doing nothing to penetrate the sorrow embedded in my skin.

"Emersyn," she snapped, losing patience with me.

"I don't know anything," I responded, staring at the floor.

She stood up and came to sit next to me in the other armchair. "We want to help you. We're the good guys. You've been given another chance in life." She was trying to be charming, but I didn't think there was anything she could say that would actually stand a chance of getting through to me.

When that didn't work, she tried the silent treatment. She just stared at me for what felt like an hour, waiting for me to crack.

What she didn't realize was that I was already cracked. I'd never been whole to begin with, thanks to my father, but with everything that had happened since that point, the cracks had only deepened. There wasn't anything left for her to break.

Someone called out loudly to a friend, and I glanced around the college campus where I ate, breathed, and slept. I guess it was generous of the government to send me to Fervian University instead of Reject Island, all on their dime, but it had been a rough adjustment. I'd been holding out hope that news would come in that they had been found alive. But anytime I asked the government agents that had been assigned to me, the answers were always the same. There were no survivors. I'd finally stopped asking last month. That was progress...right?

At first, Fervian University made me think of Caspian surprising me with the news that I'd gotten into Shifter Falls University, which only made me more depressed. But then it was catching up in school when I only had a sixth-grade education and the random books I'd read as my background. It was feeling out of place and everything somehow reminded me of them. It was getting calls from the therapist every week to see if I'd decided to open up more about my time with the Khan pack.

It had taken me a while to open up and actually talk to people, and I still felt like I was just going through the motions. I didn't have the happy background that most of the people around me did. I'd never been able to laugh as freely, to dream as freely, to live as freely. I felt like I was playing a part. A part where I smiled on command and gave robotic responses to try and fit in with the normal people that surrounded me every day.

I wondered if my whole life would feel that way after everything I'd been through.

"Hey girlie! How are you today?" my friend Kelly asked. Or I guess she was my friend. Could you call someone a friend if they knew nothing about you? She was one of the happy people that I had nothing in common with, but she was genuinely kind, and she'd stuck around the last few months, even when I'd given her very little to work with. She was in half of my classes as well, and she had tons of friends. So it had been nice to have a study group to work with without having to find one myself.

"I finished my assignment last night for Taylor's class," I responded with what I hoped passed for a smile. "So I'm doing much better than I was last night when I hadn't written a word."

"Pff. He has the biggest crush on you. He'd give you an A even if you wrote 'Professor Taylor is an idiot' five hundred times and turned it in."

I shifted uncomfortably and forced out a laugh. "Right."

Professor Taylor did have a crush on me. He was the youngest professor at the school and objectively attractive. His classes were always full of girls, all trying to get his attention. If I was normal, his charming smile might have done something to me.

But every time he flirted with me, or asked me to stay after class so he could talk to me about my assignment...aka what my plans were for the weekend, I didn't feel anything.

Sometimes I wondered if I was suffering from Stockholm Syndrome, because at night I would see them. I would see Hendrix's light blue eyes. I would run my hands through his messy locks. I would feel River's hands stroking my skin. I would hear Caspian's laugh. All night I'd be haunted in my dreams with them.

And when I woke up, I was always alone.

"Syn?"

I glanced at Kelly, realizing that I'd been lost in my thoughts...once again.

"Sorry," I said apologetically. "What were you saying?"

"I was asking if you'd come out with us on Friday."

"Oh, dangit. I have a study group that night," I automatically lied.

"Syn," she chastised. "You always say that."

"I'm so behind everyone."

"Maybe that used to be the case. But you've worked your ass off the last few months. You've more than caught up."

I opened my mouth to give another excuse, but she gently grabbed my elbow.

"Look. I know you haven't told me very much about where you were before this. But it's safe to assume there's a bad relationship in there somewhere. When are you going to allow yourself to start living?" she asked gently, her curly blonde hair blowing in the breeze.

I bit my lip. I did have a bad relationship in my past. The worst. But that wasn't why I felt this way. I honestly wasn't sure why it felt like this. We'd never said "I love you." We'd never even come close. Hendrix had told me he wasn't capable of that. And that last night...what he'd done...

Maybe it was time to push past whatever this was.

Or at least that's what I tried to convince myself.

"Okay," I finally relented, trying to sound excited. Trying being the operative word. "I'm in."

She did a little fist bump in the air, drawing the attention of other students walking past us. "It's going to be amazing."

"Yeah. Amazing," I answered lamely as we continued to walk to class.

///

"What the hell am I doing?" I muttered, straightening the silky black camisole that Kelly had let me borrow, and smoothing back my hair. It felt like a hive of bees had taken up residence in my stomach, and I was a little afraid I was going to throw up the minute I got to the bar.

Come on, Syn. You can be normal for one night, I told myself as I took a deep breath and opened the door to the *Fangs Me Later Bar.* I'm sure the owners thought they were hilarious for coming up with that name, or maybe they didn't care because they made so much money off all the college students that frequented the place. I'd passed by it a million times while walking between the apartment where I'd been set up on the edge of campus, to class, but I'd never been in before.

One foot in and I was already having flashbacks of the bar in the Hallow Sector. It was a different experience walking into a bar to socialize rather than work, that was for sure. The floor was made of rough, wooden planks, and it was littered with peanut shells from the baskets of nuts on most of the dark wood tables. There was a long, smooth bar along the back wall with a mirror bolted on the wall above it with neon shelves hung all across it loaded down with every alcohol under the sun. Above that, there was a glowing neon *Fangs Me Later* sign. The music was a mix of Top 40 hits and old favorites, and the lighting was dim.

Not that I had any experience, but it seemed like the quintessential college bar, or at least what I imagined one would be like.

"Syn," Kelly yelled loudly, cutting through the music and drawing stares, as usual. She was waving at me like a lunatic from one of the booths to the right of me, with three guys and a girl by her side, all staring at me, of course.

I gave her the best smile I was capable of and walked towards the booth, weaving in and out through tables filled with people, narrowly missing being clotheslined by a waitress carrying a tray loaded down with hot wings, fried pickles, and beer.

"I was afraid you were going to chicken out," she screeched as she threw her arms around me. Evidently, she'd already had a few.

"Here I am," I replied lamely.

"I'm so excited to introduce you to Logan. He's so fucking hot. You guys will be the hottest couple ever." I flinched with how loud she was talking because "Logan" could definitely hear every word she was saying. I glanced over her shoulder and the guy who I assumed was him gave me a charming smile and a head nod.

Even with how messed up I was, I could admit that he was cute. Maybe I'd even go so far as to describe him as hot. His hair was a dirty blond color that swept down across his forehead like he was from some kind of cool indie band. He had an eyebrow piercing above his spring-green eyes, and a tattoo sticking out from the collar of his shirt. Add in the leather jacket, and he was definitely yummy.

But I couldn't help but compare him to Hendrix, River, and Caspian...who had been the epitome of male perfection.

He didn't hold a candle to that.

You're not thinking about them tonight, I told myself harshly.

"Logan. Meet Emersyn. Isn't she gorgeous?" Kelly asked, a slight happy slur to her words.

Logan had slid off the bench and had a hand held out for me to shake. There was a beer in front of where he'd been sitting, but his eyes were clear, busy devouring every inch of me.

"Hi there. I've heard so much about you," he greeted smoothly.

Okay. I could work with this. It didn't need to be a burden to hang out with a hot guy for the night.

"Nice to meet you," I murmured, proud that my voice sounded normal.

Kelly introduced me to Gary and Diana, who were obviously together, and to Nate, who was Kelly's date. Next time I was definitely going to ask ahead about what she had in mind when she said "go out." Because this was definitely a triple date.

Logan had me slide into the booth first, and then he joined me, sitting awfully close for a first encounter.

"What do you want to drink?" he asked, flashing super white teeth. Were my teeth that white? Or was he thinking they were yellow as he stared at me? And he was really staring—

"Syn!" Kelly said loudly.

Oh right, he'd asked me what drink I wanted.

"Vodka Bang," I answered quickly, having read the menu before I left my room. "And some fried pickles."

"My kind of girl," he replied with a wink, raising a hand at the waitress who was passing by.

After he ordered, he turned around...and started talking about himself.

Evidently, he was an alpha, but a younger son, so he wasn't going to be inheriting his father's pack.

The fact that I learned that about him in the first five minutes of meeting him was a little weird. But at least he was pleasant to look at.

"So enough about me," he chuckled...like he'd said something funny. "Tell me about Emersyn."

This guy was kind of full of himself. And not in the *I'm the biggest badass in the room* kind of way that Hendrix had been full of himself. Logan was just kind of full...of hot air.

"Not much to tell. I'm from the south. Been going here

for about five weeks—" My voice abruptly cut off when I saw a flash of black curly hair on a hulking man disappear down the hall towards the bathrooms.

Before I knew it, I was pushing at Logan's leg. "I'll be right back," I murmured, once he'd let me out, not glancing back as I strode across the room.

It was just from the back, but the man's form had looked so familiar. I just had to check.

The hall was empty save for two girls giggling by the women's bathroom entrance. "Did you see a huge man with black hair go by a second ago?" I asked, interrupting the conversation they were having about some guy named "Alonso."

One of the girls hiccuped and pointed down the hall. "Some hottie went through that exit," she slurred. "I asked him to bone me." The other girl snorted like "bone me" was the funniest thing she'd ever heard. Honestly, I didn't know that was even a thing people said anymore.

But whatever. I practically ran to the exit door and threw it open, searching frantically around for any sign of Hendrix. I mean—not Hendrix—but whatever guy had looked like him from behind. The hair had been longer, but....

The alleyway was empty except for an employee leaning against the brick way across from the door, smoking a cigarette under a dim security light. He glanced at me, surprised.

"Did anyone just come out here?" I asked, searching the shadows desperately.

"Nope," he answered, popping his "p". "But I wouldn't mind you—"

"Thanks," I answered quickly, slamming the door to the outside and slowly walking up the hall towards the main area of the bar.

Feeling like a fool.

I was just out of the hallway when I ran smack into a

broad chest. Looking up, I saw a guy with similar colored hair to Hendrix.

Most likely the man I'd just been chasing.

"Excuse me," I murmured dejectedly, heading back towards the table and wondering how weird it would be if I just left. I'd thought I was getting better, recovering from whatever this obsession was with them. But that—that was just pathetic.

Logan looked weirdly relieved when I arrived at the table, and Kelly asked loudly where I'd run off too, but everyone resumed talking after the awkward excuse I gave about seeing a girl who was flaking out on a group project.

"Let's start over," Logan suddenly offered as soon as I sat down. I picked up the drink that was waiting for me on the table and took a big gulp as I glanced at him quizzically.

"I know I'm sucking at this date thing, but I've been looking forward to meeting you for weeks. Kelly talks about you all the time, and you're really pretty, and...it's been a while since I've been on a date," he rambled anxiously, kind of looking adorable without the smugness he'd been demonstrating before my fool's errand to run after a stranger.

"That sounds good," I smiled, inwardly yelling at my brain that I should give him a chance.

He held out a hand. "Hi, I'm Logan. Average student, expert chocolate eater, and an all-around awkward guy. What's your name?"

I snorted and shook my head, my smile becoming genuine for the first time tonight.

"Hi, Logan. I'm Emersyn—Syn. I'm also an average student, expert chocolate eater, and an all-around awkward girl. It's nice to meet you."

He grinned and we were able to talk more normally, digging into the food that the waitress set in front of us, and joining in the conversation with the others.

It should have been fun.
It should have been a new beginning.
But all I felt was fucked up.

It was one a.m. when I finally felt like I could tear myself away. I was a little drunk, so I didn't say no when Logan asked if he could walk me home. Waving goodbye to an extremely drunk Kelly, who tried to kiss me on the cheek before she left and instead kissed me on the lips, we set off down the sidewalk, back to the campus apartments just down the street.

There was a slight nip in the air and I could smell the ocean air coming in from the coast.

Neither of us said much as we strolled...I was honestly just trying to walk in a straight line. Finally, we made it to the front of my apartment.

"Can I see you again?" he blurted, reaching out and playing with some of my hair that had fallen from my ponytail.

"Oh," I drawled, honestly surprised he wanted to after experiencing me the whole night. "Sure."

"Awesome," he murmured, before leaning forward.

Fuck. He was going to kiss me.

At the last second, I turned my cheek, not sure why I couldn't let him kiss me, but knowing it at least wasn't happening tonight.

The deepening wrinkle between his brows made it plain to see his disappointment when he pulled away from my skin, but he still asked for my number and said he would call before striding into the night.

I'd made it to my front door and had just opened it when I heard thundering footsteps coming up the stairs towards my landing. Logan appeared.

I frowned. "Hey, everything okay—"

Without warning, he grabbed me and pushed us inside, slamming the door behind him. I was up against the wall, his lips smashed against mine, and his stale cheese tongue invaded my mouth as his hands assaulted my body.

I pushed against him frantically. "Logan, w-hat, the f—"

Suddenly he was ripped away and thrown almost across the room by a furious looking...

Hendrix?

I collapsed against the wall, watching in disbelief as Hendrix snapped Logan's neck with ease and threw him to the floor, not bothering with another glance at him as he stepped over him towards me.

His chest was heaving as we stared at each other.

I was a trembling mess, trying to figure out if I'd finally lost my mind and this was all a figment of my imagination.

Please say it wasn't.

"Hendrix?" I whispered, my hands balled into fists in front of my chest as I devoured the image of him.

He was larger somehow, more bulked up...something I hadn't thought was possible. His hair was longer, his waves touching his shoulders and falling in his face. There was a long scar on his cheek now, which only added to the perfection of the package, and I could see some shiny pink skin peeking out from underneath his collar.

A burn mark.

"Please tell me I'm not dreaming," I gasped.

"I'd never let you leave me, little wolf. Not even death could take you from me." His gravelly, familiar voice washed over my skin, and I was afraid I was going to faint. He lifted an eyebrow at me in challenge, and I launched myself at him, whimpering as I breathed him in.

It was official...something was wrong with my head. This man had bought me, kidnapped me in the middle of the night just because he could, and kept me prisoner on his island.

He'd forced me to orgasm when I'd been furious at him...and yet...

I'd never been happier to see someone in my whole life.

My world the last few months had been trapped in shades of grey. And just seeing him now, it was like it had suddenly exploded into color.

I flushed when I realized he was staring down at me in the same way that I'd been looking up at him.

"You're alive," I whispered, my eyes filling with tears.

"Syn," he murmured, but I'd buried my face in his chest. "Syn," he repeated.

I sniffed and peered up at him. And as soon as I did...

That was it.

His mouth crashed against mine. His tongue licked at my lips desperately until I let him in to tangle with mine. Hendrix groaned, and he slid his hands in my hair, holding me in place while he devoured my lips.

I was lost in his taste, in the feel of him. I was still half-convinced that this wasn't real, that this was another one of my dreams, and any minute now I'd wake up and he'd be gone.

He bit my bottom lip and I cried out against him, waves of lust reverberating through my body.

"I'd almost forgotten how you tasted. So fucking good. Like nirvana," he breathed as his hands trailed down my body, pausing on my breasts as he squeezed and massaged them for a moment before continuing down my body until they were at the bottom edge of my dress.

He pushed the skirt up, his talented fingers quickly sliding under my panties and caressing my folds as I whimpered against him, my cries lost in his mouth.

His fingers began to work inside of me, and I squeezed my eyes shut at the sensation. He worked them in and out of me, and I moved my hips against him as if it was his cock fucking me and not his fingers.

His thumb worked at my clit while he slid another finger into me. I arched against the wall, my lips ripping from his as I panted desperately as he stretched my sopping wet channel.

"Have to taste you, little wolf. I've dreamed about this," Hendrix purred before removing his fingers and sinking to his knees. He draped my left thigh over his shoulder and licked at my slit through my panties, burying his nose in my core and moaning loudly.

It might have been the hottest fucking thing I'd ever experienced. His index finger shifted into a clawed point and he swiped at my silky underwear. As soon as I was bare to him, he began to lick and suck at my folds, going back and forth between my clit and spearing me with his tongue. I gripped at his hair, riding his face like I'd been possessed. His hands reached around me and squeezed my ass, pulling me forward until I was sitting on his face and his tongue could reach even farther into me.

"Hendrix," I moaned breathily, the sound of my voice seeming to reverberate around the room as it combined with the erotic growls he was pressing against my skin. I writhed against him as he ate me. Devoured me. Owned me.

"Please, please, please," I cried out as my insides tightened while he suckled on my clit and his fingers massaged the perfect place inside of me.

I erupted, the pleasure tearing through me until tears were falling down my face from how overwhelming the sensations were. He sucked and licked through my orgasm, sending off tiny shockwaves that kept the pleasure going. Hendrix continued until I was literally screaming and on the verge of having another one.

And then he abruptly pulled away, pulling at his belt and undoing his pants.

"My perfect little wolf," he hummed throatily as he

slipped my leg off his shoulder and stood up. His eyes were blown out, the black completely overtaking the light blue.

Hendrix's hands were all over my body, like he couldn't get enough. His lips were sealed over mine again, and I could taste myself on his tongue. It turned me on even more.

He was licking and biting all over my skin, making sure I could feel him afterwards. My core was throbbing, still desperate for more even after the incredible orgasm he'd already given me.

His forehead rested against mine.

"I have to fuck you, baby," he growled, sounding desperate as his fingers dug into both my thighs. He wrapped them around my waist while he surged into me.

I threw my arms around his shoulders, unable to keep myself from gripping his silky hair as I gasped for breath. Evidently, my body had forgotten how huge he was.

"Tightest perfect pussy," he breathed against my skin as he buried his face in my neck, his tongue licking at a bead of sweat on my skin. I shivered as we held still like that, feeling like a part of my soul had returned to me.

My insides were clenching at his cock, sucking it in as needy hunger spiraled through me. I wanted him closer, as close as I could get him.

"I was dying without you, little wolf," he murmured, and I shivered at the ache in his voice. Hendrix had been so hot and cold on the island. Telling me I was his one moment, and then saying he could never be mine in the next. I wanted to feel like he'd been hurting while away from me just as much as I had.

He pushed further, expanding even more inside of me, although I didn't know how that was possible.

I was biting my bottom lip from the stretch, and he softly rubbed my clit, magically relaxing my muscles so he could slip in all the way.

"Syn," he moaned as he withdrew, and then slammed back

into me, the force of it silencing my breath as I choked out his name.

"Love how you take me, baby." He stroked in and out of me, hitting the entrance to my cervix every time.

"I'm so close already," he breathed as he paused for a moment and brushed his lips against mine. His forehead met mine again as he slowly fucked me, the moment so intimate and offsetting that I felt the inane urge to weep from the joy crashing into me. He licked at my tears, every move fucking me so deep I was more than getting my wish for him to be closer to me. I could feel my wetness slipping down my thighs as his heavy sack hit me with every thrust.

"Baby," he growled, as his strokes grew more intense. He gripped my thighs and slammed me down on his cock until I was crying out with every thrust.

"I'm so close. You need to cum. Show me how much you've missed me. Show me how much you need this."

"I need this," I gasped as the tension built inside once again. I was gripping his hair so hard, it was a miracle he still had any as I moved closer and closer to an explosion.

"I'll kill any creature that dares to touch you again, Syn. You're mine. Mine!" he seethed. And honestly, his possessive words just did it for me. The flutter that had been building turned into an outright hurricane inside of me as I catapulted over the edge into the most intense orgasm I'd ever had. He slammed into me hard, his tongue wrapping around mine as he gasped into my mouth.

"You're fucking choking my cock, baby." He buried his face against my neck again, and his rhythm faltered as he let out the hottest fucking sound I'd ever heard as he spurted inside me, over and over. So much that it joined my wetness seeping down my thighs.

The feel of it sent another orgasm ricocheting through me, and I was full-on weeping by the end.

We just stayed there for a long moment, our breaths combining, the sensations of pleasure still wrapping around my body.

It was official. This had to be real. He was still here. He was still with me.

I wasn't alone anymore.

Hendrix groaned as he withdrew, and I mewed in dismay at how empty I felt.

I realized there were a million questions that needed to be asked, but I really just wanted him to hold me.

Now that he was here, I realized even more how I'd just been holding onto sanity by a thin thread this whole time. Maybe most would have seen this as my chance to start over, but I'd been changed on that island. I didn't know it was possible for me to ever truly live a normal life.

I needed the edge of danger and pain that they gave me.

Speaking of they...

"River! Caspian! Are they alright?" I asked frantically, wanting to slap myself for being so focused on the fucking part of the reunion when I wasn't even sure they were alive.

He gathered me back in his arms and softly stroked my hair. "Shh, little wolf. It's okay. Caspian and River are fine. I just won the toss to come get you while they watched over things at home."

I opened my mouth to finally ask how he'd survived—and where he'd been all this time...and then I saw Logan's body on the floor.

"What are we going to do with the body?" I asked with a frown, knowing I should be feeling something about Hendrix having killed him...maybe some anxiety at least. But I felt nothing other than annoyance...because now we were going to have to get rid of him instead of spending my time doing what I really wanted with Hendrix. Which was getting in bed with him and staying there for the foreseeable future.

"What the fuck were you doing on a date, Syn, is the better question? That boy signed his death warrant the second he sat next to you tonight," Hendrix growled, kicking Logan's body to the side as he strode towards the bathroom.

"You were at the bar," I accused with a frown as he reappeared a second later with a wet washcloth that he used to clean me up. Since I was still just standing there with cum dripping down my legs.

I flushed, wondering how the clean-up process could feel more intimate than the sex part sometimes.

He tossed the washcloth on the kitchen counter to the right of us before tucking himself back in his pants.

"It took us a while to track you down. Now, answer the question. What the fuck were you doing letting someone else touch you?"

"It's been five months," I whispered to him in answer, wanting to cry all over again just thinking of everything that had happened. His gaze softened and he gently stroked my cheek, brushing a soft kiss against my lips before I continued. "But tonight was supposed to be a hangout. Definitely not a date. That was a surprise. And judging by how he tried to rape me at the end, a huge mistake..."

Hendrix swept me up in his arms and strode towards my tiny bedroom, pulling my sheets down before laying me on the bed. He kicked the door shut before he sat next to me and pulled out his phone.

"I need a cleanup," he snapped abruptly into the phone before ending the call and tossing it on the nightstand.

Then he stood up and began to strip, reminding me belatedly that he'd been fully clothed the entire time he'd fucked me against the wall.

Why was that so hot?

"Take your dress off," he ordered and I found myself

obediently slipping it off as I watched inches of his tan skin be revealed.

I frowned when I saw another new scar across his chest, and I softly ran my finger across it. His body trembled at my touch.

"Do you—think they're hideous?" he asked roughly, his finger gesturing to the scar across his face.

"I think they just make you hotter," I admitted truthfully, and his answering grin was almost blinding with how beautiful it was.

He got into the bed and slipped behind me, wrapping his arms around my body until I felt like purring. My wolf was lazily moving around inside of me, completely calm for the first time since everything had happened.

Hendrix reached over me to turn off the lamp and then continued holding me. I heard my front door open outside the bedroom and I jerked.

"It's just the crew to get that asshat's body," he murmured soothingly.

"How do they have my—never mind. Of course you would have it figured out to have your team already have the key to my apartment. Why would I think otherwise?" I said. And he chuckled against me, his tongue licking at the back of my neck. I shivered, trying to decide whether my aching pussy was actually capable of going another round.

It was literally aching from the pounding he'd just given me. And the million orgasms.

I absentmindedly stroked his arm as we laid there in the dark. Fifteen minutes after they'd come in, I heard my front door close. At least I wouldn't be sleeping near a dead body tonight. Although with Hendrix, I'm not sure that would even affect me.

"So, tell me what happened," I finally said, my mind

whirling as I thought about that day on the island. The explosion. Searching for their bodies. The aftermath.

"We were fine after the first blast. But the second one...it trapped us under a section of the house. All three of us." His grip tightened on my body as if he was afraid that I was going to be ripped away from him once again. "We were passed out for who knows how long. All I know was that by the time our team of soldiers got there for backup, the government had already been there, grabbed the bodies, and set up a bomb to get rid of any they missed."

I gasped. "They told me that the bodies were in pieces. That there was nothing they could do."

He laughed roughly, the sound of it sending shivers falling down my spine. "Maybe there were pieces, but there were infinitely more pieces when they blasted the island to smithereens once again. We were on the beach, being loaded into a boat when it went off. He snarled. "I lost five men in that blast, and Caspian's concussion was so bad from being thrown into the side of the boat, that he didn't wake up for another few days."

"But you said he's okay, right?" I asked, fidgeting around in his arms until he loosened his hold enough that I could turn and face him. He stroked my hair again, and I closed my eyes with a sigh.

"He's fine. We're all fine," he murmured once again. "But it took a while to recover enough that we could find you. One of my soldiers had seen them loading you on one of the boats, but by the time they dug us out from under the rubble of the house...and the third blast went off...you were long gone."

"I searched everywhere for you before they came. I screamed out your name. You were probably not that far away from me the whole time," I gasped, the terror of that evening and night spiraling through me.

"We wouldn't have been able to hear you. We were all

knocked out. The only reason that my soldiers could even find us was because I have a system on my watch that monitors my vitals and sends out a signal of my location if they get too low."

I nuzzled my face against his chest, thinking of them trapped under a building, how close I'd really come to never seeing them again.

I wonder if my life would have ever recovered, or if I would have been stuck in that weird state of mourning forever.

"Do you have any idea who set off those blasts?"

"No," he fumed, and I could feel his body trembling under mine at the thought.

"I'm glad you're not dead," I murmured, and he growled approvingly while petting my hair.

"I can tell, little wolf. That's a very good thing."

My body was warming again, and I was ready to throw all cares about aches and pains out the window. I was sure he could make it feel good.

His eyes gleamed knowingly as he stroked down my face. "There's much, much more I want to do to you, but we need to leave tonight."

"Tonight?" I asked. I glanced over my shoulder at the clock. It was almost three a.m.

"Tonight," he confirmed, his gaze tracking me, something unidentifiable in their depths.

I sat up in bed, glancing around my meager little apartment, at the small amount of belongings I'd collected in almost half a year. I thought of the classes I'd been taking...and Kelly. Who I guess had set me up with a rapist.

Really, not much to miss.

"I think I just have a few things I need to throw in a bag," I finally announced. He seemed to relax, and I cocked my head at him, wondering what he was thinking.

I got out of bed and dressed in a pair of yoga pants and a

slouchy tee, before throwing things in a bag. Hendrix lazed about on the bed, his eyes tracking my movements.

I felt like prey.

But then again, I always had kind of felt that way around him.

I stopped suddenly at the end of the bed, trying hard not to just stare at his sculpted, perfect body in admiration, and actually concentrate.

"Will things be different?" I asked haltingly, my hands reaching down and tugging on the end of the blanket awkwardly.

He cocked his head, his gaze ever intense. "Different?"

"Will I be a member of your household...or will I be a prisoner?"

He leaned forward, his ab muscles flexing with the movement.

"You'll be mine," he stated simply, as if that explained everything.

I opened my mouth, not liking his answer, and he leaned forward, grabbing onto my hands.

"Little wolf, I've learned what it's like to lose you. I'm never going to do anything to jeopardize that again. These last few months, not knowing where you were, worrying you could be dead. I ached for you. I thought about you every second. I—" His voice trailed off for a moment, and a hint of vulnerability crossed his features. "I couldn't breathe without you," he finally finished.

That was perhaps the closest to a "love you" that I was going to get from Hendrix. It certainly felt as heavy as those words.

"Okay," I murmured.

He blinked. "Okay?"

"Yeah. Okay," I grinned. He wrinkled his nose at me In

confusion, but brushed a soft kiss against my lips and released my hands.

"Okay then."

I finished packing my things and then I stood staring at my apartment, my rational self saying I was making a huge mistake...but my heart...living on cloud nine.

He'd gotten out of bed by that point and slid his clothes back on. Once I said I was ready, he took my bag and my hand and we left. I paused at the doorway, looking back at the little apartment once more, wondering why it had never felt like home.

"Come on, little wolf," he encouraged softly. "It's time to go home."

There was a limo waiting for us outside the building—of course—and I felt a wave of appreciation as I slid into the creamy leather seats. There hadn't been much luxury living on the government's dime. It had been kind of embarrassing how used to the finer things I'd gotten. You could say this much for an alpha warlord, or at least the Hendrix, River, and Caspian type of alpha warlord...they lived in style.

I sighed as my head lolled back against the cushioned seat and the air conditioning softly blew on my face. Hendrix was staring at me again, as if he couldn't bear to look away. His hand tangled with mine and warmth flooded through my veins at the simple touch.

"You're too far away, little wolf," he growled as he pulled me onto his lap.

"Much more comfortable than the leather seat," I murmured, not really joking at all since my body was craving his touch constantly.

The limo pulled away and my thoughts drifted to River and Caspian.

"What were Caspian and River's injuries?"

"River had a concussion and a broken arm, but that healed quickly once he could shift. Caspian had a concussion...and his leg got hurt."

My insides chilled hearing that. Caspian didn't have a leg to spare...

"His leg?" I asked, heartbreak in my voice.

"He broke it in three places. And it got infected while we were stuck under there since the bone almost pierced through the skin. It was touch and go for a while. But he pulled through. He has a more noticeable limp, but it's better than the alternative." Hendrix's fingers grazed my skin soothingly, helping to push away the tension I was feeling at their injuries.

We were all fine. That...was extremely lucky.

"Tell me about your life the last few months. I want to know everything," he ordered a few minutes later.

I winced, because it wasn't that exciting. But I still told him anyway, and he listened avidly as if I was sharing the most enthralling story on earth.

Thirty minutes later, we were at the pier where the boat was docked that would take us to the island. Hendrix had detailed how security had been tripled around the compound, something I was actually happy about for once.

As we stood on the dock to get on the small yacht, I glanced at the city in the distance. "Hendrix," I started hesitantly.

"Yes, little wolf?"

"What would you have done if I hadn't agreed to come with you?"

His hand wrapped around my neck, his thumb caressing my pulse as he stared at me intently.

"That was never going to be an option," he murmured,

using his other hand to open up his leather jacket to reveal a syringe full of red liquid in the pocket.

Right. He would have drugged me.

Unease and anger coiled in my gut.

But because I was off in the head...I was slightly turned on too.

"You're mine, little wolf. Never forget that again, and we won't have any problems," he said, right before he pulled me in for a dragging, lazy kiss that destroyed all my defenses.

As we pulled away from the shore, I stopped looking behind me.

I was finally going home.

CHAPTER 7

CASPIAN

I paced back and forth on the shore, keeping my eye on the horizon where the boat would be coming from, ignoring the pain still stabbing me in my leg.

A small price to pay for being alive and getting another day with...her.

"You're driving me mad," River complained, but I ignored him. I hadn't missed all his anxious tells that told me how desperate he was to see Syn either. He just had to be the ever stubborn bastard. Even after almost dying.

Finally, I heard it. A boat approaching from the distance. Soldiers all stood at attention, ready for danger. But I wasn't worried. I knew it was her. It was like there was a golden string tethering us together and I could feel her getting closer.

Adrenaline was pulsing through me as the boat became clear, and I could see that it was, in fact, one of ours.

My wolf was dancing around inside me like a pup.

It was ridiculous how...happy I felt just thinking about seeing her again.

I'd known that I was falling for her. But having her ripped

away from us like that...it had made me realize I was far past the point of falling for her. I was desperate for her. Obsessed with her. I needed her to be whole.

I glanced over to see that River was watching the shore just as avidly as I was, his body practically trembling in anticipation and tension. Like a livewire about to explode.

When the boat was just a half-mile out, I sprinted towards the dock, wincing at the limp to my steps that was more pronounced than ever. There was now a large indent in my leg, thanks to the blast, which had magical properties in it preventing complete healing. I'd been trying not to worry about if she'd think I was still attractive or not.

But I guess she had wanted me even with one leg, so what was another deformity?

She came out on the deck, and all worries and thoughts in general disappeared. I hungrily eyed her, taking in every feature. Her hair was longer, and she was thinner than she'd been that night before she'd been taken. There were more shadows in her gaze.

She was the most gorgeous creature I'd ever seen.

I was limping forward without thought, and she hopped off the boat the second it was close enough to the dock, much to Hendrix's displeasure.

We crashed against each other, my arms snapping around her, I'm sure squeezing much too tight. But I couldn't help it. Something inside of me snapped into place. The ache was gone. She was here.

My lips slammed against hers as I pressed her even closer to me, loving the soft moan as it passed from her lips to mine. Had she tasted this good before?

My teeth ached with the urge to bite her and claim her as mine forever. My heart was threatening to beat out of my chest, like a locomotive charging down a hill, out of control.

I realized it then. I was in love with her. That's what this was. This desperate, aching, mourning for something outside of you to be yours. It was love.

She moved away from my lips and I chased her, eliciting a delicious giggle that I wanted to grab onto and put in my pocket.

I didn't recognize myself. I'd been transformed from the teetotaling playboy that got blowjobs by the pool, to an obsessed being who found it hard to breathe when their mate wasn't right next to them.

Mate. I rolled the word around on my tongue, loving how it felt. Would she freak out if I all of a sudden spat out that I loved her and then begged her on bended knee to let me bite her so I could be with her forever?

Not that I would ever be able to let her go again. She'd just have to get used to the forever part. Sneaking a glance at River and Hendrix, they were staring at her with the same rapt fascination and desperation that I was sure was written across my face.

They wouldn't be letting her go anywhere either. The thought comforted me, because if anything, the events of the past few months had shown me that it might take all three of us to keep her with us.

As painful as that was to admit.

A pitiful sound came out of River's mouth, half growl, half whimper. I smirked at him, squeezing her tighter against me...and he snapped.

In half a second, he was behind her, pulling her gently out of my arms and whirling her around to face him. He just stared at her for a long moment...and then he buried his face in her neck.

Syn's eyes were wide, her mouth open in a cute little 'o' at his actions. I didn't blame her; River had been so hot and cold with her that his behavior would have been completely shocking. She hadn't seen him fall apart after we'd woken up in the rubble and realized she was gone.

"Um...hi," she murmured, a small giggle escaping her even as a tear trailed down her beautiful face.

And then we were all giggling...or laughing, I should say. I definitely didn't giggle...and just imagining Hendrix and River giggling had me laughing even harder.

The laughter, of course, was tinged with hysteria, but that was to be expected considering everything we'd been through.

I'd always considered myself a hopeful, positive person. It was the only way I'd survived when I lost my leg...or when my father had drowned me. But the last few months had brought on a darkness that I'd never experienced before. Losing Syn, thinking I might never walk again...I couldn't see the end of the tunnel at points.

She was here, though. I could walk. I was fine. I muttered the reassurances to myself, hoping I would eventually feel better.

"She needs to eat," Hendrix barked after the ridiculous laughter had subsided and River still hadn't let her go.

A territorial growl ripped from River's throat, stunning us all. Syn peered up at him, studying his features with a cocked head, before she stood on her tippy toes and brushed the softest, most tender kiss I'd ever seen on River's lips.

I heard his hitched breath as her lips moved away, and he closed his eyes as if he were savoring the sensations he was experiencing.

I'd never been a particularly jealous person, at least not with my brothers, but I'd experienced flashes of it since Syn had come into our lives.

Right now though, I just felt fucking happy for my brother. That after being such a boarded-up mess for so long, he could experience this kind of happiness. That Syn could make him feel that way.

Hendrix, however, didn't seem to be feeling quite so bright and shiny. He finally stormed over, grabbed Syn from River's hold, and cradled her in his arms as he headed to the estate.

Well, then.

River glared after them, but Hendrix didn't bother looking back at us.

"You'll get plenty of time with her," I murmured to River reassuringly, trying to hold back the strange, blind panic I was experiencing as she got further away from me. Like she was going to disappear again forever if I let her out of my sight.

As I hobbled after them, I wondered just how long I was going to feel like this.

I was staring at her while she ate. I kept telling myself not to be so fucking creepy, but I couldn't help it.

And Syn, of course, noticed. There was a flush to her cheeks and she kept catching us staring every time she lifted a spoon to her mouth. Had she always been so hot while she was eating? I was sporting a woody watching her sip her soup.

That was kind of...weird.

She cleared her throat and had just opened her mouth to say something when a blur of movement burst past me and Syn was almost tackled out of her chair. I reared out of my seat, calming only slightly to see that it was Eliza who had her arms wrapped around Syn.

I ignored the fact that my skin was itching seeing Eliza touch her. Evidently, my line where I shared Syn with others only extended around my brothers.

I was proud of my self-control, because after a minute that felt like an eternity, Hendrix barked, "That's enough."

Eliza jumped back from Syn, terrified.

"Let her eat," he commanded more gently, or at least he tried more gently. The fierce scowl on his face probably wasn't giving off those vibes.

Eliza got the message though, and she scurried out of the room.

"She's my friend," Syn chided, her chin upturned in that stubborn way that I loved.

"We're going to be territorial for a while, love," I explained, pushing the bread bowl towards her since she'd lost far too much weight in our separation. "It's an alpha thing."

Hendrix snorted, and I winked at her. Because we all knew that possessiveness wasn't something that would just go away. But I could pretend, right?

Syn seemed shy as she ate, casting us furtive glances as we continued to watch her.

River grew more sullen and withdrawn as the meal progressed for some reason, and as soon as he finished dessert, he stood up and excused himself from the table, striding out of the room without a glance back.

She watched him, with hurt and confusion marring her gorgeous features. River might need to talk to her about his issues...

Nighttime was falling rapidly, and I knew she was probably tired. But I was desperate for more time with her.

"Want to take a walk?" I asked, soaking in the warmth of her answering smile.

She nodded. "That sounds perfect."

I moved to her chair and held out my arm. She stood up and linked arms with me.

Hendrix stared at us grumpily. "You got your alone time

with her already," I jabbed haughtily. "And I'm sure you used it."

That perked him right up, I'm sure thinking of the hot sex he'd had with her most likely the moment he'd seen her again.

Or at least that's what I would have been doing. I was hard just thinking about it. All of my instincts were telling me to do it now, but I was trying to be a gentleman.

We would see how long that lasted.

Hendrix huffed as he stood up from the chair and sauntered over to where we were standing. He gave me a wink before abruptly pulling Syn away and laying the deepest, wettest, most erotic kiss I'd ever seen on her lips. She moaned, pressing into him.

And I didn't even try to be discreet as I adjusted myself, growing harder just from watching her get so turned on.

I was really debating if our walk needed to end in the bedroom.

I coughed loudly when Hendrix's hand slid up her shirt. Syn pulled away from him and glanced at me sheepishly. I chuckled at the dark blush to her cheeks. What was she going to do when we started taking her at the same time? I didn't know if River was going to be into it, but I could see Hendrix and I playing that game.

Fuck. Okay. We needed to go on that walk.

I wrapped an arm around Syn's waist and led her to the exit, holding a middle finger up above my head so Hendrix could know exactly how I felt about his little show.

Asshole.

We made it outside and Syn threw her head back, inhaling deeply. "I'd forgotten how good it smelled here. The city was so..."

"Noxious. Annoying. Smelly?" I offered, cheering at the laugh she gave me.

"Well, it certainly didn't smell like flowers."

Vulnerability gripped my insides suddenly at the faraway look in her gaze. I knew she was thinking about her time in the city.

"Will you miss it?" I asked tentatively, trying to withstand the urge to grab her, haul her over my shoulder, and lock her in a room somewhere with me so she couldn't ever leave.

She cocked her head, deep in thought as she stared at the waves as we got to the path on the edge of the compound that looked out over the water. "I think something's wrong with me," she finally said. "Because I don't think I will."

"Why do you think something's wrong with you?"

She shot me a look, like it was obvious. But I didn't see anything wrong with her falling for me...and my brothers. I was quite happy about that, in fact.

"You know as well as I do that I didn't exactly come to this place under the most ordinary of circumstances."

"Hmm. I'll have to make a note in my journal that kidnapping isn't considered normal in your eyes."

She shot me a glare, and I winked, loving how her blush extended down her neck and all over her pretty chest.

Don't think about her boobs, Caspian.

"A normal person would hate you, all of you. But I think —" her voice trailed off and she frowned, biting her lip like she was trying to hold her words in.

I slid my hands up her arms and gently turned her towards me, unable to keep my words in, even if she was trying not to say it.

"I love you, Emersyn," I murmured. Her eyes lit up in wonder, and doubt, like she didn't think someone was capable of loving her. "I love every part of you." I leaned forward and kissed a freckle on her cheek. "I love this." I kissed her collarbone. "And this." I slid down to my knees and kissed her stomach. "And this..." I said once more before gently pressing a kiss through her shorts in between her legs.

Her breaths were labored, her gaze tracking my movements as I stood and laid a kiss over her heart. "And I definitely...love this."

A tear slid down her cheek and I kissed it away reverently, feeling like my heart was going to explode with how much fucking emotion I was experiencing.

It reminded me slightly of the Grinch character in that Christmas book; hadn't his heart grown a few sizes?

Mine felt like it had grown at least that much, if not more.

"I—" A slight sob burst out of her chest before she cleared her throat and stood up straighter. "I love you too, Caspian." She pressed against me, her entire body quivering. I wasn't much better. I was struggling with the overflow of emotion.

I'd never said I love you to anyone else. I tried to think if anyone had ever said it to me. Definitely not my brothers— they struggled with emotion just as much as I did. And obviously not my bastard father—may his soul rest in hell.

Had my mother loved me? When I thought of her, there was just a blurry face and a warm feeling.

Nothing like this.

It was like my soul had begun existing outside my body.

"I'm going to kiss you now," I murmured. And she sighed as my arms draped around her and lifted her towards me.

Syn

I was breathless as his lips touched mine. His tongue slid into my mouth sweetly. This wasn't the dominant kiss I was used to from him...but it was just as effective. I was melting as he intertwined with my tongue, a soft flush of arousal floating through me. It was a sweet, slow, dragging kiss that sent shivers cascading across my skin, as if his kiss was actually all over my body...and not just my lips.

I was giddy as he pulled away, a glow emanating from my insides in wonder at what had just occurred.

He loved me.

And more importantly...I loved him.

I hadn't actually thought it was possible, honestly. I'd thought the part of me capable of such a feeling had been killed off. First by my father and the loss of my family...and then by my asshole of a mate.

But here I was, in love...

And not just with him. I pushed that thought away. I definitely wasn't up to admitting that at the moment.

"I'm pretty sure I'm addicted to your lips, love," he murmured as he dragged his against mine once more.

The endearment suddenly had a whole new meaning. "I'm pretty sure I don't mind."

We were both grinning like loons when we finally separated and continued walking along the gold-burnished path. The stars were coming out, faint twinkles of wonder shining in the inky black sky.

"I'd forgotten how beautiful it was here," I whispered, wondering at how everything just seemed...more right now. It was like every possible sensation had burst across my synapses and I'd become truly aware of my surroundings for the first time.

"Did you ever go to the beach in the city?" Caspian asked curiously, his eyes on me instead of the beautiful view spread out before us.

"No," I admitted, frowning as I thought about how lonely I'd been in that city surrounded by hundreds of thousands of people.

I guess I knew that already though, that it didn't matter how many people surrounded you...what was most important was who the people were. I was pretty sure I could be stranded alone with Caspian for the rest of my life, and be ridiculously happy.

Well, Hendrix and River should probably come along too.

"I don't think I care that we started out wrong," I told him haltingly. "I—ached for you, thinking you were gone. Maybe the moon goddess knew the only way for us to get it right, was to get it all wrong first."

Caspian gave me a lazy, sunny smile that made my heartbeat quicken, and then he kissed me again before we continued walking.

As we strolled, he told me stories of how terrible River and Hendrix were as patients, making me laugh at his impressions of them. I noticed he didn't say anything about how he'd been while recovering. And I couldn't help but observe his very pronounced limp. When it grew more noticeable, I suggested we head back, and I didn't miss the flash of relief in his eyes at my offer.

Fuck, I needed to pay attention to that. Knowing him, he'd never tell me if he was in pain. The words burst out of me before I could stop them.

"How badly does it hurt?"

He stiffened, and then I watched as he forced himself to relax. "Here and there," he lied.

I frowned. "Okay...."

"Shit," he cursed under his breath, before pulling me to him once again. "It hurts right now. As you obviously noticed. It's just—hard for me to talk about. I came to peace a long time ago with only having one leg. I guess I never thought about the chance of losing the other. And I came really fucking close on that island." He squeezed his eyes shut and looked away.

"Hey," I whispered, gently grabbing his chin and bringing his face back to me. I was shocked at the vulnerability I saw there.

"I love you. I would love you no matter what. I swear on it." His gaze brightened, like my words had magic in them with the power to vanquish his insecurities for good.

"Just to be safe, I'll try not to lose any more limbs," he joked with a wink.

I rubbed his strong arm and pressed my head against it as we continued our walk home.

Chapter 8

Exhaustion hit me the moment we made it to the house. I realized once more how I'd never really fallen into a deep sleep for all these past months. It's like my body had to stay alert just in case they returned. Now that I was back with them, I had the urge to sleep...for days if I could get away with it.

We arrived at my door, and Caspian opened it with a flourish. It was exactly the same. A breeze blew in from the window, shifting the sheets on the mattress as if we'd walked into a dream.

A lot had happened in this room...but it said quite a bit for my tiredness that I could care less at the moment. I just wanted to be in that bed.

Caspian hovered in the doorway as I walked towards the bed. I glanced back at him over my shoulder. "Are you coming?" I asked casually, not bothering to hold in my yawn.

I didn't miss the spark of relief on his face and how he practically lunged for the bed, throwing off his shirt as he went.

He bounced onto the mattress eagerly, shooting me an impish grin that was ridiculously sexy.

Heat stirred inside of me...but also...I was so fucking tired.

I yawned again and he snorted. "I'm sorry," I apologized. "I'd love to seal our whole 'I love you' thing, and I really can't wait for you to fuck—"

"Make love to you," he corrected, pulling me into his arms and throwing the covers over us. He was like a mother hen, moving me around until he was content with how I was situated. Which was perfectly nestled against him. And then he sighed—blissfully, it sounded like–as he cuddled his chin over my head.

"We can sleep, baby. I'll try not to ravage you in the middle of the night. I probably need all the sleep I can get as well."

I was already drifting off when he murmured, "I love you."

My eyes flew open. I didn't think I was ever going to get used to that. I didn't want to get used to that. I didn't ever want to take for granted the idea of his love. I knew firsthand how hard it was to find. And no matter what I did, I was going to remember that.

"I love you too," I whispered back. "And just for the record, I'm fine with fucking still being on the menu, along with making love."

He groaned, rubbing his hard-on against my ass. I opened my mouth to say something else, but before any words could come out...I was drifting into a deep sleep.

I sat up with a gasp, a nightmare where I was back on that island, screaming for my men, still clawing at my mind. I reached for Caspian, wanting him to hold me so I could reassure myself that the dream wasn't real, but I realized he wasn't there.

Frowning, I looked around the room, leaning over to see if he was inside the bathroom. But he wasn't there.

All of a sudden, he appeared in the doorway and I jumped, my hand over my heart in surprise.

"Casp—" I started, before realizing he was just standing there, staring at my wall. I frowned and slid out of bed. His attention never moved to me even as I walked towards him.

He was sleepwalking.

I bit my lip, wondering what I should do.

River was suddenly in the doorway, making my heart once again leap out of my chest. But he was definitely not sleepwalking, judging by the way his eyes were focused on me.

"He's sleepwalking," I whispered, gesturing to his brother.

"Climb back in bed," he ordered before placing his hand on his brother's back and leading him towards the bed.

"I didn't know he did this." I frowned. I knew River had before. So was this some kind of genetic thing?

"It started after the blast," River murmured, leading Caspian back to the bed. He obeyed without ever coming back to consciousness, his eyes still locked in front of him.

I sat on the bed, biting my lip, unsure of what I should do.

Caspian murmured my name, his eyes finally closing.

I glanced at River who had moved to the foot of the bed. I couldn't read the expressions on his face, they were flipping so fast from one to the other. "Care to join?" I asked, patting the other side of me. He opened his mouth, that same yearning I'd seen on Caspian's face shining through in River's.

But then he shook his head and walked towards the door. "Goodnight, Syn," he whispered in a pain-filled voice as he left the room.

My thoughts were spinning as I settled back into bed, sighing in relief when Caspian's arms wrapped around me and he whispered my name once more.

As tired as I was, it was a bit harder to fall asleep this time.

River's pain echoed in my thoughts for hours, and daylight was breaking by the time I finally went to sleep.

When I woke up hours later, still tired, Caspian was still in bed with me despite the late hour.

"Hi baby," he beamed, his fingers trailing across my cheek...and down my neck...and then—I caught his hand before he could get to his destination.

"How are you feeling?" I asked, concerned.

"What do you mean?" Caspian's forehead was lined with confusion.

"I woke up and you were sleepwalking last night. River had to get you back in bed."

Caspian bit his lip sheepishly. "Ahh, yes. Should have mentioned that."

"River said it started after the blast?"

He shrugged his shoulders. "It's not a big deal. I think it's just from the unknown, and worrying about where you were. I suspect I'll stop now once I can convince my head you're not going to disappear on me."

"Okay," I murmured, getting the hint that like his injuries from the blast...this wasn't something he wanted to talk about.

Caspian brushed a kiss across my forehead and squeezed my hand gently. "I'm going to take a shower and get dressed." His eyebrows lifted up and down like a cartoon villain. "Unless you want to save some water."

I giggled and made a show of licking my lips and dragging my eyes up and down his body. "I'm always up for conservation," I said in what I hoped was a sexy voice.

I'd never really tried to be sexy before. Hopefully I didn't look like an idiot.

Caspian seemed to like it, because his finger was rubbing

his bottom lip and his pupils were blown out. I slowly slid off my shirt, shrieking when he ran at me and hoisted me over his shoulder before trotting towards the shower.

And once inside, with the hot steam floating around us, he indeed made love to me...against the wall.

So maybe there was some fucking involved too.

And I don't think any water was actually saved...

The next week may have been the most blissful week of my life. Whatever "warlord" business they usually conducted, seemed to be on hold as the three of them were around almost constantly. And I wasn't complaining.

We spent days lazing about in bed. Or eating picnics on the beach where they would take turns feeding me. We went for walks. And swam in the pool. I lazed about under the sun while River read to me.

It was just perfect.

Every night Caspian would appear, no matter if Hendrix was in the bed or not. He'd take whatever side was free and snuggle into me like an overgrown puppy. River never joined, but sometimes I would wake up and see him in an armchair near my bed, sitting there with a brooding expression on his face. Maybe it should have been creepy, but it wasn't, not to me. Whatever River was working through, at least I knew he was as desperate to be close to me as I was to be close to him.

Some nights Caspian would sleepwalk again, but I hoped he was right, and eventually his mind would relax enough to know I wasn't going anywhere.

I was happier than I'd ever been, doing my best to ignore the voice that told me my happiness never seemed to last...

CHAPTER 9

When I woke up, my bed was warm. Caspian lay on his side, hugging one of the pillows to his chest, the bed sheet tangled around his legs. Hendrix wasn't with us tonight as he had warlord business he had to finish.

I found myself staring at Caspian. The man was a beautiful and dangerous temptation I couldn't resist. Even when he breathed heavily and snored, I found him gorgeous. It could have something to do with him insisting on sharing my bed when Hendrix wasn't in it so I'd never be alone again.

In fact, all three brothers were more possessive than normal since I returned. It might have annoyed me in the past, but after what Brayden had done to me, and then when I ended up in Fervian City, I welcomed their protection. Around them, I felt safe and loved. And I could tell they missed me terribly. Just as I'd missed them.

With all of that on my mind, and the past refusing to leave me alone, I quietly climbed out of bed and padded across the floorboards on bare feet, needing fresh air.

I glanced behind me at Caspian who took up two-thirds of the bed, his hair messy around his face, and each time I gazed at him, I remembered the trembling expression on his face when Hendrix brought me back to his brothers. How I couldn't tell if I would go crazy or burst out crying at seeing them. Plus, Caspian had always been the kindest of the three brothers to me, the most affectionate too, but no less possessive.

I drew open the balcony doors gently, to not make any sounds, and stepped outside, closing it behind me.

Cool night air swished through my hair, and I moved to the edge of the railing, holding onto it, staring out beyond the front gates to the sea. The full moon reflected off its dark surface, the waves calm and silent. I tried not to think about the last time I spotted River out there and where it got us.

Now, guards stood at their posts.

Silence. It was eerie, and yet I struggled to forget the past or move past the heaviness in my thoughts. I craved peace, and the need for it welled inside me, growing bigger with each passing day.

I listened to the silence for a while, trying to calm my mind, and part of me could still feel the warmth of Caspian's lips on mine before I fell asleep in his arms. Just by the deep echo inside me when I was apart from the brothers, I could tell that I'd let myself feel deeply for them. More than I expected.

Someone's voice drew my attention to the grounds down below. I looked over the railing to a large man, hair so dark it blended into the night, flowing wildly in the breeze. And I knew instantly it was Hendrix.

The sight of him filled me with heat and excitement.

I studied him as he mumbled something to himself, the sound drifting on the breeze as he kept studying the yard around him, then wandering slowly, not seeming to go anywhere specific. But the longer I watched him, the more it became clear he was pacing up and down the front yard.

Guards watched him too, but none approached him.

Was he drunk? He wasn't stumbling, and each step seemed controlled.

How odd to watch him marching as he grumbled to himself. Something about seeing him in this worried state made him appear fragile. That wasn't the Hendrix I knew. So what would cause a man as powerful as him to behave this way?

Unable to help myself, I retreated into the bedroom and hurried to the door across the room. Caspian didn't stir, so I let him sleep while I rushed downstairs. Worry played through my thoughts that something bad was happening and Hendrix hadn't told me.

Of course, my mind ran amok with scenarios of another pack coming to attack us, or the government tracking him down and deciding they were coming for me.

My pulse thundered at the thoughts of being torn from them again. With it came an anger that ignited deep in my gut at the idea of anyone making decisions for me.

I moved with haste down the stairs and across the empty foyer in the dim lights. Silence and shadows followed me, while only Hendrix consumed my thoughts.

In an instant, I hauled open the heavy door and stepped out onto the front marble steps and into the night.

Darkness permeated the yard with no sign of Hendrix. Something in my stomach clenched, and I stepped forward, scanning the place left and right. Empty.

Where did he go? Back inside?

I retreated, shutting the door behind me, and just as I turned, I ran into someone.

A small cry came from the girl I almost bowled over. We

both stumbled on my feet, and only when I really paid attention did I realize I stood in front of Eliza. As the chef's daughter, she'd been one of the few people I befriended here when I first moved into the mansion.

"Syn, I'm so sorry. I never look where I'm going. Are you alright?" The sweet girl, only seventeen, was rambling, which I noticed she did a lot when she was nervous.

"I'm the one who should be sorry for running into you." I glanced around the foyer. "Did you see Hendrix come this way?"

She shook her head while patting down her golden-wheat-colored hair and pushing it behind her ears. She still wore her cream dress but it was without an apron for a change.

"That's so strange," I murmured mostly to myself.

"What's that?" she asked.

"I just saw him from my balcony pacing in the front yard, and when I came down, he was gone. I just don't want something to have happened to him."

Her eyes softened, almost seeming to take pity on me.

"Do you know something?" I asked desperately.

She nodded. "Are you hungry?" she asked suddenly. "I could eat something."

I guessed I could eat something, though I did prefer to just find out what she knew. She took my hand and dragged me behind her as we rushed through a side door and then several more passages. I smiled when we emerged into a grand kitchen with all the latest appliances. It could have been one of my favorite rooms in the place since this was where her mother cooked all the delicious meals I got to eat.

Eliza pulled up a stool on the middle island in the room and patted it for me to sit. "Mother made bread and butter pudding, a recipe handed down to her from our family. It's fucking good. I just need to warm it up for us."

While she busied herself around the kitchen, I hopped up on the seat, admiring for what must have been the millionth time how enormous the kitchen was. At the gas ovens, the stainless steel fridges, the wall of sharp knives hanging off the wall, the boxes of what looked like lettuce that sat in the corner of the room.

"So, are you going to tell me what you know about Hendrix, or is this your excuse to eat more dessert?" I asked teasingly. Every time I bumped into Eliza, we always ended up eating, and I was starting to think that she sometimes used me as her excuse to eat what her mother forbade her. Not that the girl was curvy. Quite the opposite, but I'd say everyone at the mansion remained loyal to the three brothers to a fault and wouldn't indulge in their supplies.

"Give me a sec," she said, and it wasn't long before she sat alongside me on a stool and placed a warmed-up plate of bread pudding in front of us with two forks. "Dig in while it's warm. It's delicious."

The smell alone, sugar and cinnamon, had me salivating, so I took a bite and moaned. If there was such a thing as comfort food to make you forget every worry in the world, it was this. "Oh my goddess, this is amazing," I said and took another bite.

"Told you. And I needed an excuse to get you away from the main foyer where anyone could hear us talking."

I peered over at her smirk, now understanding. Being heard gossiping about Hendrix, the lord of his mansion, would not be in her favor. "So tell me, what do you know?"

"Well, for the past few months since you've been gone, things have been a bit strange in the mansion with the three master alphas."

"Strange like how?"

She shrugged and pushed another forkful of food into her

mouth. Once she swallowed it, she said, "We keep seeing them acting strange at night and in the mornings. You were saying you spotted Hendrix in the front yard. That's been going on for a while now between the brothers. They pace through the mansion randomly in the dark."

"And what's the reason?" I asked, my fork slipping out of my grasp and hitting the marble island counter at hearing her words.

She half laughed and it sounded strained. "Oh, that's not something you'd ask an Alpha. No one in the mansion would dare ask them. Their affairs are not our business. But a few people have tried to approach them when they are pacing, but they don't seem to acknowledge you. It's like they are in their own heads only."

"Like they're sleepwalking," I muttered.

"Everyone watches them. I can promise you no one would allow them to get into danger. But most mornings, if you ask the brothers how they slept, they tell you they were fine or change the topic. It's not our place to push the topic unless they raise it with us first."

What was going on with them? And why did it affect all three of them? "So, Hendrix is safe?"

"Yes. He is being watched and has always returned back to his room."

A sense of relief came over me, even if I still didn't understand their behavior.

"You shouldn't be wandering out of your room, Syn," Eliza said, almost scoldingly, which was strange considering I was a bit older than her. "It's how people get hurt. Just last week, one of the kitchen helpers had a portion of the ceiling fall on her. Luckily, she just had a slight concussion. And weeks before that, a guard stepped into a ditch that wasn't there earlier on the grounds and broke his leg. There's something strange going on in this place."

"To me, that sounds more like the mansion needing repairs." I tried to smile at Eliza, but the hardness of her expression wasn't budging.

"I'm serious. You need to stay safe in your room at night, okay?"

Taking another mouthful and swallowing the food, I replied, "Fine, as long as you take the same advice."

Her hard exterior finally cracked and she laughed lightly. "Oh, you sound just like Mom."

We kept on eating and chatting about lighter things like her starting to do gardening, and how last week a local fisherman caught a great white shark just off the island's shore.

Once we were done, she walked me to the top of the stairs to my room when I turned to her. "Okay, I've got it from here." I couldn't help but hug her. "Thank you."

She blushed when I broke away. "I love having you back home with us. I missed you." Then she spun and darted down the steps.

Home. It was still crazy to me that this was my home now.

Eliza was adorable, and I made a mental note to spend more time with her during the day.

Once I walked back into my room, I shut the door and found Caspian lying on his back with the bed sheets kicked off. He'd insisted on sleeping in the nude, and right now he was having a super erotic dream.

It was obvious by his tented cock, thick and hard. My cheeks burned up at the sight. Caspian was the biggest of the three brothers, in all respects. My nipples pebbled in response seeing him this way, and a whisper of desire flared over my body, igniting something within me.

While I might have first guessed he was laying a trap for me, with the way he was heavily breathing, I doubted that was the case.

It was crazy how much these three men turned me on.

While what I'd just learned about their strange actions at night had me wanting to shake Caspian awake and ask him about it, I also contemplated waking him in a very different way. He had a way of always pulling crazy stunts that I never expected. Maybe it was time he tasted some of his own medicine.

On soft steps, I closed the distance toward the bed and stood at the end, staring down at the powerful alpha. Butterflies burst in my stomach with excitement to know I had an upper hand over him. Was this why these powerful men always loved to take charge? The adrenaline was addictive.

My breath picked up as I got onto the bed, crawling between his spread legs. I kept glancing at his face, half expecting him to jerk upward and scare me, and then my attention would dip to his cock, which sat like a flagpole, waiting for me.

I licked my lips, taking in his enormous size, my mouth watering with the thought of tasting him. Crouching in front of him, I wrapped my fingers around his shaft, surprised by the satisfaction burning through me.

Holding him, I leaned forward and slipped my lips over the tip of his cock. He smelled intoxicating, so masculine that it covered me in delicious tingles.

I kept my eyes on him the entire time, loving how the deeper I slid my mouth over his huge cock, the more his breaths sped up. His snores morphed into growls, his chest arching.

He was magnificent in this state and totally under my control.

I drew him deeper and deeper between my lips, the aggressive part of me wanting to make him explode in my mouth while he still slept. To wake up just as he came and discovered I was his little wet dream.

I wanted more, so I worked him in until his tip touched

the back of my throat. I paused, catching my breath, and attempted to open my throat a bit more, my lips tight around his cock. He was so warm in my mouth, salty and musky.

With my gaze on him, his breaths were quickening, and teasing him was doing something to me too. My pussy was drenched, and as I licked the underside of his shaft, I imagined what it would feel like to have him fuck me. Excitement drove me wild, and I had my ass in the air, my pajama shorts clinging to my wet pussy the more I sucked on him.

Running my tongue over and over along the bottom of his dick, teasing him, I felt him thicken, sensing the long vein on the front swell up. Oh, he was close, and I pushed him deeper, pressing past the tears in my eyes. I wanted to give him something he'd never forget.

It was only when I felt the rocking of his hips, thrusting deeper into my mouth, that I jerked my gaze back to Caspian.

Eyes open, he stared at me with the most incredibly wicked grin. My heart thundered in my chest at being busted.

"Well, hello there, baby," he moaned, gasping for breath.

My entire body trembled, my desire flaring.

Just as I felt him harden, he shifted his hips and pulled out of my mouth, a loud popping sound echoing around the room.

"Hey, I wasn't finished," I teased, sitting back on my heels and wiping my mouth with the back of my hand.

"You're amazing and so fucking beautiful, but do you really think if you wake me up by sucking my cock, I'm not going to go crazy until I fuck you?" He raked his fingers through his hair, his eyes flashing with lust. "Take your clothes off and spread your legs. Show me your perfect pussy and how wet sucking me off made you."

I shouldn't have been shocked, but his dirty mouth always did that to me. I might have made a muffled sound in response, forgetting for a moment that I'd just had the upper hand. With savagery in his gaze and the arousal painted over his expression, I doubted I stood a chance of controlling this beast.

And maybe I secretly didn't want to. I let the dynamic change between us, the pleasure he rose in me aching for release. He hadn't even touched me yet and I felt like I could come.

But I also didn't want to give in too easily, either.

I climbed off the bed, leaving him lying there with the world's biggest boner. "I'm tired now," I teased him. "I think I'll go to sleep."

"Oh, Syn, you've been a very bad girl, haven't you?" He pounced at me. One second he was in the bed, the next he towered over me.

His fingers slid across my shoulder, and he yanked my shirt up and over my head. The cool air teased my hard nipples. I didn't even fight him...I didn't have it in me.

Then he dropped to his knees and tugged down on my shorts. I barely had a chance to step out of them before his long tongue lapped across my drenched pussy.

I shuddered, crying out, my hands clasping on his shoulders. There was no gentleness about the way he ate me; he took what he wanted, tasted me, pulled at my lips. There was always something burning hot about having this dangerous man on his knees in front of me.

Suddenly, he pulled away and got to his feet. "I'm going to fuck you now, sweetheart. But because you misbehaved and didn't show me your pussy when I demanded, we're doing this my way."

I blinked at him, half scared to ask him what he meant by that.

"I love seeing you shocked," he murmured.

"As much as you were when you woke up?"

He laughed, the sound sending a buzz down my spine.

"Do you have any idea what you've awakened?" he purred. "How I'll be dreaming of that moment for months to come now, expecting that sweet little mouth over my cock all the time."

"Is that what you want? For me to take your big dick back into my mouth? To suck you until you spill down my throat?"

"Ok. Fuck. I love when you talk like that."

Before I could respond, he swept an arm around my ass, and he had me up and off my feet. Then we were walking onto the balcony. A slight sense of panic came over me, and he must have sensed my tensing.

"No one will see you from up here," he soothed.

"Yes, they will, because I can see them."

"Then next time show me your sweet pussy," he whispered in my ear before placing me back onto my feet. In one movement, he spun me away from him, my face plastered to the glass doors.

"Now be a good girl for me and spread," he growled. His hand swept between my legs, to where desire dripped down my thighs.

"Tell me how much you want me to fuck you," he demanded in my ear, his tongue swirling around my earlobe while his finger plunged into me.

I moaned, my back arching.

"I want to hear what you want me to do to this naughty little cunt."

"Fuck me," I said defiantly, sticking my ass out toward him. "I'm ready for you." These Alphas, they brought something out of me, a confidence about my body I'd always lacked.

Instead of fearing how they would react to the burns on my back, I was enjoying Caspian fingering me while running his tongue across my shoulder blades where the skin wasn't smooth from the burn marks. He loved every inch of me just the way I was, and that made my heart flutter.

"Are you going to enjoy being punished? Or will this make you misbehave even more?"

"All depends on how good you are," I teased, knowing I would gladly misbehave if it led to this every time..

He pulled out of me and stroked the length of my slick pussy all the way up to my ass crack. Then, in an unexpected move, he slapped my ass hard, the sound resonating through the silent night air.

"I'll obey," I whimpered, amid a moan at how good the slap felt.

"Good girl, because all actions come with consequences."

"Where's the consequences for your actions?" I blurted out as he stepped between my legs, his heavy cock sliding up and down my ass.

"Fucking you to teach you a lesson."

I laughed at him, which only resulted in him roughly handling my hips and pulling them out as he pressed the tip of his cock at my entrance.

"Are you ready to scream for the guards down there, so they know exactly what I'm doing to you?"

I twisted my head to sear him with a fiery glare just as he pushed a bit more into me. "Asshole."

"Your cunt is so fucking wet. I'm having some control issues right now."

"Fuck control," I whimpered. "But I'm not going to be screaming."

His laugh that time in my ear was pure evil, then he pressed into me. Squished against the glass door, the coldness against my breasts felt tantalizing, but nothing compared to his huge cock forcing itself into me.

I moaned louder than I intended as he surged into me without any pause. And suddenly I forgot we were on the balcony, forgot I had intended to tease him, forgot that I wasn't going to scream.

He felt amazing, stretching me to the point of pain, filling me to complete satisfaction. The way Caspian fucked made me feel like I was the center of his universe, every inch of him was attentive to all my needs, to claiming me. He ripped the heart out of my chest with the passion he put behind his fucking. Surrounded by him like this, I felt like the most loved person in the universe.

Powerful hands gripped my hips, and he pounded into me from behind, his balls slapping me each time he drove deep. The stinging ache from his size and force only added to the exhilarating sensation.

I shook, my muscles trembling with how well he wielded my body under his control.

Suddenly, I was lifted off my feet and swung around to gaze out over the yard. Slight panic struck until he set me back down and ran a hand up my spine, pushing me forward as I held onto the railing.

"I need to go deeper," he growled. "I want to sink all the way in, need you to remember my cock inside you."

I groaned as he slapped harder and reached parts of me I thought weren't possible to touch. With the way I was bent over and the vines growing across the railing, I was hidden from any eyes down below, but there was no mistake in what we were doing. Especially with the way Caspian roared like a beast, surging into me savagely.

Bent over, I breathed heavily, the pounding in my ears escalating the faster he went.

"You're so beautiful," he groaned. "Everything about you makes a man go crazy."

I had no ability to speak with my body rocking back and forth, and every inch of me tensing as the build-up climbed through me. It came at me fast too, and I wanted to prolong the sensation, to drown in it.

I shattered, all of my muscles tightening, shuddering. That scream I'd tried so hard to tame burst past my lips. My voice echoed through the night across the yard, across the ocean. And I didn't care.

Capsian growled, and jammed his rock hard cock all the way inside me, unmoving. I could feel his explosion inside me. My walls constricted around him, squeezing him, milking him for every last drop.

I forgot how long we were tangled, gasping in tandem until I caught my breath. Caspian pulled out of me. Instantly, I felt the warm spill of his seed rolling down the inside of my legs.

"Spectacular," he murmured. Then, in a move I hadn't expected, he ran his cock along my inner thighs and pushed it back into me. "But I want my seed to be buried deep inside you, not wasted."

I smiled at his action and twisted my head to gaze at him over my shoulder. "So, what's your suggestion? We stay out here all night like this?"

"While tempting, I have a better idea." Wrapping his strong arms around my middle, he lifted me off my feet and walked us back into the bedroom. Somehow, he managed to maneuver us to lay back on the bed with him still pressed inside me.

Now, we laid on our sides, him behind me, cradling me against his body, his lips on my neck. "Fuck, Syn, you have no idea what you do to me. How much you mean to me. I never want you out of my sight. I want to stay like this...always."

Curled up in his arms, exhaustion crashed over me. The sex had been rough but incredible, and it left me feeling completely consumed. "I like the feel of you inside me," I admitted truthfully. "It's like I'm never alone."

"Baby. You'll never be alone ever again. I'll never let you out of my sight." His soft kiss on my temple melted me. Large hands held me locked to him, and for now, I closed my eyes, wanting to pretend that I'd remain safe like this forever. That I'd finally found someone who adored me, someone who didn't want to hurt me.

CHAPTER 10

I paced back and forth in the hallway outside of Syn's bedroom, waiting for her and Caspian to...finish.

Finally, I couldn't take it anymore. I was too anxious to see her and get our date started. I threw open the door, coming to a screeching halt when I saw that Caspian had Syn on all fours on the bed, and he appeared to be fucking her...ass.

I wanted her ass.

Fuck. That was so fucking hot. Caspian grinned at me and gave me a mock salute, but he made no move to stop, and Syn didn't seem to be in any hurry either. Although I was tempted to try and join in, I walked over to the armchair beside the bed instead and undid my jeans, pulling out my painfully hard shaft, thinking I'd just watch.

Syn's erotic moans filled the room, and just at the sound of them, I was pretty sure I could cum.

The smack of their skin against each other, the sway of her breasts as he pounded into her over and over...

I was dying.

I was about to take matters into my own hands, when

Syn's heavy-lidded gaze focused on me. "I need you," she cried, sounding almost like she was in pain. I quickly jumped out of the chair and stood next to the bed, sliding my hand gently down her spine, admiring her beautiful skin that had grown golden through all her hours spent in the sun.

"I want — to taste you."

Caspian and I exchanged grins. I wasn't about to object to that. I pulled my pants down a little more and got on the bed.

She reached out and grabbed my dick, not bothering with any niceties as she licked at the head before wrapping her fucking incredible lips around it and sucking up the copious amounts of pre-cum I was gushing.

She moaned around my cock, and Caspian cursed, slapping one of her ass cheeks as his other hand gripped her hip tighter.

"None of that, love," he groaned. "I'm not near done with you, and you're going to make me cum if you keep on making those sexy little noises."

Syn's lips...were made for blow jobs. That might've been a weird thing to say, but I'd had a lot of women's mouths wrapped around my dick, and not a single one had looked as painfully erotic as what I saw every time I had the pleasure of receiving one from Syn.

She was teasing me, continuing to lick and suck at the head while the rest of my cock was desperate for her. I grabbed her ponytail and wound it around my hand, pulling on it slightly so her gaze danced back up to mine.

"Sure you want to tease me, sweetheart?" I purred. "I'm sure Caspian would have no problem teasing you right back."

At that remark, Caspian slapped her ass again.

"Fuck, she just gushed. It's dripping down my balls," groaned Caspian, and she gave me a naughty wink before finally sliding her mouth farther down my shaft. Syn wasn't able to reach the bottom at first, but she tipped her head back like the good girl she was and relaxed her throat, and then she was deep throating me like a motherfucking champion.

I couldn't help but take over, slamming my hips a few times roughly into her perfect fucking mouth.

She moaned again but didn't tap my thigh to stop me.

"You feel so fucking perfect, sweetheart. I want this mouth...and your pussy forever."

"Haven't I said that before?" Caspian barked with a laugh, but it was cut off when her orgasm clamped down on him. I could feel her trembling against me.

"Fuck. You're choking my dick," he breathed as his head fell back and he moaned loudly as he came.

I was getting close, but I decided right then I didn't want to finish in her mouth. I missed her pussy too much.

I pulled out of her mouth, enjoying the long draw of her tongue against the underside of my cock as I did so.

Caspian had pulled out of her ass by then, and I wasted no time flipping her around and sliding my dick in her sopping wet channel.

She was fucking perfect.

"Such a dirty girl turned on by getting her ass fucked," Caspian drawled, leaning against the bed and watching us with his hands behind his head.

I forgot all about him as her warm heat clenched around me, her soft sighs echoing my own thoughts that this was where I belonged. I lifted her up and down on my dick, adjusting her hips so I could find just the right angle to make her scream.

I slid my hand to the front of her and started massaging her clit in the way that I knew always made her cum. I knew Caspian had already taken care of her with most likely several orgasms, but she was going to cum again.

"It's too much," she cried out, and I licked at her neck, my teeth aching from the urge to bite down and claim her forever as mine.

But we needed to talk first.

I set out for today to be sweet, but look at what she and Caspian had made me do.

"Cum," I growled, pressing on her clit with a little more pressure.

That was enough to set her off, her walls strangling my shaft as she came, sending me catapulting over the edge. I would've loved to fuck her longer, but she just felt too good.

I moved her up and down my cock a few more times, enjoying the sensations, until it became too much. I slowly slid out of her and laid her back down on the bed, stepping off so I could walk to the bathroom and grab a washcloth to clean her up.

"You get five minutes of rest and then we're going on our date," I called over my shoulder. I laughed when I saw her waving her hand, too worn out to say anything back.

She was probably going to need a nap after what had just happened. It would be a hardship to lay there wrapped around her, but I thought I was up for the job.

"Time to get up," I murmured, stroking her hair as she nuzzled closer into my chest with a soft whimper that had my cock hardening again. Caspian was on her other side, as usual, laying on his back, staring up at the ceiling while he twirled a piece of her hair. I was going to need to talk to him soon. I could see the panic every time he wasn't in the same room as Syn. I felt similarly, but I was afraid that she was going to feel like she needed space soon.

And space was the one thing I was never going to let her have.

Caspian needed to back off, at least a little bit, so we never got to that point.

I softly kissed her lips, thinking again how perfect they looked wrapped around my dick.

Focus, I chided myself.

Glancing out the window, I could see the sun was going to be setting soon, and I wanted to be out on the water as that happened. Just so we could get the full effect while I confessed my feelings for her. I don't know why I was so fucking nervous. It's not like I couldn't tell she loved me. It was in the way she moved, and the way she gazed at me...the way she touched me. The way her eyes tracked me across the room.

She was all in.

I just needed to make sure she knew that *I* was all in.

But even knowing the end result of this conversation, I was still freaking out.

"Come on, little wolf," I cajoled. "I've got your favorite dinner for tonight."

Caspian sighed in mock aggravation as I gave my best attempt to lure her out of bed. And evidently, I'd done well at the mention of steak, because she popped up like a damn Jack-in-the-Box, a gleam of excitement in her eyes.

A girl after my own heart.

She gave Caspian a lingering kiss, and slid out of bed, her movements graceful and sensual without her even trying.

"What should I wear?" she asked as she walked towards the closet we filled a little more each day, it seemed.

"Whatever you want," I answered, ignoring the pulse of longing I felt to follow her into the closet after she disappeared from sight. Caspian sat up, I'm sure to do that, and I gripped his arm.

"Time for you to go," I grinned, and he huffed and stuck his tongue out at me. I could see the debate in his eyes; he was wondering if he could convince Syn that he should come with us, but after I shot him the death glare, he came to his senses and got off the bed.

Just like I had done too many times, he walked into the closet and dragged her into the entrance before leveling her with a kiss she wouldn't soon forget. For some reason, we all felt the need to imprint ourselves on her before she was with the other. I wasn't sure that territorial lust was going to fade with time. It hadn't so far.

Caspian reluctantly left the room and I tried to get a hold of myself while waiting for Syn to emerge from the closet. What felt like forever, but was actually only a few minutes later, Syn came out dressed in a striking white dress that clung to her curves. I loved white on her, probably because it reminded me of the wedding dress she'd be wearing soon. A wedding was a distinctly human thing to do, but something inside me craved it almost as much as marking her with my bite. I liked the sentiment of it, a whole crowd of people seeing that she belonged to me.

But I was getting ahead of myself, once again.

"You look gorgeous, little wolf," I purred, loving how she flushed at my compliment. I needed to remember to give her more of those. When she grabbed her sandals, I grabbed her hand and led her out into the hallway, catching a glimpse of River creeping nearby. It would be nice if he could stop torturing himself and just give in like the rest of us had. A little wave of guilt crashed over me thinking of the fact that I was one of the reasons that River was so messed up. But I pushed it away. This wasn't like that. It was never going to be like that.

A golf cart was waiting for us since I didn't want to waste time walking as the sun was beginning to set. We took off, heading to the dock where one of our smaller yachts floated. Syn stared at it excitedly, yelping when I scooped her into my arms and walked her down the wood planks and up the steps into the boat where our small crew was waiting.

They'd been given strict instructions to make themselves scarce besides serving our meal, and after they'd nodded a welcome to Syn, they quickly disappeared into the ship's interior.

Syn squealed when she saw the elegant table waiting for us, two place settings with elaborate white and gold china, champagne flutes, and delicate silverware. There was an ice bucket next to the table with her favorite champagne.

"This is amazing," she gushed, almost bowling me over with the force of her hug.

My little wolf was easy to impress, evidently. She hadn't even tasted dinner yet.

The boat took off, keeping a steady pace until we were a couple miles from the shore with just the open sky as our landmark. I helped her to her seat after pouring her a glass of champagne, and we sat and watched as the colors lit up the sky and the staff brought out our meal. Crab cakes and grilled shrimp for the appetizer. Medium steak with purple carrots and her favorite mashed potatoes for the entrée. And then, of course, Caramel Brule for dessert topped with blackberries, since Syn had an orgasm every time the cook made it for dessert.

It was crazy how much I enjoyed being around her. We sat there throughout dinner, the silence never awkward, the conversation never boring. Out of anyone I'd ever met in this world, she was the only one who I could spend hours upon hours with without wanting to throw them off the boat, my brothers included.

I found everything about her fascinating, from the way that she moved her hands as she talked, to the sound of her laughter when she thought I'd said something ridiculous. Considering she hadn't had much life experience, she was remarkably learned, and she ate up everything I told her about places I'd traveled around the world. Her eyes teared up, like she was about to cry when I told her about my plans to take her to the Isles.

"That's where those little huts are out on the water, right?" she said excitedly, hope and surprise gleaming in her eyes.

"Yep. Part of the floor is glass-bottomed so that you can watch the fish underneath you even while you're in your room."

She swayed a little in place, and I was a bit afraid she was going to pass out with the news. I chuckled and shook my head.

When dessert was brought out, I had trouble following the conversation thanks to the little sexy noises she was making every time she took a bite. I made a note to ask the cook to make the Brule much bigger next time so I could listen to her even longer.

And then...dinner was over, and I was the one who probably looked like I was going to faint.

It was getting darker, the sun almost completely slipped from sight, and the clouds filled with a pink glow. This was my moment; I just needed to tell her...

"Hendrix, are you all right?" she asked as she came up beside me, where I was clenching the handrails on the side of the boat.

I opened my mouth, thinking I'd just blurt it out, but then I lost my nerve. This wasn't romantic enough. I needed to keep with the plan.

I signaled to one of the staff on the top deck and he nodded. Soon, the sound of Frank Sinatra's crooning voice filled the air.

Maybe some people would've called Frank Sinatra corny, but I couldn't think of music better to set the mood. To me, it screamed romance, and by the way Syn had just melted into my arms, she agreed.

We swayed to the music, her head resting against my chest,

the soft breeze brushing against our skin. I wished there was a way to capture a moment in time, to be able to have it as more than a memory, to be able to actually go back and experience it.

Because if there was ever a time in my life I wanted to capture, it was that moment.

We danced as the sun closed its eyes and the moon made her appearance. We danced as the stars flickered above us and the waves softly rocked the boat.

And finally, I couldn't hold it in. I had to say it.

"Syn," I murmured.

"Hmm?" she answered in a soft, languid voice.

I stopped dancing and lifted her chin so she had no choice but to look at me.

"I love you."

Her eyes were twin flames as she stared at me, her mouth slightly open like I'd said something totally unexpected.

"I love you too," she breathed. Tears gathered in her eyes, sparkling like diamonds, and I wondered when I'd started thinking such ridiculous things.

I leaned down and kissed her. "I know."

She sighed and shook her head in mock exasperation, but I knew she liked it when I was contrary.

"When?" she asked in a small voice, her head back on my chest as we began to sway again.

"When?"

"When did you know?" she clarified.

"Maybe I've always known. Maybe I knew it the moment I saw you in that bar. I just didn't know what it was. I didn't want to admit it to myself."

I thought about that first night, and all the nights since then. I'd been a bastard for most of it. I should consider myself lucky that she loved me, even though I was never going to give her another option. There was no way for the story to end, but with her in love with me, not when I felt like this about her.

"I'm...sorry," I said in a halting voice. She stopped swaying.

"What are you sorry for?"

"That night. I lost my mind. I hurt you."

She finally peered back up at me, and I was relieved to see there was only love in her eyes when there could've been condemnation.

"Don't do it again," she murmured.

I nodded and then we continued to dance under the stars. And I promised myself that I would do my best to keep her love for the rest of my life.

There wasn't any other option.

"We've never talked about it..." She didn't answer, so I continued on. "We've never talked about how you feel about a claiming bite."

She missed a step but then quickly regained her footing.

"You mean, a mate bite?" I couldn't read how she felt about it. Her voice was completely blank, and she wasn't looking at me. Nerves twisted my insides.

This again was one of those... non-negotiable things. She was going to be my mate. I just needed to convince her of that.

"Yes," I finally answered after a pause.

She still didn't say anything, but she was still in my arms. We kept dancing. That was a good sign...right?

"You know, there's a story that they tell. I don't know who *they* are. But someone out there has told it." I bit my lip. "I'd like to believe that it's true."

"What is it?" she asked in that same still, blank voice.

"The story I heard as a little kid, about the moon goddess. In the story, the moon goddess was fated mates with the sun, but in their brief moments together, in those days where they both could be seen in the sky, he rejected her."

She stopped swaying. She was just standing there, listening to me talk.

"The story goes that the stars eventually came to her, and they were able to become her love even though she was fated to another."

Syn's breath hitched as she leaned against me.

"At the end of that story, they always say there was never a love that shone so bright as when the moon finally let the stars love her."

"Do you think that's how our story can end?" she finally asked. "Do you think there's a happily ever after if I let you love me?"

I pulled her tighter into my arms, breathing in the scent of her hair as I buried my face against it.

"I know there's going to be a happily ever after if you let me love you the way I want to, give yourself to me, and let me all the way in," I promised her, feeling perfectly confident I could keep that promise.

"I'd like that," she finally answered.

Her voice was full of confidence, but when she gazed up at me, there was so much hope that it took my breath away.

I could work with hope.

"See you later, Syn," Eliza called out from the back door of the kitchen as her mother yelled for her to hurry up and peel the carrots. She quickly vanished inside, and I smirked to myself.

For the past week, I seemed to have fallen into a comfortable routine which I had absolutely embraced.

My life had never been dull. It had always come at me with the force of a storm, ripping me apart and reminding me that I just didn't fit in anywhere.

Well, until now, that was.

The sun beat down on my shoulders, birds sang from the palm tree branches, and the salty smell of the sea was a constant reminder that I lived on a dream island. Sure, my home was with three dangerous alphas who killed for a living, but I never said anyone was perfect. And definitely not me.

But damn it, I deserved happiness too. I would never wish my old life upon anyone, and now I just hoped the bad shit that seemed to follow me disappeared.

I strolled away from the back door of the mansion, following a small path through the lush jungle of the island.

Greenery everywhere, and the sound of the lapping waves on the shore in the distance kept me company.

It wasn't long into my walk when a faint whistle caught my attention from my left. Past the trees and shrubs, I spotted someone in the distance.

I stepped aside to get a better glimpse at who was deep in the forest, whistling while looking like they were digging something up.

The mansion lay behind me, and up ahead were some of the huts where the locals lived. But for some reason, I couldn't stop watching this man with chestnut brown hair fluttering in the breeze. There was something familiar about him. It was only when he pulled up and wiped his brow with the back of his hand that I caught a glimpse of his face.

River.

He stood at least fifty feet away, but I'd recognize him anywhere. Curiosity burrowed through my chest to work out what he was doing out there all by himself.

Without thinking, I found myself traipsing off the beaten track and into the woods, trampling over the foliage. I side-stepped a huge palm tree and kept my attention on River.

He didn't seem to notice my approach, or at least pretended not to as he kept working.

My chest squeezed as I glanced at the hole he'd dug in the ground.

Wait! Had he just killed someone? The memory of him shooting Joe, the gardener who'd turned out to be a psychopath, flashed vividly in my mind. I'd witnessed the horrific event, and my stomach clenched just thinking about it.

So who had River killed now? Was there another crazy person on the island they had to eliminate? A shiver wormed down my spine as Eliza's warning from the other night came to light.

You shouldn't be wandering out of your room.
It's how people get hurt.

I shook her words from the forefront of my mind since her examples of those injured sounded more like accidents rather than someone intentionally hurting others.

Still moving forward, I was adamant on finding out the truth and not being kept in the dark. River had been acting distant with me ever since I arrived back to the island. I'd like some answers for that as well.

He lifted his head in my direction before I reached him, but I wasn't exactly trying to conceal my approach either.

"Syn," he said promptly, and I felt the sting of displeasure in his voice.

"Am I interrupting you?" I asked lightly. It wasn't like I could accuse him up front of burying his latest victim, but his standoffish welcome had me rearing my shoulders back and wanting to grill him.

He returned to digging the hole, not responding right away. He wore a checkered shirt with sleeves rolled up to his elbows and dirty blue jeans, easily reminding me of a lumberjack or cowboy. Everything screamed handsome, and my mind ran even more with questions on why he was pulling away from me.

Once I stepped closer and onto the patch of open land where he worked, I observed the large round hole, deciding it didn't resemble a grave.

"How about you give me a helping hand?" he asked, gesturing to a potted frangipani tree blossoming with beautiful white flowers sprouting large petals I hadn't noticed a few feet away. Its roots were wrapped up in a plastic bag.

"Oh, you're planting a tree?" I blurted out, which gained me a laugh from him, so I took that as a positive step forward.

"Why? Did you think I was going to bury someone?"

I walked over to him and helped him carry the tree over to

the hole. "It crossed my mind."

River crouched down and, with his switchblade, slashed at the plastic bag, wrestling to remove it from around the tree roots. I jumped in and helped him.

"It's a fair assumption to make, all things considered," he responded, and his laid-back response reminded me why I should be cautious around him. He was unpredictable.

"I'm going to place the tree in the hole, and I need you to hold onto the trunk to ensure it remains upright while I fill the space around it with dirt."

"Okay. I've got this." Down on my knees across from him, I followed his instructions, and once we put the tree into the hole, I sat back on my heels, while he pushed the loose dirt around the roots and began patting down the earth.

He was completely focused on the job, and he didn't once lift his gaze toward me. Part of me wished he'd just look at me with a smile on his lips...

"Why are you out here? Surely there's someone else who can plant trees?" I asked.

"I enjoy getting my hands dirty. Besides, trees don't give me shit or try to kill me if they disagree with what I do." Despite his attempt at being funny, he wasn't exactly smiling.

"I find this therapeutic," he admitted out of the blue, grabbing the watering can and spraying the soil. He began to whistle again, and it was a strange feeling to be with someone, yet feel like you weren't really there with them at all.

"River, is something wrong, you know, between us?" I asked, hating how much my chest clenched.

The bluest eyes raised to meet mine with a tight pinch across the bridge of his nose. "Not at all."

He was back to his calm exterior self, while my own insecurities were going off the charts. I liked River, more than liked him, and having him pretend all was okay when it clearly wasn't, hurt me.

Swallowing the thickness in my throat, I went for it. "You've been distant since I returned." I wanted to be honest and not play games. The feelings I held for him were real. "I just thought you cared for me like I do you, but maybe I was just imagining it." I licked my dry lips nervously, wishing I could desperately retract those last words back into myself.

A beat of silence swept between us, and I felt heat crawling over my cheeks that I'd dared to open up. I started to get up, needing to leave before I did something crazy like start crying.

"I care a lot, maybe too much and that's the problem," he murmured, pausing me in my tracks as I stood several feet from him. He set the watering can back down and turned to me. "I've got work to get back to."

When he started to turn away, my chest ached, and I was drowning in emotions. A breath escaped me as I stepped up behind him.

"River." I reached a hand to his arm, and he paused.

My internal voice urged me to talk to him about this, while my heart worried I'd get rejected. "I'm confused," I finally acknowledged. "Please, don't push me away."

The thumping in my chest quickened when he twisted around to face me with a frown.

"Maybe we can talk later," he suggested in a nonchalant voice, which only irritated me. His eyes narrowed on my pinching lips.

"What do you want me to say? I've been busy," he finally snapped.

"Don't lie to me, River. Have the decency to be honest. Why have you been avoiding me? Did I do something wrong?"

While he didn't respond right away, his widening eyes confirmed I'd struck a chord.

For a long pause, neither of us said a word. But his dismissive words drifted to the surface, and they haunted me while he stared at me blankly.

I was close to just storming away, refusing to push him if he had no intention to make an effort, when he said, "Okay. Come with me." He stuck his hand out, waiting for me to accept it.

Staring from his hand to his eyes, something had shifted behind them. Gone was the hard exterior, and instead, something painful reflected back from his blue gaze.

I gingerly took his hand. His fingers curled around mine, and a buzz of warmth from his touch shot up my arm, filling me with an excited anticipation. My relationship with River had been combustible since we first met, but when we came together, the fireworks exploded. And with the way he gazed at me, the way he'd fucked me, I knew it wasn't just one-sided. It couldn't be.

"I want to show you something," he announced softly, and holding my hand, he walked me through the jungle. We traveled for a long while, mostly climbing upward on the ascending landscape. I played with words in my mind, trying to decide what to say, but I kept doubting myself. I hated feeling this awkward around someone I was so drawn toward. But I knew the reason for it...

I was terrified he'd reject me. Had I fooled myself this whole time to believe he wanted me as much as I did him?

After our hike, we emerged out onto a narrow ledge that overlooked a shore of jagged rocks. The ocean rushed up onto it, spraying water upward, a few sprinkles kissing my face.

"It's spectacular here," I mused with a small smile, staring out at the crystal water that sparkled like a treasure in a chest. The breeze swished through my hair, tugging on my clothes, and I enjoyed its cool embrace.

"I've always struggled with trust," River admitted, which surprised me. I watched him and let him speak. "I grew up believing those who loved you hurt you and that they'd abandon you. Of course, my brain was fucked up as a kid from my father, and living with my brothers has helped me heal a lot. But apparently not enough."

He paused, and I wasn't too sure where he was going with all of this, but I understood feeling like I could never remove all the loneliness from my heart, all the scars people left, all the desperation to escape those things that gnawed on me for years.

"When we first moved to the island, I was going through some heavy stuff. I spent many nights sitting out in this very spot alone, wondering how long before I lost my shit and just threw myself on the jagged rocks. To finally end all the fucked up hell in my head that tortured me constantly."

My heart constricted, and I gasped as I took his hand in mine, lightly squeezing it so he knew I was here for him. "I'm glad you didn't do anything."

He turned to face me, his other hand sliding along my cheek, staring deep into my eyes. "I hadn't felt that way for a long time, Syn, but when we couldn't find you for those few months, I lost myself again. And I ended up back here during the nights. Those dark thoughts rose in my mind," he continued, the corners of his mouth tightening. "I'm not telling you this to gain your pity, but so you understand that you mean the fucking world to me. That I never realized how much I let you crawl into my heart and bond with my wolf until you were out of reach. Not until I thought I would never see you again."

I blinked up at him, tears pooling in my eyes at hearing the heartache in his words. To see the agony he felt at losing me left me shaken as though an avalanche of emotions had just crashed into me.

He leaned in and our lips suddenly crushed together, all the moments we'd spent together playing over my mind, how much I'd missed the way he held me, how he smelled, how he tasted. I wanted it all.

River held onto me, his kiss deep and passionate, his tongue sliding into my mouth, taking ownership. My toes curled and I knew this wasn't just a normal kiss. It was a kiss from someone who cared about me...who might even love me.

His body shook against mine. He'd hurt a lot and still did.

"It's okay to be afraid," I finally whispered against his mouth. "That doesn't mean you should stop living. We all fall apart, and I'm a complete mess most of the time. But maybe we can start from here to put each other back together again."

"You don't understand. I lost my mind without you, Syn. I went to a very dark place," he muttered, still holding me possessively against him.

I grasped onto his shirt, curling my fingers around the fabric so there was no chance of him going anywhere. "I'm not going anywhere."

We stood on the edge of that cliff, the most beautiful scenery surrounding us, but we only had eyes for each other. I let him hold and curl a hand through my hair.

"I'm sorry for being standoffish, but I *was* scared," he confessed, his brow furrowing. "Shit, I'm still scared that one day you'll be gone again. What if we don't find you? What if..." His words faded, and I noticed the glistening in his eyes.

He lifted his head, blinking the tears away.

"It's okay," I said to him, nestling myself close to him. "I'm not going anywhere. But I would rather live a shorter life filled with love, than one where I wake up fearful every day."

The smile stretching over his mouth was captivating. Warmth spread across my chest, and he pulled my mouth to his once more. That time we kissed like lovers, like each breath depended on one another.

My heart gave a jolt at the passion he showered on me. That was when I decided I never wanted to come back up for air from River's kiss. I wanted to feel the soft caress of his lips forever. He could have all my breaths. I was good with that.

I woke up that night with a gasp on my parted lips. River had been on my mind, the softness of his mouth on mine. I turned in bed, reaching a hand toward his side where he'd embraced me until I drifted off to sleep.

His side felt cold under my fingertips, and I looked around the room, finding no signs of him. Only the door to my room was slightly ajar.

"River," I whispered quietly into the night.

The moment I lowered my feet from the bed, instead of the cold floorboards, I stepped on something small and velvety soft.

Looking down, I saw there was a myriad of white flower petals under my feet, along with a path that led around my bed.

So pretty and sweet, it made me smile. Did River do this?

Curiosity had always been my weakness, and right now, I followed the trail of petals out of my room. The hallway had a light on as if on purpose, illuminating the trail left for me.

I lifted my head and gazed at the petals in front of me.

They led to a door I knew went upstairs to the open roof. Eliza had shown it to me last week.

Uncertainty surged through my chest that this might be a trap, yet I also couldn't help but think of River who had been planting a frangipani tree today with these exact flowers on its branches.

That thought alone made me hurry past the door and upstairs. I pushed the door open and stepped out onto a small courtyard that sat toward the rear of the roof, the space surrounded by a framed railing. The scene from here was spectacular, taking in the forest behind the mansion.

Despite the darkness, there was a tiki torch flame flickering in the breeze several feet from me, and that's where I spotted a double recliner seat up near the railing that had the best vantage view.

"Hey gorgeous," River's voice came from my left in the shadows. "I was starting to wonder if I had to come and wake you up." He emerged from the shadows, dressed just in slacks which hung dangerously low on his hips, below the V-shaped curves that always drove me wild.

Sharp angles and valleys of muscles covered his chest and abs, biceps drew my attention, and his smile melted my heart. His hair sat messy around his Adonis face, and my knees felt weak just looking at him.

"What's going on?" I asked, catching my breath.

"I wanted to start making things up to you." He took my hand, our fingers interlacing. It was crazy how within the span of the same day I could feel angry, heartbroken, and smitten... all with the same person.

He brought us around to the outdoor recliner, noting that the table next to us was decorated with glass flutes and a bottle of bubbly, along with a bowl overflowing with individually wrapped chocolates.

"Tonight is what many call a blood moon," River

explained. "With our island being far from the cities, there isn't a lot of light pollution and the skies are crystal clear for a perfect view of the universe."

I didn't waste a moment and raised my head to the sky just as the moon slid out from behind the clouds. I gasped aloud. "It's actually red." Of course, I sounded silly repeating exactly what he'd told me, and he just laughed at me. But I'd only ever seen the moon in its silvery hue.

But this..."Wow. How? It looks like someone has painted it with blood."

River guided me to sit beside him, and we both reclined to stare up. He slid his arm around me, and I pressed myself against him, his skin on fire against me and distracting.

"Blood moons occur about twice a year, and are actually total lunar eclipses."

"Why's it red?" I found myself pressing closer to him, loving the way he smelled so sexy, how he gently caressed my back.

"It's a similar phenomenon that causes colorful sunrises and sunsets, and also what makes the sky look blue. It's more complicated than that, but in its simplest form, it's nature at its most perfect self."

"Sounds a lot more boring when you say it that way," I teased.

River chuckled and brushed a kiss across my temple. "Then let me tell you one of the scarier myths associated with the blood moon."

"Oh? I'm ready then."

"Some say there's another reason for its name. One that comes from the sport of hunting shifters like us. A long time ago, humans believed the red moon was an omen placed on them by their god. So, to ensure he didn't strike them down, they made him an offering twice a month. In other words, sacrifices."

I gasped. "They hunted shifters to sacrifice them?"

"Yes. During those two days a month, no shifters were safe. There was a saying that the darker the moon, the angrier the god, and as such more blood had to be spilled. Now to many, the darker moon is associated with death, while the bright silvery moon is about rebirth to our Moon Goddess and salvation. Many believe this is why wolves howl to the bright silver moon, but on blood moons you'll never hear a wolf howl."

"That's...intense." Huddled against River, I lay on the roof of the mansion, staring up at the red moon, reflecting on his myth and wondering if it was real or not. "Sometimes I think that I've missed out on so much in life, hidden away in a cage like those twirling ballerina jewelry boxes. She only sees the world when someone wants to watch her dance, and not when she longs to come out."

River squeezed my hand, his lips on my brow. "That just means we have a lot more to show you. Speaking of which." He pulled away from me, reaching for something on the small table with the drinks. Then he returned holding a small velvety pouch in his hand.

"I got you something for those times when the past haunts you. This will remind you of how bright your future is. Stick your hand out for me."

"I never get gifts." I told myself to not get sentimental, but my heart was thumping louder in my chest as I offered him my palm raised upward.

He opened the pouch and turned it upside down. From inside, a golden chain tumbled out along with a white opal clasped to the necklace by a small golden claw. A play of colors danced across the stone's surface against the night, but more so, it appeared to be almost projecting a luster from the inside.

"Oh, River. This is really for me?" My mouth had fallen

open, and tears were already racing down my cheeks, my throat thickened.

"You deserve the world to sink to their knees for everything you've been through." He leaned over and tried to kiss me softly, but I practically threw myself on him and kissed him back, peppering his face. "Thank you so much. This means everything."

"Then let's put it on." I loved how much he smiled at seeing my joy.

Giving him the necklace, I sat up and lifted my hair for him to clasp the chain around my neck. The opal felt cold against my chin and it had enough weight to remind me it was always there, nestled just above the valley of my breasts.

"They say opals represent faithfulness and confidence," River whispered in my ear, his arms sliding around my middle and drawing me back against him. "So when you're having a shitty day, hold onto the opal and remember that you are a shining light who is meant for amazing things."

Okay, that time I became a blubbering mess.

"Baby, don't cry. I wanted to make you smile." He had his chin propped over my shoulder, his arms wrapped around me.

"Oh, these are happy tears. I never grew up with anyone saying things like that to me. I never received a gift for my birthday or Christmas. So, what you're seeing is me bursting with joy."

He chuckled softly in my ear just as the sky overhead rumbled with thunder. I shuddered at the unexpected sound and pressed myself tighter against River. Glancing up, the moon slid behind a heavy storm cloud. And in the distance, the streak of lightning danced across the heavens.

"Not a fan of storms?" he asked.

"Thunder makes me jump. It's always made me a bit uncertain."

"Let's see what we can do about that then, shall we," he

whispered against my ear, his breath like fire on my skin. When his tongue stroked across my neck, I came close to falling apart from that simple touch.

I shouldn't melt so easily, but with his massive body against me, and his hands sliding under my top, finding the heat of my stomach, things turned hot very quickly.

He dipped his head, and his mouth was on the curve of my neck, nibbling at my skin while his hands drove my shirt higher. There was no waste in time as he pushed his large hands higher and cupped my breasts, squeezing them. He pinched my nipples, and I let him have his way with me. I needed this desperately.

He growled as he yanked the top completely off me with the aggression I'd expected from him. "Mine," he snarled. "All mine."

"I love the way your touch feels," I murmured between raspy breaths and the scorching heat he awoke in me.

Half-twisting around, I leaned in and our mouths clashed. We kissed like the approaching storm. Deep and fast, our wolves growling for more. The man claimed me aggressively, and my core clenched with the heat drenching between my thighs.

"You are everything, Syn," he purred, then shifted to kneel beside me. There was no pause, only his hands tugging down on my shorts and ripping them off me.

I lay naked in front of him, and I reached over to the tent in his slacks.

But he brushed my hand away, making a tsking sound. "Nope, baby. Tonight you are mine to do with as I please. And you can't touch. I need you to understand how much I adore every inch of you, how much my heart thunders for you. I want you drowning in my love."

I tripped over my own breath. "Love?" Did he just say the four-letter word?

With the evil grin curling the corners of his mouth, he stood up and dropped his pants, standing naked in front of me. Of course, my attention immediately fell on the massive cock that hung heavily between us. Thick and long, the tip glistened with his readiness.

"I'm about to show you how much I love you, Syn." Just as he finished, the skies grumbled once more.

I flinched at how loud it boomed.

I trembled while River lowered his body over me. "Open for me, little one. I want to see it all."

The hungry lust in his eyes intensified, his wolf rumbling in his chest. I buried my hands into his hair, drawing him closer, spreading my legs for him. He moved his mouth to my nipple, pulling it into his mouth, sucking hard, then lightly biting down on it.

I arched against him, the pinching sensation deepening, driving me crazy with need. He moved to the other breast, teasing me just as much. He positioned himself between my legs, his hand under my ass, lifting me to give him easier access.

"I'm going to worship you," he purred as he pressed his cock against my entrance. I gyrated my hips to meet him, to welcome him while his hands slid under my back, me slightly off the recliner.

Then he pushed into me, only an inch, then pulled back out.

I groaned in protest, wrapping myself around this god. "I need you, River," I moaned. Every touch, every kiss covered me in goosebumps.

He grinned at me like he knew something I didn't. He leaned down and licked my breasts, while I tried to hook a leg around his hip to bring him back down to me.

"Is this your new kink? Holding out on me until I pass out?"

He laughed at me and spread my arms away from his

chest, pinning them on either side of me. He hovered over me. "You're mine to do with as I please tonight. And we're going to play a little game."

"Oh, really?" I said lustfully, because to have him keeping me spread open while his cock just teased me at the entrance was just cruel.

The crack of thunder grew louder, closer. I practically jumped in my skin, starting to wonder if we were even safe out here. "Maybe—"

He cut me off with a kiss. "Let me reacquaint you with my cock."

I swallowed hard because he meant every word, already pushing into me without ceremony. I was so excited, my heart beat crazily.

With savagery, he plunged into me, widening me, filling me up completely. He hammered into me, almost to the tune of the thunderous growls overhead.

He kept my hands pinned by my side as he drove into me, and I cried out from how incredible it felt. The guy was hung like a beast, and with each stroke, he ignited a fire between us.

"You're strangling my cock, baby. Keep doing it," he growled.

Then he suddenly pulled out of me, and there was nothing but silence. For a second, my mind struggled to understand what he was doing, especially when the climax building inside me had me humming with arousal.

"River!" I protested, wanting to cry at his teasing.

"What is it, my baby girl?"

"Are you fucking with me?"

"Actually, I'm fucking you to the tune of thunder. I want you crying out for it, not fearing it." His grin was pure evil.

My eyes bulged at his confession. "Are you crazy?" The thought of him constantly pulling out was going to kill me.

I breathed deep, drawing more air into my lungs while I stared at him, trying to work out if he was serious.

"Don't mess with me," I muttered, working to wriggle and free myself. Except, he wasn't releasing me.

"But it's so much fun," he whispered, and I noticed that wickedness in his eyes, the one where I knew a crazy alpha lived inside him.

Crackling thunder snapped overhead. With a grin, River plunged back into me, rutting me madly. His rush was driving me wild, and I wanted to shove him aside, but why the hell did he feel so good inside me?

My heart gave a tremble as he rocked both our bodies with a fierceness, his balls slapping my ass from his aggressiveness. I knew that tomorrow I'd be sore. But I didn't care.

Again, he withdrew, and I groaned loudly that time. "You're going to be the end of me. In fact, maybe get off me."

"Did you notice something?" he asked, releasing my wrists.

"What's that?" It didn't stop me from shuffling backward because two could play this game.

"The storm is getting closer. The gap between the thunder is closer."

"Well, let's see how that works out for you." Hurriedly, I rolled over to get off the seat just as the heavens came to life with a show of spectacular lightning spearing across the sky.

The boom came right on its heels. I scrambled, but large hands grasped my hips and tugged me back. His cock must have been magnetized to my pussy because he slipped right back into me, spreading me.

"River, no more teasing," I threatened.

I cried out with how amazing it felt, as he fucked me doggie style, going deep. I was a walking contradiction because I wanted him inside me, but I also wanted to make him suffer too.

On hands and knees, I stuck my ass high and he plunged into me while his thumb played with my ass, before pushing into me.

My lips curled, a snarl on my lips. "More, please, more," I demanded, rocking my hips back to meet each one of his slaps.

And for the first time, I prayed for more thunder. My pulse boomed in my ears, desire owning me.

"Please don't stop, please. Fuck me harder," I pleaded, just as my climax tore through me. Shuddering, I screamed out as the sky lit up once more and thunder ripped across the island. I didn't care but instead jolted beneath River who pulsed inside me.

I lost myself to the high, feeling nothing but River buried inside me.

"Fuck yes, take all my cum," he growled as he flooded me. My body ached in the most incredible way, my pussy slightly stinging at his roughness, and yet I craved more.

Once I finally came down from my high, I collapsed onto my stomach, and he pulled out of me. Lazily, I rolled onto my back to face him, and he made sure to spread my legs and kneel between them. His gaze dipped to my swollen pussy as he bit down on his lower lip.

"I love watching my cum seep out of your cunt. It's so fucking hot."

I gasped when I tried to find my voice because the things he said to me had me tingling all over again. His thumb was on my clit, rubbing the sensitive nub. I squirmed beneath his touch.

"Baby, keep your legs open. I want to see it all."

"You're crazy, you know, pulling that stunt."

"You're welcome."

My attempt to appear angry failed as a moan slipped past my throat. "What for?"

"I've helped you overcome your fear of thunder."

And only then when another cracking sound filled the night sky did I notice I hadn't flinched.

"But I think just in case you're still scared, I'd better fuck you again," he told me as the first trickle of rain hit my face.

"In the rain?"

A devious expression came over his face. "Yes...fuck yes. I want you dripping, then we're going in the shower."

"God, you're going to kill me," I whispered to him. "You'd better fuck me hard, and don't even think about stopping this time."

He laughed, the sound so addictive, and I knew then that I had finally found my forever home.

"I love you, River," I whispered, holding onto him.

He leaned over me, his lips hovering over mine. "I've loved you from the first moment I laid eyes on you."

I groaned as someone opened the window and light poured into the bedroom.

"Rise and shine, my beauty!" Eliza called out cheerfully.

I groaned again.

"Go away." I opened my eyes and glared at her.

"My mom made a huge breakfast to celebrate Caspian's birthday. Everyone's waiting for you."

I sat up with a start, my heart hammering. My head was spinning, and I tried to remember if I'd drank anything last night. I hadn't even had a sip of wine, but this certainly felt like a terrible hangover.

Wait a minute...Caspian's birthday?

"He never said anything," I said anxiously, dragging myself out of bed. "I haven't gotten anything ready. I haven't gotten him a present!"

Eliza set her hand on my shoulder. "Syn, settle down. Caspian doesn't really celebrate birthdays. We don't ever make a big deal out of it, but my mom at least makes his favorite foods that day."

I put my hands over my face. "I'm a horrible girlfriend," I moaned before grabbing clothes off hangers and undressing.

"Girlfriend, ha? Feels a little bit more serious than that," she teased. I leaned over to put on the skirt, and my head started spinning again.

"Are you all right?"

"Just feeling a bit off this morning." I finished pulling up my skirt. Eliza examined me closely.

"You do look a bit like shit. And I'm pretty sure you weren't feeling well yesterday either," she commented.

I scoffed. "Thanks a lot," I drawled.

"I'll see you out there," she sang, walking towards the door. "And stop freaking out. How were you supposed to know it was Caspian's birthday when no one ever told you?"

I should've asked, I thought to myself. But I guess with the whole kidnapping thing and reuniting, we hadn't exactly gotten to that point.

After I had clothes on—although my appearance was far from respectable based on the fact that my skin looked pale and my eyes were slightly bloodshot—I walked out to the hallway and down into the dining area where Hendrix, River, and Caspian all sat discussing something.

As soon as I walked in, all three of them practically bounded out of their seats to greet me.

I took a step away from them and shook my pointer finger in the air. "Nope. I'm mad at all of you. Why didn't anyone tell me it was Caspian's birthday?" I snapped half-heartedly.

All of them winced with varying degrees of guilt, but it was Caspian who swept me into his arms and walked over to the table carrying me. "I never really had a reason to celebrate before," he murmured, smacking a perfunctory kiss against my lips.

"And why didn't anyone wake me up earlier?" I

complained as some of the staff filed in with an array of delicious breakfast items they set on the table.

Caspian was a big fan of food, and it showed based on this birthday breakfast. There was everything from caramel apple pancakes to chocolate chip waffles to omelettes to eggs Benedict. Really, everything you could possibly want. Caspian moved some eggs Benedict in front of me, knowing it was my favorite. I took one sniff of it, and that was it. I turned my head at the last second, puking all over the chair next to me. The room went silent and then there was a bustle of movement as all three of them crowded around me.

I waved my hands in the air, wanting them to get away from my vomit, which smelled so bad that I was about to throw up again. At that moment, one of the girls came in carrying a loaf of banana bread, and...nope.

I lurched out of my chair and stumbled from the room, barely making it to a hall trashcan before I puked up everything else in my stomach. I sank to my knees in front of it, moaning in agony.

The guys' anxious voices filtered down the hallway as they rushed towards me. "You're sick again? What's going on? What do you need?"

Just then, Eliza's mother strode into the hallway, her hands on her hips. "Why aren't any of you eating?" she scolded before her words faded away. She saw me on the floor, basically hugging the trashcan. She cocked her head. "What's wrong, Syn?"

In answer, I groaned again. And then I leaned forward and wretched. But there was nothing in my stomach, so I was mostly just dry heaving.

Which was almost worse.

She clucked her tongue and pushed the guys out of the way as she moved towards me, squatting down and pulling some of my hair out of my face.

"How long have you been sick for?" she questioned.

"I've been feeling off the last couple of mornings, but today...today, I feel like I'm dying."

"Um... And your symptoms, besides throwing up?"

"Nausea, vomiting, dizziness... And feeling like my period's on the way. Without it actually happening."

The guys were silent as they listened, and although I didn't usually talk about my cycle in front of them, the symptoms were an apt description for how I'd been feeling.

"And when was your last cycle?" she asked.

I opened my mouth to tell her last month, but then I promptly closed it.

Because I hadn't had my period last month.

With everything that was going on, I had just kind of brushed it off, not really even paying attention. I pulled my phone out of my pocket and scrolled through my calendar, looking for the last time I'd marked the start of my cycle.

Holy fuck.

It had been over two months. But I was just stressed, right? She was watching me knowingly, something I didn't appreciate right about now because I was flipping the fuck out.

"What is it? What's going on?" Hendrix snapped, sounding like he was ready to tear the world in half if it would help me.

My stomach was in knots, and it wasn't just from the nausea. It felt like if I said it out loud, then it would be true.

When I thought about it, it was all there. The swollen boobs, the bloating, the morning sickness, I'd even had some weird cravings... peanut butter-covered carrots anyone? And I thought I'd just been gaining weight from actually having regular meals, but what if...

"I think I need a pregnancy test," I blurted out. I squeezed my eyes closed when I said it, in fear of what I would see written on their faces. I mean, surely this was going to freak them out more than anything else. We were definitely not ready for a baby. When it was so silent that I wasn't quite sure they were still standing there, I peeked open one eye to see all of them looking like they'd just had the biggest surprise of their life.

Which, in fairness, was probably true.

It was Caspian who moved first, sinking down to his knees in front of me, his gaze caught on my stomach.

"You think you could be...pregnant?" he gasped, a sort of reverence in his voice.

I could feel the heat in my cheeks, from what I wasn't quite sure. Maybe anxiety?

"I've missed two months worth of periods, and stress has never really affected me like that before. So..."

Hendrix turned and lunged forward, basically screaming at the top of his lungs. "I need a fucking pregnancy test right now," he growled as he stormed down the hallway.

One of the maids, Rosie I think was her name, came bustling from the kitchen, a pregnancy test in her hand. This was becoming a freaking spectacle.

I reached my hand out, trying to ignore the nausea building up, but Hendrix brushed it away. Instead, he leaned over and scooped me into his arms, before hustling down the hallway towards my room. I didn't have any energy, so I just leaned my head against his chest, wondering when I was going to stop feeling like I was going to puke up my insides.

Hendrix sat me down on the marble floor of my bathroom, and I swayed in place.

"Okay, little wolf. I've got you," he soothed, pulling me into his arms once again and walking towards the toilet. He sat me down in front of it and then pulled up my skirt.

"Um, what are you doing?" I asked in horror.

"Just helping you get ready to take the test?" His brows

pinched in confusion, like he couldn't possibly understand why I would think it was weird that he was trying to help me pee.

I shook my head. "Absolutely not. Go over there and wait," I all but shrieked.

"But..."

Just then, River and Caspian appeared in the doorway, anxiously glancing from the pregnancy test in my hand, to me, to the toilet. It was almost comical watching their eyes bounce around like they'd gone crazy.

I stared at the ceiling. "Moon Goddess," I cursed before glaring back at the Three Stooges in front of me. "That's it. Out!"

They all began talking at once, and it felt a little bit like I'd entered an alternate reality where my cool, suave, warlord alpha lovers had suddenly become bumbling idiots.

I leveled them with another look and pointed out the door, and they reluctantly left. Well—River and Caspian left, Hendrix just leaned against the wall and folded his arms, glaring at me in challenge.

I shook my head and sighed, but didn't bother pushing him. Glaring at him defiantly, I pulled down my underwear, shaking my head at the rush of heat in his gaze as he saw my panties slide down my legs.

Seriously, he was such a horn dog.

I ripped open the packaging, staring at the stick like it held my life in its hands. I didn't know what I was feeling at the moment. Unprepared. Terrified. Hopeful...

I pulled off the lid to the stick and awkwardly stuck it between my legs before peeing on the white fiber tip. Hendrix was watching me closely, an inscrutable spark in his eyes.

When I thought I'd done it long enough, I shook it off a little and then pulled it out before snapping the lid quickly back on.

"What do we do now?" asked Hendrix, taking a step towards me.

"Look away," I complained.

Waiting for him to turn his head before I wiped, I took care of things and then hopped off the toilet and washed my hands. Once my clothes were back in place, and I'd brushed my teeth, I finally felt like I'd delayed long enough and I examined the stick I'd set on the counter.

A second later, Hendrix was beside me, staring down at it. "Two lines, what does that mean?" he asked, a thread of panic laced in his voice. He grabbed the instructions and started to read them. His shoulders suddenly sunk. "Two lines. That means you're not preg—"

"Look," I gasped, pointing down where another line was appearing to create a plus sign. I grabbed the sheet of instructions from Hendrix, even though I was pretty sure I knew what that meant. I picked up the stick and examined it next to the instructions...just to make sure.

A second later, the stick and the instructions both clattered to the floor as I dropped them in shock, and I sunk down to the tile with them.

I was pregnant.

There was a...baby in there.

A rush of overwhelming love and protectiveness flushed over my skin, and I braced my hands on top of my stomach, realizing for the first time that the slight swell there was actually a baby.

"I can't believe it," I gasped.

Tears were streaming down my face as I got the courage to peek up at Hendrix. I didn't care if they didn't want a baby or not. Now that this had happened, I suddenly couldn't imagine it any other way.

"I know this wasn't what you all had planned," I began.

"But I can raise the baby alone, if you could just help me get on my feet first—"

"Shut your pretty mouth, little wolf," Hendrix ordered in a choked voice, tipping my chin up to meet his beautiful eyes.

He was...crying. Hendrix was crying.

"I've never been so happy in my entire life," he murmured through his tears, right before both his hands went to my cheeks and his lips were crashing against mine, our tears combining together as they streamed down our faces.

A rush of nausea flashed through me and I gently pushed him away, taking a deep breath to try and combat it.

Caspian and River both burst through the door, coming to a halt when they saw us both lounging on the bathroom floor...in tears.

"Syn? Are those good tears..." River blurted out.

"The best," I sobbed as a fresh wave of them crashed over me.

"You're pregnant?" River's voice was thick with disbelief.

I nodded, and he crashed down on his knees in front of me, his hands both going to my stomach reverently. He gazed up at me. "Thank you," he murmured, his eyes now becoming glassy as well.

"Well, one of you played a hand in this as well," I joked.

He chuckled and shook his head. "I don't even care whose it is. It will still be mine in every way." He took a deep, shuddering breath. "You gave me a family." I didn't point out that he'd still had his brothers before this. Because he was right in a way, we had become a family. The three of them had been a sadistic bunch of merry assholes before I'd come in the picture, with wounds that weren't healing.

And now, here we were.

Once again, I was a mess, but I glanced at Caspian standing there by the door, a blank expression on his face. A knot formed in my stomach. What was he thinking?

"Caspian?" I asked hesitantly.

He shook his head, his hands clenched tight. "I'm just trying to soak it in, so I can remember this moment for the rest of my life," he whispered, his gaze glued to my face. "You've just taken one of my worst days and made it the best."

I cocked my head to the side, wiping at the tears on my face even as Hendrix and River continued to paw at me. "Why is your birthday one of the worst days of your life?"

Caspian's jaw clenched, and he looked away, obviously trying to control his emotions.

"It was the day our mother disappeared," answered Hendrix, and my insides clenched in sadness, thinking of them as three little pups...their mother just gone one day.

No wonder Caspian had never celebrated his birthday since then.

It flashed in my brain then, that moment with Hendrix where we talked about all our bad moments leading to this life we were now building with each other. Maybe it was true. Because every day I didn't think I could get happier, and the next day somehow beat it.

"Can you come over here?" I asked softly. He pushed himself off the wall that he'd been leaning against, and quickly strode over, sinking down on the floor on the free side of me. He held my face in his hands, his palms gently stroking my skin as he searched my gaze. "Sometimes I can't believe that you're real. I'm afraid I'm going to wake up and realize that this was all a dream."

"I'm thinking if you were dreaming, you probably wouldn't be sharing Syn with us," River interjected dryly.

Caspian wiped at a tear that was falling down his cheek with the back of his hand.

"You know, it's not so bad sharing with you assholes. As long as I always get her ass." He winked sexily at me. "Plus, think of the diaper duties that we get to split up, and the late-night feedings," he mused.

Hendrix and River nodded in agreement, almost identical expressions on their faces as they scrunched up their noses, obviously both in deep thought about what lay ahead of us.

"We should move this party into the bedroom. I never thought that one of my brightest moments would come by the toilet," I mused.

Caspian startled and lifted me in his arms. I could get used to the whole not walking thing, and I didn't really have to worry about them not being strong enough to hold me when I got as big as a whale. I was pretty sure shifter arms were good for that sort of thing.

Caspian laid me down on the bed and went to sit on it.

"Wait!" River cried frantically, throwing his hands up in the air.

We all looked at him in alarm. "She's not supposed to lay on her back, I don't think. The book—"

I pursed my lips in question. "What book?"

River resembled a fish as he opened and closed his mouth repeatedly. He was shifting around on his feet, obviously embarrassed about something.

"What book?" Hendrix pushed, crossing his arms in front of him, an amused tilt to his lips.

River ran a hand through his hair sheepishly. "I may have bought a baby book," he mumbled under his breath.

"What was that?" Caspian smirked.

River threw his head back with a loud, exaggerated sigh. "I bought a baby book. Okay? But at least I'm going to be one step ahead of you assholes in knowing what to do to help Syn get our baby here."

Okay...finding out that River had bought a baby book was quite possibly the most adorable thing I'd ever heard.

If I hadn't already been pregnant, my ovaries would be

demanding that I drag him to the bed so he could make it happen.

Caspian cursed under his breath, and then I watched as he pulled out his phone and frantically typed on it.

"What are you doing?" I asked, wondering if he had friends he hadn't talked about that he was giving the news.

"I'm ordering a baby book," he said perfunctorily, as if I should've expected that.

My gaze bounced between the three of them, my heart so full that it might burst if they did one more wonderful thing. Their response to this was more than I could have ever hoped for. They might have been more excited and happy about this than I was, and I wasn't sure how that was even possible.

I burst into tears once more. All three of them stopped what they were doing and came rushing over to me, alarm on their faces.

"Little wolf, what do you need?"

"I'm just so happy," I cried. And then we were all laughing and crying again. And I wondered if we could possibly stay this happy forever.

Hendrix was glaring at the doctor as she walked in, even though she'd been their doctor for years, taking care of all the various injuries they'd gotten in their line of work...including their recovery after the blast.

Right now, he was staring at her as if she was a random stranger off the street who'd offered her medical services.

"And you're qualified for this?" he pressed, for what must've been the millionth time since she walked into the room.

Dr. Clayborn brushed her hair out of her face, taking a deep breath as she obviously tried to control her annoyance.

"Yes, Hendrix. My specialty in residency was gynecology. I just got sidetracked a bit in emergency medicine once I got to my fellowship. Your mate's in good hands."

I noted that none of them made a move to correct her, so I didn't either. Plus, I really liked the sound of that. Mate. And judging by the grins on all of their faces, they liked it too.

She walked out into the hallway and a second later wheeled in a large machine that she pushed next to the table I was laid out on.

I'd already peed in one of her special cups, and I was definitely still pregnant.

So that was a good start.

"Are you ready to see your baby?" the doctor asked with a smile, ignoring the two out-of-control alphas behind her. Fireflies sparked to life in my stomach and I nodded, finding that I'd suddenly lost the ability to speak.

I lifted my shirt and she squeezed some warm goo on my skin before moving it around with a wand-shaped device. She twisted some knobs on the machine, and a second later, the most beautiful sound I'd ever heard came out of the speakers.

A heartbeat.

It echoed around the room and time seemed to stand still. Hendrix, Caspian, and River had stopped growling and grimacing, and they were standing there, dreamy looks in their eyes. I'm sure it was the same look that was in mine.

A hiccupped sob burst out of my mouth when she pressed another knob and a black and white picture came up, with a tiny, squirming gummy bear-shaped creature moving around inside of a kidney bean-shaped space.

My little gummy bear.

"I'd say you're about eleven weeks along already, mama," the doctor cooed, typing some buttons on her computer and then taking some measurements. A moment later, images started printing from the machine and she handed them over to me, eliciting another sob as I softly traced the image of our child.

Caspian was suddenly by my side, and without a word, he just buried his head in my hair, his arms carefully wrapping around me.

River looked like he was about to start crying again.

And Hendrix, he appeared to be freaking out.

The doctor used a wipe to clean off my stomach, and with a few more instructions on foods I should be eating, vitamins to take, and some tips for my constant nausea—I'd thrown up in Hendrix's hair this morning, and I wasn't keen to repeat that—she turned to leave.

Hendrix cleared his throat, looking awkward for the first time since he'd come storming into my life. I raised an eyebrow, wondering what was going on.

"Sex?" he blurted out, stopping the doctor in her tracks.

"Pardon."

"Is sex...good?" he mumbled, his cheeks turning pink.

She chuckled, and I was impressed, because very few people outside this room would dare to laugh at my scary alpha.

"Yes. Sex is good," she answered reassuringly. Her gaze flicked between the three of them, and then back to me, a faint blush now blooming on her cheeks.

"Although maybe..."

"Yes, Doctor?" goaded Caspian, obviously enjoying making her embarrassed after the attitude she'd been giving them.

"Caspian," I chided, but he just shot me a sexy wink.

"Maybe the group activities, if there are any," she rushed out, "could be relaxed a bit."

"Okay," I squeaked, thoroughly embarrassed, especially thinking of how I'd been spit-roasted between Caspian and Hendrix just this morning.

"Okay," the doctor repeated, in the same embarrassed tone that I'd just used. Then she pushed her machine towards the door and left the room as quickly as she could.

The second she was out of the room, their gazes were back on the set of pictures in my hand. They crowded around me, staring at them in awe.

"Our little bean," cooed River. I shook my head and he raised an eyebrow at me questioningly.

"Our little gummy bear," I corrected, and Caspian chuckled.

"Okay then, our little gummy bear," he repeated, softly rubbing my stomach, so much love in his gaze that I was about to cry...again.

1 Month Later

"Ready to go, little wolf?" Hendrix asked, looking sexy as he leaned against the doorframe while I finished packing my bag.

It was our one-year adventure. One year from the time he'd first seen me in that bar. And it said a lot for how far we'd come that this was something I was willing to...celebrate. I was sure that most kidnapped women did not have such a positive attitude about their capture date.

But I couldn't deny it. I was happy. Blissfully so. One of the worst moments in my life had somehow turned into one of the best.

So because that date was now something I deemed celebratory, we were going out on the yacht and spending the night, just the two of us.

Hendrix babied me all the way to the boat, barely letting me walk at all...a fact that was annoying and endearing all at once. They'd been doing that. About everything. I think I hadn't lifted anything heavier than a washcloth since we'd found out a baby was coming.

The sex had still been good...but they'd definitely taken the doctor's words about relaxing seriously.

Tonight, I was determined to shake things up.

After an amazing dinner in the sunset, reminiscent of the evening he'd first confessed his love, I made my move.

The staff had been instructed to retire early, and not leave the lower deck until morning. So while Hendrix's back was turned as he fiddled with the speaker system, I slowly slipped off my clothes, until I was standing completely naked right behind him.

"What are you in the mood—" His voice cut off when he saw me, his eyes widening, lust already building.

Exactly what I was going for.

"Fancy a swim?" I teased, stepping backwards toward the ladder that led to the water off the yacht's side.

He bit his lip. He wanted to, desperately by the looks of it, but I could also see he was warring with himself about it.

I trailed a finger around each of my nipples before sliding it into my mouth and then down, down...

"Okay," he said roughly, moving towards me with fire in his eyes as he stripped off his shirt to reveal the perfect planes of his chest.

Fuck he was hot.

"But no jumping."

"Yes, Daddy," I quipped, sticking out my tongue.

"You're in trouble now," he growled, continuing to prowl towards me.

I quickly scrambled down the ladder into the balmy water, thinking belatedly that the ship's shark deterrent system better work.

Probably should have thought of that before.

Somehow I felt safer the second he was in the water with

me, all thoughts of scary ocean creatures disappearing as he slid his body against mine, allowing me to feel every inch of his hard cock.

I shivered at the sensation. "Are you feeling neglected, baby," he murmured as his fingers slipped through my lips, separating them as he massaged my clit.

"So neglected," I moaned, my breathing escalating as he softly kissed me. I wrapped my legs around him as his cock replaced his hand between my legs. He teased me as we made out, his slick dick sliding between my folds, but never going where I wanted it.

"Please," I cried out, and he finally pushed inside.

"Such a perfect, tight pussy," he growled as he pulled out, and then slammed back in again. His pace was a little slowed by the water, but it was no less effective in driving me crazy.

His mouth lowered to my nipple as he moved, sucking and nipping at the sensitive flesh until I was helplessly crying and moaning. My breasts had become crazy sensitive since becoming pregnant, so this was giving me sensations almost as good as his dick. His teeth, tongue, and lips continued to work on my nipples, going back and forth between each one until I was clamping down on his cock, an orgasm ripping through me. The sound that came out of my mouth was akin to a desperate howl, but he seemed to think it was sexy because he kept going.

"Come on, sweetheart. Give me another one. This was what you wanted, right?" he murmured in a gravelly voice as he moved his attention back to my lips.

I'd lost the ability to speak. Apparently, all I could do was moan and shriek. His tongue dove in my mouth, fucking me in the same rhythm that he was with his cock.

"You want my cum, little wolf. Choke my cock one more time and I'll give it to you."

Hendrix and dirty talk was the perfect combination

because I exploded with a burst of heat that lit up my insides right as his dick jerked inside of me and he spilled into my core.

We breathed together under the stars, me wrapped around him as we floated there.

"Happy Anniversary, Hendrix," I murmured, pressing my forehead against his.

"Happy Anniversary, little wolf," he whispered back.

I woke up with a start, a sharp metallic smell burning in my nostrils.

Hendrix was gone.

Something was wrong. I could feel it. I slid out of bed, checking in the bathroom to make sure he wasn't there, but it was empty. I grabbed his shirt off the floor and pulled it over me before moving out of the bedroom and into the hallway.

Everything was perfectly quiet, but I could still feel the strange darkness in the air. I wandered up the stairs, to the lower deck, but I didn't see him anywhere.

And then I heard a splash.

I darted over to the railing and screamed when I saw Hendrix sinking beneath the midnight blue waves. Without a thought, I rushed over to the opening and jumped into the water, swimming towards him the best that I could in the water. I dove down where he'd disappeared, a burst of bubbles bleating from my mouth as I screamed in horror at how far he'd sunk already.

I propelled down, grabbing onto his hand that was floating above his head. Fuck, he was so heavy.

I called on my wolf who was growling and snarling desperately inside of me, begging her for help. I pulled and pulled, but even with my extra shifter strength, I wasn't making progress.

He was just too big.

My oxygen was gone, and a sob burst from my lips, echoing in the water. Because...what could I do? I couldn't let go.

But our little gummy bear.

I tried to slap his face, but he wasn't responding.

When I'd just thought all was lost, his eyes suddenly snapped open. It took him a second to realize what was happening...which was when I started to lose consciousness, but then he grabbed me around the waist with one arm and we were bursting towards the surface.

We broke into the cool night air, both of us taking deep gulps of oxygen as we clung to each other.

"Hendrix," I cried, when I could finally speak. My whole body was trembling, realizing how close to death we'd both just come. He pulled us up the ladder and gently laid me on the deck before laying down next to me.

"What happened? You weren't waking up. That wasn't normal sleepwalking." Tears were streaming down my face as adrenaline rocked through me.

"I—don't know," he stammered. "Something's wrong. It's been wrong. I—" His face suddenly lit up with horror. "Did you jump into the water to save me?"

"Of course I did—"

"Get this fucking boat back to shore," he was suddenly screaming. He kept yelling until the captain was stumbling up from his quarters, half asleep. He tried to ask something but Hendrix cut him off, ordering him to get the boat moving.

"Hendrix, what—"

"The baby. You jumped into the water," he growled desperately.

"I'm fine," I tried to soothe him.

Except, suddenly, I smelled that dark metallic scent again, and a sharp pain ripped through my stomach. I felt something wet and warm dripping down my thighs. Shaking, I glanced down, hoping it was just water, but knowing it wasn't.

"Hendrix," I cried. He scooped me into his arms, his body shaking as he sat in a chair and rocked me back and forth.

"It's going to be okay. It has to be okay. It has to," he repeated over and over again all the way back to shore.

"I'm sorry. There's nothing I can do," the doctor said in a choked voice after she finished her exam. "Your body is rejecting the baby. I've given you every medicine that I know of. It's just—these things happen sometimes. I'm so sorry."

The doctor had been working on me for three days now. The blood would come and go, but just when we thought it was gone, there would be more.

"It wasn't from her jumping in the water?" Hendrix asked in a tense, devastated voice, for what must have been the millionth time.

"No," she said reassuringly. "It's just a random coincidence that it happened so close together. I don't know why this is happening, but it certainly wasn't caused by that."

There was a ringing in my ears, and I felt like I was back underwater. Everything was distorted around me, and it was hard to breathe. Like the air had grown thick like soup around me.

An oxygen mask was forced on my face, and I sucked in the air as sobs ripped from my chest. I laid there, gasping for air, until I felt a warm body settle in next to me, strong arms wrapping around my waist.

Caspian.

He held me as I cried, and Hendrix and River gathered around me. The doctor had left who knows how long ago. But I couldn't move. I was stuck in this place, this terrible place where all I could feel was grief and pain.

"The lake," said River suddenly.

"What?" Caspian asked, lifting his head from the bed.

"We need to take her to the lake." His eyes were wild, out of control. "It saved us then, it could save the baby now."

"The lake?" I asked, confused a moment before remembering the guys' so-called "origin" story of how they became who they were now.

I tried to sit up, gasping when another pang rocked through my stomach.

"Look at what it did to us," growled Hendrix, grabbing at his hair in frustration.

"Better a monster than gone," argued River.

My mind was whirling. If there was any chance...I would do anything to save my baby. Anything.

"Please. Take me to the lake," I begged. "We have to try." My voice was hysterical, strange...desperate.

Hendrix's lips were pursed, a tic in his cheek. He was obviously torn.

"Please," I pleaded again.

"Fuck," he muttered. "I'll call for the boat—the speedboat. Make sure she walks as little as possible." He strode out of the room, his shoulders hunched and tension laced through his form.

The guys had been almost silent as we raced through the waves. At the last minute, right before I'd stepped onto the speedboat, Hendrix had freaked out that the bumps would be too much for my condition. So he'd had the staff retrieve one of the bigger boats.

Not the yacht from that fateful night, thankfully. I thought it would be a long while before I could get back on it...if ever.

We'd been on the waves for several hours, going as fast as the boat could without the rocking getting too intense. As the miles passed, all three of them became more and more somber. Hendrix was managing his tension by asking me every five seconds if I was all right. River was standing at the guard rail, his hands clenched around the metal, his features tight. And Caspian, he hadn't stopped moving, walking around the boat over and over again without speaking, ratcheting up my anxiety.

"Do you remember very much about the lake?" I finally asked hesitantly, wanting to prepare myself for what was ahead. I was kind of picturing this green glowing, scary-looking water with magical properties. But that probably wasn't right.

He shrugged his shoulders, not liking the subject matter obviously. "It was near our childhood home. I'm sure the mansion we grew up in is still there...falling apart. There was no one on the island except for us and the servants. We had crops on the property, and whatever we couldn't grow ourselves, we had shipped in. My father didn't let us leave the property very often. His paranoia was too much for that."

His thumb was softly stroking my skin as he stared out at the water.

"I remember that day as if it was yesterday. I remember him calling me a 'demon,' how he broke my nose before he drugged us all. I remember being dragged out into the cold water and sinking into the blackness. I remember when I began to die."

His body shivered and I shivered right along with him, thinking of my father the night of the fire. If there was a hell, I was certain that they were both down there.

"I don't remember anything standing out about the lake. We didn't talk to enough people to know if there were any stories about it. I just remember feeling warm, fire licking at my insides, and then, all of a sudden, I wasn't dying anymore."

I rubbed my bump softly. "You don't remember thinking anything at the time? I'm just wondering if there were like magic words or something that triggered it."

Hendrix shook his head. "There were just three dying boys, thinking it was the end."

Land rose up sharply in the distance then, and Caspian stopped his pacing, going eerily still as he watched it grow larger.

Its beauty grew the closer we got. It was a large island, filled with emerald valleys, sharp mountain spires, and jagged cliffs aged by time.

"What's the island called?" I asked, marveling that they'd grown up in that place without anyone around.

"When we lived there it was called *Isla de Cascada*. We've called it *Isla de la Perdicion* ever since that day."

"Hmm," I mused, cringing when my stomach cramped again, and I leaned over, gasping in pain.

"Syn," Hendrix barked, panicked.

I took a few deep breaths and straightened up. "I'm fine. Let's just get there."

Hold on, gummy bear, I mentally pleaded with our baby.

I scrunched up my face as we got closer, wondering if I was having a hallucination—was that mist around the shore...glittering?

"Um—by chance, are you seeing anything strange?" I murmured, wanting to make sure I wasn't going mad.

"Sparkly fog—I don't remember that growing up," answered River in a blank tone that held none of the emotion it should have.

I shot a glance over at him, noting how pale his skin was from its normal golden color.

If this idea didn't work, I wasn't quite sure what parts of us would be left when all was said and done.

The existing dock was obviously rotten and decaying, so we anchored as close as the boat could get, and then we took one of the small safety rafts to the shore.

My unease grew the closer we got to the mist.

"There hasn't been any blood," Caspian said quietly as he gripped my hand.

I gave him a sad frown, because I just hadn't told him about it. He'd already looked worried enough.

Caspian's skin grayed. "Fuck," he muttered under his breath, his hand squeezing harder on mine like I was his lifeline.

Hendrix hopped out of the raft first, followed by River, and then they helped me step out onto the powdery white sand. In front of us, the mist glimmered like diamonds.

It stretched as far as we could see, so it didn't seem like we could find a way around it.

The only way was through.

Hendrix approached the mist tentatively, his hand outstretched as he reached a fingertip towards the fog.

A boom reverberated through the air as soon as his fingers grazed the haze, and Hendrix stumbled back when the mist began to shift and stretch...until a moment later a woman's outline was standing in front of us, formed by glittering mist.

"You've returned," an inhuman voice echoed around us.

The voice didn't seem to be coming from the form, it seemed to be coming from...everywhere.

We were all silent, staring at the woman in shock and awe. I certainly had no inclination to talk back to it.

You couldn't make out any facial features, but I had the strange sensation that she was smiling at us.

"But are you still worthy of the gift you've been given?" the woman continued. "We shall see. If you can complete your three trials, you can reach your heart's desire. Enter the lake one at a time and we shall see who you are."

A breeze blew past, scattering the melody of the voice away, along with the strange being who'd just been visible in the mist.

And then we were all alone.

The bitter wind licked across my skin, stealing my warmth.

"Trials?" I murmured.

"What the fuck for?" River snapped, his arms holding Syn tightly by his side, while Caspian stared into the air where the apparition had been seconds earlier.

"We should do as it said," he suggested. "We all know there's something special about this water. The three of us have abilities from when we almost drowned here." Caspian turned to me. "Never look a gift horse in the mouth, brother. If that fucking thing wants us to do a trial so we can save Syn, then fuck it, we do it."

"I'm not saying I wouldn't do everything for Syn, but I'm also not going to go into this blindly," I snapped, before taking a deep breath. "Let's head to the lake." I peered around us with distrust. "The sooner we can leave this place, the better."

Everyone nodded and I scooped Syn into my arms and walked into the thick jungle of trees. It had been years since I'd been here. But I still remembered it as if it was yesterday. The three of us trudging from the lake to the shore as boys, completely lost and alone.

We were all silent as we went along, the occasional squawk of a bird the only thing disrupting the silence.

It was only about a mile from the beach to the lake, but it seemed to last forever.

At last we breached the trees, and there it was, spread out before us, a still sheet of blue water. It was placid and serene, no sign of the magic beneath its depths...or whatever trials that being had mentioned.

I set Syn down on the rocky shore bed and took a deep breath.

"Want me to go first?" River asked, squaring his shoulders and taking off his shirt, but I instantly shook my head.

"No, I've got this. I will find out what we're dealing with for all of us."

Syn stared into my eyes with a painful expression on her face, and I couldn't help but reach for her, cupping the sides of her head. "I promise everything will be okay, little wolf. For you, I'd find a way to pluck the stars out of the sky. There's nothing we wouldn't do to save our baby." My insides hurt with the heartache at seeing the misery on her face and knowing that something beautiful we'd created with her might be taken from us.

I lowered my hand to her stomach. "We will save our wolf pup."

Tears rolled down her cheeks and she nestled in against my chest. I felt her fragile body tremble, and my heart constricted. "Please, be safe and come back to us. Okay?" Her shaky voice gave me the resolve to do whatever the fuck it took to fix this.

"I give you my word." Reluctantly, I broke away from her warmth, then I slipped my boots off and stripped. The lake was cold as I entered.

Trepidation snaked up my spine as I took another step

forward, the sediment on the lake floor squishing between my toes. My mind flooded with memories of the past , of my father dragging us out here. Of him trying to kill us.

I'd had nightmares of this place, woke up screaming, and yet here I was again. But for some reason, I wasn't the crumbling mess I'd always imagined I'd be if I returned here. Standing in the water with a greater purpose for my coming back, something else came over me.

A strength that reminded me this had nothing to do with me, I was doing it for her. I was doing this to protect our future and those I loved the most.

"Hendrix, please be careful," Syn called out, drawing my attention back to the ache in her eyes, the worry, but I also noticed the way she clutched her middle and scrunched up her face from the pain. The more she hurt, the more determined I was to rip the world apart to find a solution.

The woman I loved carried our child. I never understood true terror until now, until my unborn child was on the brink of losing their life.

Lifting my chin, I said, "Keep fighting, little wolf. I won't be long. Caspian and River, take care of her until I return." I walked in deeper, the gritty floor descending fast, and when the water lapped up to my chest, I threw myself forward, diving headfirst into its cold embrace.

Eyes open in the murky water, I swam forward, figuring whatever my trial was, it may be lying in wait under the surface.

And fuck being snuck up on. My beast lingered just below the surface of my skin, feeling the tension, knowing we were headed toward danger.

Kicking through the water revealed nothing. A muddy floor, dead branches, but nothing else. Not even fish.

I pushed myself back up, my head breaking the surface as I sucked in air to fill my lungs.

"Anything?" Caspian called out.

"Nothing," I replied, spinning on the spot in the water, seeing nothing out of the ordinary. What the hell did I miss?

With another lungful of air, I dove back under, kicking furiously when a spear of light caught my attention from up ahead. A green glow grew bolder the closer I swam, and soon I discovered I was looking at a small underwater cave. I guessed that was my cue to follow.

Kicking savagely, I glided closer and pushed myself through the gap, quickly realizing that one side of the wall resembled a set of steep steps that had been carved into the stone. Faint light led me along the upward passage, and the longer I swam, the tighter my lungs ached for oxygen.

Giving up wasn't an option, not even close, so I kept going until I emerged from the tunnel into a new cave filled with water. The kind that sparkled and was as crystal clear as the ocean around my island.

Driving myself upward, I broke free and gasped for air.

Dark cave walls and ceilings glinted with a green hue, while light poured inside from a fissure running the length of the ceiling.

Silence.

Everything was too peaceful, too calm, which gave me the creeps.

The abrupt scraping sound of stone rubbing stone flared up from behind me, raising the hair on my nape. I jerked around in the water to find what I guessed was my trial.

A monstrous beast clung to the side of the wall on all fours, talons scraping over the stone each time it moved. His skin was weathered and leathery, the color pasty white as if it had never seen the sun. Its head resembled a skull with no eyes and only a mouth full of razor sharp teeth. It paused there, hanging off the wall, hissing at me, its round head lowering in attack pose.

"You fucker, get down here. Don't know what you are, but if your death means saving my Syn, then you're about to become extinct."

It suddenly scuttled across the wall, making a terrifying bug-like scratching sound that had my skin covered in goosebumps.

Fuck that. I frantically scanned the enclosure for a way out of the water. I wasn't exactly made to fight in water, but considering I came up short, I'd make it work.

The beast hurled itself into the water with me, and panic laced through me.

Desperately, my beast poured out of me, my spine bowed as I followed the race to change, fur spurting out, my body stretching.

Fighting to stay above water was another problem mid-transformation, but the moment I embraced my form, I roared. Anger pummeled into me, and I dove underwater to find the monster.

Just then, something brutally crashed into my back.

I growled, the pain zipping up my spine. I kicked the thrashing water to face the beast.

It was gone.

Fuck!

Another jab at the back of my legs. I snarled, heart hammering, and I was getting pissed. I'd worked out its attack mode. Always from behind.

Gotcha.

And just as I felt the faintest of currents across my back, I spun around with all my strength, snatching the piece of shit by the throat underwater. I squeezed while driving my fist into its chest. Talons clawed at my chest and arms, the sting excruciating, but I never let it go. I stared at the bony face, constricting its throat as it snapped those sharp teeth at me.

"Nothing you do to me compares to what I'll lose if you don't die."

And we attacked each other, clashing, claws and teeth. I wasn't holding back. Blood tainted the water, but I fought with everything I had.

In a flash, the creature had me by the chest and moved us with such speed through the water, it was terrifying. He slammed me up against the jagged wall, the stone cutting into my back. I lashed out and fought, but when he bit down on my shoulder with those teeth, I bellowed.

With all the terrifying agony thumping in my shoulder, the burning sting of flesh tearing, a voice flared over my mind. And it wasn't mine.

"Are you prepared?" he seemed to almost hum the words. "What are you willing to sacrifice for the girl with child? What would you do to save the ones you love, Hendrix?"

I paused momentarily at hearing this beast say my name, to speak so clearly.

A sudden jab came out of nowhere, striking my ribs like steel. Pain pierced deep, and I groaned, but when another strike came, I was thrown backward through the water with such force that I had no way of stopping myself.

In a heartbeat, the pressure around my legs eased and I was no longer being dragged. I swam to the surface and sucked the air into my burning lungs.

My insides squeezed tight as I looked around to find myself surrounded by a thick, green mist. The longer I padded around in the water, searching for the creature, the more my vision blurred.

I blinked and rubbed my eyes, but nothing focused. It got worse. My sight darkened.

I turned in the water, splashing my face with water, but nothing made it better. The tunnel vision darkened. Goddess, what was happening to me? Was I going blind?

I couldn't breathe, couldn't think. I only splashed madly, unable to see where to go, how to escape. And instead, I felt like the world was pressing in around me, suffocating me, locking me away in darkness.

Goosebumps raced, and my beast retreated just as quickly. I floated there, and with a single blink, my vision vanished.

Terror raked claws down my back.

Nothing but darkness filled me.

I spun, and the cave felt like it spun. But the agony of what I'd lost slammed into me.

With my heart beating in my ears, shock throttled me. I had to remember my mission.

Syn and the baby.

Then the beast's words came to mind.

Sacrifice.

What would you do?

The words swam over my mind, while I kept kicking to stay afloat, trying my best to not lose myself to panic.

I kept repeating his words, realizing I had to make a sacrifice to save Syn and the baby. With it came the dreadful reality that the cost to me would be my vision.

I didn't move for a long time, knowing without a doubt that I'd give my life for Syn's. I'd give her everything I had, and if that meant I would never lay eyes on my beautiful woman or see the smile on our baby's face, it was a sacrifice I'd accept.

Warm tears rimmed my eyes, and I wasn't a man who cried. I had been dealt a hard life, but these tears weren't for me. I would give Syn everything she wanted. I was broken...fucked.

Something suddenly grabbed my legs and yanked me downward. I was thrown left and right, and that was when I smacked into the wall with the steps, recognizing I was being dragged back the way I'd come.

The whole time, a voice repeated in my ears, "Someone among you betrays you."

Frantically, I grasped for the stairs, but my hands slipped, lost on what he was saying let alone what was going on with me.

I hadn't taken a full enough breath either, and now my chest burned for air. When my legs were finally released, I kicked, waiting to hit the surface. When I did, I sucked in the oxygen, beating my legs to stay afloat.

Still, I saw nothing but darkness.

Reluctantly, I called out, "Caspian, River." My voice echoed around me as though I remained inside a cave. As much as I told myself that I'd be alright, a terror-stricken fear came over me that I'd be lost in this cave for eternity. No one would find me. And I'd never discover the way out.

Worst of all, I'd never again lay eyes on Syn or our child.

***

Caspian

"How long has he been gone?" I paced in front of the lake, grinding my back teeth.

"Thirty minutes," River answered.

"You think he's okay?" Syn asked, the frantic tone of her words adding to my own growing trepidation.

I shook my head, unable to stop moving. "This was a shit idea," I blurted. "I should have gone with him rather than go alone. Fuck. Fuck. Fuck."

"He'll be alright," River said. "He's a tough sonofabitch."

When I glanced at him with a hard glare, I noticed his arched eyebrows and stiff expression as he kept looking down at Syn in his arms and then back at me. Our poor girl was barely holding on, and here I was losing my cool.

Great job. Shit.

"You're right, he'll be fine." I lied terribly because even Syn looked unconvinced.

"Okay, fine, I'm going in," I finally announced. "I'll bring him back out."

Stripping, I stepped into the water, leaving the bottom half of my synthetic leg in place. I had no time to remove it when an ominous feeling suffocated me that something was wrong with Hendrix. I couldn't bring myself to voice the worry in front of Syn, but my growing sense of dread had me rushing deeper into the water until I was deep enough to dive in.

It didn't take long to find myself following a bright light through a cave opening only to find myself in a narrow tunnel with the strangest fucking upward steps on the wall. What the fuck created those? Yep, I already hated this shithole, but Hendrix was in here somewhere.

Pulling myself up through the water, kicking and moving my arms, I finally reached the surface and found myself in a cavern, barely able to catch my breath, and something white rushed at me.

It came so fast, I barely had time to react. I threw my arms up, but the hard strikes at my body were like blades. I was thrashed in the water, swallowing it while fighting to keep my head up.

It was only when I ducked my head under, punching ferociously at whatever the hell was attacking me, that I saw the bastard.

Some kind of freakish, skeletal thing. Fuck me but it looked like some alien creature straight out of the movies.

We whipped around in the water, but the thing moved too fast. I wasn't a fool to not know when to count my blessings and when to know shit was going sideways for me. Hendrix... was he in here somewhere, floating dead after we'd been conned to come into the lake?

Lashing out, my punches weren't as effective when striking underwater, but the moment I saw the gaping mouth with razor teeth coming for me, my life flashed before my eyes.

He bit into my neck, moving so fast, I couldn't even deflect the attack.

Like steel, the bite tore at my flesh, and the wisps of blood floated in the water around us.

I screamed, fighting like a motherfucker against him, when a voice called out into my mind.

"Caspian, are you ready? What are you willing to sacrifice for the girl with child?"

The fuck? I breathed heavily, my head just bobbing over the surface, while the monster remained attached to my neck. And no amount of punches would dislodge it.

"Are you my trial?" I gasped, spitting out blood, the pain in my neck burning like fire.

It hummed in my mind, saying, "What part of yourself will you give up for her safety?"

I stared at the bony head with no eyes. "What the fuck?"

Then a strike to my gut knocked all the wind out of me. The next thing I knew, something snatched my feet and I was hauled back under with such speed, that the creature vanished in the blink of an eye.

Then it whispered once more in my ear, "Someone among you betrays you."

Writhing for escape, I reached for anything, kicking my legs while my lungs screamed for oxygen. They were empty and I was going to drown.

Fear engulfed me, and only when I'd been released did I finally drive myself upward through the water, desperate for air.

Hitting the surface, I gasped for oxygen, my chest pumping furiously. Desperation clenched my throat at what I'd just seen, and only then did I notice the thick green mist surrounding me. I could barely see my own hand in front of my face, let alone where the hell I was.

"Hendrix," I cried out.

Nothing, yet something felt odd. I tried beating my legs, but I found myself dipping under the water's surface, struggling to stay afloat.

I dipped my head low, gaze piercing through the water, convinced something still held onto my legs.

Wait! What the hell? My legs were gone. Both missing from below the knees.

I yelled underwater out of pure shock, staring incredulously and kicking the stumps I had left.

Fuck no, fuck no. Darkness reached out with sharp fingers, grabbing me by the chest and squeezing. My lungs were burning for air as panic shuddered through me.

Coming back up for air, my pulse thundered like a storm in my chest, and I felt myself drowning now from the inside out.

It took me a long time to accept the loss of my leg when I was younger. Years of fucked up shit that made me hate myself, but this... this was both legs gone. What the fuck good was I now?

Swallowing hard, I thrashed in the water, amid the green mist, I was losing the battle of fighting the rising panic. Instead, it filled me. With it came the creature's words...

What part of yourself will you give up for her safety?

Was this real?

My girl was carrying our child, and to save them, this was my sacrifice. These weren't trials of battle, far from it. I realized that now. I'd give her everything...but it didn't make the sting hurt any less. Or the fact that I'd be useless to my brothers and her now. What was I going to do?

And what did it mean by, "Someone among you betrays

you." My brothers would never backstab me. No reason to... My head hurt.

I roared and a flash of agony cut through me as I felt the wounds of my past ravage my mind. For so long I assumed I'd escaped my father's past, and yet coming here reminded me that I would always suffer.

With it came a wave of anger, and acid slipped into the back of my throat.

Syn.

For you, I'll fight, I'll give you everything.

***

River

"Something's wrong," Syn murmured, shaking against me.

"It's going to be okay," I reassured her, rubbing her back, though my stomach clenched tight because she was right. It had been an hour now since Hendrix went in and neither he nor Caspian resurfaced. The fucked up thing was, I had no idea what to expect to go in prepared rather than walk right into whatever trap they'd most likely fallen in.

"I'm going to have to go after them," I said, turning to my gorgeous Syn, needing her to know I had no choice.

"I know." She blinked away the tears that broke me. Despite her words, she held onto me with a death grip. "I'm scared of losing you all. I've never felt this about anyone. Never found anyone who loved me, so please, whatever you do, don't die."

Her sincerity tore at my emotions, and the ache she brought out in me made me gasp for air.

"You've got it." And I kissed her, needing to taste her. I memorized everything... the softness of her lips, her honeyed scent, her quickened breaths. I imprinted them on my mind.

My heart raced for her, but I also had to do this for her like my brothers did. "We're going to have a future together." I slid my hand down to her stomach, overcome with emotions I never thought I'd feel about becoming a father.

Everything about Syn reminded me of how real love felt.

With a final kiss, I left her side and moved around the lake as darkness slithered inside me. But instead of walking right in after stripping, I skirted the water's edge, trying to see if a different angle gave me insight into where my brothers dove into the murky water.

The surface rippled from the breeze, and in all honesty, I saw nothing. The longer I lingered on the edge, the more nerves danced beneath my skin. I had to go in, though part of me felt like I walked directly into a trap.

Trials. The word circled my mind like vultures.

With a last glance to Syn who watched me carefully, I gave her a fake smile, and walked into the lake. I guess I had no choice but to do this. To save Syn, to find my brothers.

Whatever it took.

I wasted no time and dove into the cold water. My skin rippled from its bite, and I swam around for a while, finding nothing. I came up, then dove back under, hating that I couldn't see anything.

Going back in, I instantly spotted a glowing light from an underwater cave this time, and, well, I just knew that was where I had to go.

Kicking madly, I dragged myself through it, then found myself swimming upward past some weird assed shaped rocks. I kept a vigilant eye on everything, expecting the worst.

When I broke the surface, the last thing I expected was to come face to face with a white skeletal creature with a terrifying face from anyone's darkest dreams.

"Whoa." I backpedaled instantly, thankful I kept my shoes on, and reached down for my blade. Wielding it, I hurled it at its gaping head, while kicking it in the chest.

Unexpectedly, it threw itself at me, teeth and claws coming so fast, they were a blur.

Then it struck, teeth sinking into my neck and dragging my sorry ass deep down until we hit the floor. I slammed my fist into its head, kicking the motherfucker and dropping the blade.

Pinned to the floor, the thing stood on my chest, weighing a ton. My lungs screamed for air, while the thing still held my arm in its mouth like it might tear it off. It reminded me of a damn shark, and they always poke those sonsofbitches in the eyes. But this asshole has none.

Yep, I was fucked.

"River, are you ready? What are you willing to sacrifice for the girl with child?"

The words that flowed over my mind, not from his mouth, stopped me in my thrashing tracks. Had this fucker just spoken to me in my head?

And of course, he'd be my trial. But was drowning me part of the trial?

"Release me," I bellowed in my head, having no idea if he understood.

"You once welcomed death," he stated, his voice making a clicking sound in my head, while my vision started to blur in and out from suffocation. "You called for it."

"I did," I admitted truthfully in my mind. For a long time, I didn't know if I wanted this life, if I deserved it, if I even knew how to survive in it. My father did a damn good job of making me hate so much.

"A dead man is a dead man," the creature droned one. "If you were going to throw your life away, what difference would it make if you gave up Syn and the child."

I started to convulse because I knew I was going to drown here. White dots formed in my vision, while his words ripped me to shreds.

"Fuck you. You're not taking her from me." I'd just found a reason to love, to live again.

His teeth seemed to sink deeper into my neck, striking bone. And I lost all control, my lungs giving up.

As if sensing me slipping away, the creature finally dragged me to the surface and released me, but not before it said, "Not even if it meant her and the baby's survival?"

Fighting for breath, I battled to stay afloat while desperately taking in air. And yet something inside me shifted. A sense of emptiness crawled over me. I was wrenched underwater, and I reached out for purchase on anything to stop myself.

I flew through the water the way I'd come, and moments later, I was breathing air suffocated by a green mist, while the creature's words filled my head, "Someone among you betrays you."

Treading water on the spot, the world seemed to spin with me and his words confused me.

Plus, I couldn't explain it, but deep in my gut, the sense that I'd lost Syn sat like a boulder. Loneliness came over me as if someone had broken into my house and taken everything I owned while I wasn't looking. And there wasn't a fucking thing I could do about it.

My muscles stiffened and I punched the water. I struck it, bellowing my fury.

She was meant to be mine, and I couldn't explain it, but the creature's words stuck in my mind. I had to let go to save her. I had to walk away, letting my brothers keep her.

I blinked the water from my eyes, driving myself through the water, lost in the green mist. With my heart speeding and harsh breaths escaping my lungs, a frantic sensation came over me. I moved rapidly but I wasn't going anywhere, and the whole time I slipped deeper within myself.

I'd been in that place too many times, faced death, and now he reared his head once more.

And the more I fought it, the more it blasted in my head that this had to be some cruel fucking joke, the more I felt for certain that I'd lose Syn. That she'd no longer be mine and I had nowhere to turn.

All the while, the darkness in my mind whispered, *I've been waiting for your return.*

Worry sickened me. My men were still missing in the lake.

With it came an urgency, the need to be doing something other than waiting around. The ache in my body remained, and with each harsh breath, I inched closer to the lake's edge.

Enter, a voice sang in my head, but I had no idea if it was my panicked mind or something else. Something meaning ill intent.

Silence.

I waited and it killed me.

The angry sky darkened, and from my vantage point, I could see the whole lake, the glint of green appearing on its surface, but no air bubbles. No sign of distress. Where in the world had the guys gone? Was there some kind of creature under there that had killed them?

The longer I lingered there, the more I shuddered that I wasted time. My palms were slick with sweat, and I hated how I kept losing my breath.

Finally, it became too much, and I stepped into the water

with bare feet, still wearing my clothes. The water rushed up my skin, its bite cold.

A shiver ran up my legs. I lifted my head, saying, "This would be a good time to give me some advice, ghost thing, or whatever you are."

Nothing. Of course nothing responded.

"Fine then." I huffed just as something floated to the surface of the water up ahead.

My heart thundered, and I stepped closer, making out that they were lying on their stomach. His head was submerged, spine arched. And he wasn't moving.

It had to be one of the guys.

I screamed in panic as I threw myself into the water, madly pushing through the lake. Pulse hammering, I ran as fast as I could. Then I threw myself at him, hastily, grabbing his arm and twisting him over onto his back. Hendrix!

That was when I noticed all the blood pouring from the huge bite mark on his shoulder. The purple bruises on his ribs made me sick.

He was white in the face, and my heart stopped. What did this to him?

"No, no, no." I clasped him on either side of his face. "Hendrix, don't you dare leave me." I shook him out of pure shock. I'd thought I'd lost him earlier to drowning and now this. Distraught, I wrapped an arm around his chest and hauled him across the water, needing to get him to shore.

Tears drenched my cheeks, a low snarl in my chest from my wolf growling her agony.

Echoes of my heart shattering flooded my mind when a croaky sound came from Hendrix.

Frantically, I whipped around to see his eyes fluttering open. My stomach hit the back of my throat as I cried out.

He was staring up at me, blinking crazily like something was in his eyes.

"Syn," he murmured. "Is that really you?" He reached out, his hand stroking the side of my face. "I can see you."

"Hendrix, yes, it's me." I threw myself at him, embracing him, crying like a baby. I splashed water everywhere in the process, but I didn't care.

"I'm okay. I think I'm okay," he cooed, though by the shock on his face, I suspected he'd had quite the ordeal. He looked half-dazed and kept touching me like I wasn't real.

Shifting to stand up in the water on his own, he leaned and kissed me. It was soft and tender, and I sensed his tremble. "I thought I'd never see you again," he kept repeating, and it scared me.

"I'm not going anywhere," I reassured him. "I'm right here."

He kept staring at me, looking like he was so far away. "Something strange happened in the cave. I went blind and all I could think about is never seeing you again, not being able to see our baby's face."

The guy was completely shaken, not even seeming bothered by the bruises on his chest or the vicious bite mark on his shoulder. Blood rolled down his arm and into the lake, and still, he only stared at me, holding me close.

I held onto him too, scared for him.

A sharp whine had me twisting around and spotting Caspian popping up from within the lake, seeming to splash uncontrollably in the water, his expression filled with frantic fear.

I gasped, my heartbeat completely out of control.

Hendrix and I rushed over to him, grabbing hold of him.

"Caspian," I cried out, grasping both sides of his face, trying to make him look at me while Hendrix took hold of him from behind to prop him up. But he kept pulling away from us, dunking himself underwater. Blood dripped from the bite mark on his arm.

Hendrix grabbed hold of him again, wrenching him out from under the water. "Casp, what are you doing?"

"My leg, my leg's back," he gasped, staring at us incredulously as if seeing me for the first time. "Syn?" Then he took in the surroundings, really looking around to see we were all in the lake. He gave a low whine, his gaze wide and desperate, and yet he smiled. "It's back."

"It's back? What was wrong with your leg?" I asked, not understanding. I embraced Caspian around the middle, terrified to see him so disoriented. "Your neck is bleeding. What bit you?"

But he didn't notice and instead embraced me, and Hendrix was there too, doing the same. "You are ours. And I have my leg back." He chuckled almost madly.

They clung to me, both of them shaking, like they were afraid they'd lose me.

"My good leg had been taken from me in the cave. It felt so real. Goddess, I believed it." His shoulders squared and he slowly began to look every inch the powerful alpha I loved, though fear still clung to his gaze.

"You're okay," I soothed, putting two and two together, it seemed whatever happened underwater had played a cruel joke on them.

"River, where's River?" Hendrix finally asked.

We turned to scan the water just as his body bobbed to the surface. He came up head first, his shoulders curled forward and defeated, blood pouring from a bite just like the other two.

My heart constricted at seeing him. What in the world had my men just been through?

"River," I called out to him, and he turned to us as we pushed through the water to get to him.

The moment I neared River, he stood there, not

embracing me, but blinking at me. When I reached out for him, he pulled back from me, and my insides curdled.

"River, whatever happened in the water wasn't real," I explained, needing him to snap out of it.

"We were hallucinating," Hendrix muttered. "Our trials were a test to see if we'd accept the sacrifices for Syn."

The tremble in my body intensified as I thought about how they'd hallucinated parts of them were taken for me.

River blinked, then ran a hand over his face. "So, you haven't left me?" His voice choked.

I burst out with a crazed sounding laughter, the moment of utter confusion and chaos scattering my emotions.

"I would stalk you down if you ever left me," I admitted.

Hendrix and Capsian remained by my side, pressed close, their arms wrapped around me. So I reached out for River, needing him with us.

The darkness shrouding his expression moments earlier faded, and whatever illusion blurred his thoughts seemed to clear from his eyes.

He collected my hand into his as he stepped closer.

And the moment he did, an explosive burst of water shot upward from around us, throwing us all apart. Something smacked into me too, throwing me backward.

Ghostly hands grasped me around my middle and dragged me under the water.

I thrashed my arms and legs wildly, but nothing I did lifted me back to the surface. Air bubbles rushed from my mouth, trapping my scream within them.

Movement above the water revealed my three men staring down at me, desperately hitting the water but never reaching me. It seemed as though I was in a bubble and they were locked outside, unable to find their way to me.

And I decided then that fighting this might be the wrong

answer. My men were tricked in this water, so what if this was the same?

With every inch of strength, I lay back down on the lake floor, my eyes wide and watching my panicked alphas try to reach me. My lungs screamed for air. But I tried to quiet my mind.

What do you want from me?

No response came.

Silence. It pulsed in my head as loudly as my heartbeat.

A tingle ran up my fingers, and I lifted my hands in front of my face to where emerald sparks danced around them. Beautiful. The shine spread down my arms, buzzing across my skin like ants and needles. Then it raced across my body, engulfing me, and circled around my stomach. It warmed me, stealing away the cold.

The corners of my eyes were darkening now, and I knew I was close to passing out from suffocation, yet instead of panic, a calmness came over me. And yet it was strange knowing that all would be alright.

Laying my hands on my stomach, I felt the strong kick of a baby. That simple act had me tearing up, and I desperately wanted to share it with the three men who brought love into my life.

I curled upward, wanting to scream with joy that I hadn't lost my baby. The small kick came two more times. I stilled, smiling up at the guys who frantically beat at the water to reach me.

If I wasn't in the water, they'd see my tears. I reached out, needing them.

At that moment, two things happened.

The voice in my head whispered, *you will always sense the truth in someone's heart.*

Then the water suddenly rushed around me in a dizzying effect. Suddenly, those ghostly hands pushed me upward with such force that I broke free from the water and higher up. For a few seconds, I hung suspended in the air, gazing down at my three men, the green glow centered around my stomach. Then just as quickly, I fell, causing a huge splash.

Powerful hands dragged me back to the surface. It was madness. Screaming filled the air, to not let me go, to get me out of the water. I didn't fight it and soon found myself cradled in my men's arms, peering into their frightened gazes.

I smiled to reassure them, dripping wet and trembling, and said, "I think everything is going to be alright now."

"How are you feeling?" Hendrix asked, distress painted across his features. He stroked the side of my face tenderly, and I loved it when he looked at me like only I existed in his world.

"I felt our baby kick," I gushed, and those tears of happiness came again. "I didn't lose the baby." Then I was full-on crying from all the pent-up stress and tension. "I felt the little kicks. It was so beautiful."

River and Caspian immediately reached over and laid a hand on my stomach as if hoping to catch the moment.

I did my best to hold onto whatever part I could reach, bringing us all close together.

The beaming smiles on their faces had me choking up with emotions. Hope filled me as I stared at my three alphas. "I think I'm ready to leave this lake," I murmured.

River laughed and it sounded beautiful. Yet, all three refused to let me go, so they carried me out of the lake. At the shore, they placed me on my feet.

"Okay, grab your clothes and let's never return here again," ordered Hendrix.

They moved quickly to collect clothes, and I walked over to my discarded shoes, pressing my hands to my stomach, completely smitten. I was distracted... So much so that I hadn't noticed the danger lingering right behind me until it was too late.

I sensed the prickle of something sharp on the back of my neck, and I snapped around only to come face to face with a blade coming right for my face.

My heart thundered in my ears, and I jutted out of the way, the weapon biting across my cheek and drawing blood, as it barely missed completely sinking into me. I flung my arm outward in reaction, knocking the knife out of her grasp.

I was screaming out of pure shock to find the witch who had helped me with the bracelet laced with dark magic attacking me.

What the hell?

"W-what are you doing here?" Every inch of me shuddered down to my bones, recoiling from her. The cozy, heart-warming feeling faded, replaced with fear and the terror that maybe I assumed too quickly things would be alright. The longer I stared at the old woman with gray-streaked black hair sitting wildly around her round face, the more the fear grew.

She snatched my hand, nails digging into flesh, her vivid orange eyes piercing into mine. "Bitch."

I tugged against her, clawing at her iron fingers wrapped around my wrist. "Get off me," I cried out, drawing the men's attention.

Their growls pierced the silence, but then everything happened too fast. And like I'd seen on the first night I met her weeks ago, there was a flash of brownish scales and sharpened teeth showing past the wrinkles, through whatever glamour she used.

"What do you want?" I demanded.

Ignoring me, she sneered at Hendrix and his brothers racing toward us.

One flick of her hand, and they flew backward, tumbling away. My heart sank and I cried out for them, wrenching my arm still trapped in her grasp.

"You think I'd let any of you go so easily? You greedy

assholes, coming here to draw more power from the magic lake. It's mine, only mine. Why do you filthy beasts deserve this precious magic?" She spewed the words with venom and raised her other hand towards me, while murmuring under her breath. Words I was convinced were a curse to destroy me and my baby.

My breath sharpened, and urgency to escape drummed in my veins.

Movement came from around me as my men threw themselves at us again, shouting at her. In seconds, they flew back just as quick but farther away this time.

"Get the fuck away from her," Hendrix roared, gaining her attention, climbing to his feet as his beast spilled out of him, tearing out of his body.

Twisting her head toward him, her upper lip curled over her teeth and gums. "Don't worry, I'll deal with you soon enough. Seems I was too light-handed on my sleepwalking spells. Should have guessed you three were too fucking stupid to even do that right and fall for all the traps I'd set on your island." With one snap of her hand, Hendrix flew once more away from us.

Her words struck a chord with me, with the times I caught the men seemingly wandering aimlessly. With Eliza's stories about others on the island hurt by bizarre accidents.

"You bitch," River hollered, throwing himself back up to his feet, and with his brothers, they charged at us. But like before, they kept bouncing away.

"Why are you doing this?" I pleaded, hating that I should show her anything but the fury she deserved. "We've done nothing to you."

"Oh, save your breath. Try watching for years these spoiled brothers using a power that didn't belong to them. And yet the lake gives me nothing," she screamed the words then shot a side glare at Caspian who prowled towards us like a predator, growling, his eyes already taking on his wolf form. "I even used the blood sample I took from them in the lake, and nothing. So yes, I will destroy them, take anything happy from them, including you and that furball you're carrying." Her eyes grew wild, leaving me trembling. "They need to understand suffering."

My wolf rumbled in my chest, and holding back was impossible. "You have no understanding of what suffering means." I lashed out at her, my wolf shoving forward.

The bitch wrenched out of the way, while she hurled a fireball right at my face. It slammed into my chest, the heat sizzling through the fabric of my shirt, sending me backward.

I yelled frantically, batting away the fire, ripping off my top before it spread. I stumbled back, seething as the witch marched toward me, throwing the men away from us.

Her eyes darkened, trepidation lurking in the depths of her glare. She raised her hand right in my face, muttering under her breath.

Terror suffocated me. After everything, this couldn't be where it all ended. Not when I was so close to finally holding onto happiness.

Out of instinct, I reacted quickly, shoving my hand forward, slapping my palm to her chest to shove her away from me.

The moment my palm touched her, a flash of emerald light glowed from my hand, pulsing like a heartbeat. It boomed outward in heat waves.

Her eyes widened with a shock I hadn't expected, and instead of backing away, she shuddered, her pupils rolling into her head. She frantically beat at my arm, fingers tearing at my skin, but I couldn't move. Evidently, my hand had glued itself to her chest.

"You," she snarled in my face, her brows furrowed. "The water bestowed magic on you? A pathetic wolf? Wolves don't have magic." Her chest puffed with how furiously she sucked in each breath.

"You're jealous? All of this because of envy?"

"You're so stupid. The lake gave me its power years ago, only a taste, but soon after these three idiots gained their abilities, the lake stopped working. So, the solution is easy. Remove them and the power will be redirected to me." She spoke so matter-of-factly, as though she knew these things as a truth.

I didn't believe her. How could I when she tried to kill me and my men?

My arm trembled, and a sharp pain across my forearm had me wincing. That was when I noticed the white moon tattoo forming over my skin.

I stared at it incredulously, confused and terrified. Especially with the witch now striking my hand in a panicked reaction. Her hits hurt, and I winced, shoving her to stop while I fought to rip my hand away.

Whatever was happening, I felt it calling to me, and a shot of sparks jolted up from where I touched the witch, making its way directly to the moon. Where earlier the red color fringed the top, now it dripped across the moon's surface, encapsulating it completely.

Eclipse.

The word came to my mind just as when River had told me about the blood moon.

The witch suddenly screamed, and I flinched, jerking my gaze up.

She seemed to crumble right before my eyes. Sunken cheeks, her body was shriveling, life stolen from her in seconds.

"What the hell's going on?" Hendrix growled, throwing himself once more to our side, reaching for the witch.

"Don't touch us," I snapped. Deep inside, I knew whatever was going on with me was dangerous.

The witch suddenly fell, breaking my touch, and hit the ground like a bag of bones.

I gasped, slightly horrified. Stumbling backward, I hugged myself with one arm while staring at the completely red moon on my arm as it started to fade. The image reminded me of River's words the other night when we were on the mansion rooftop.

The darker moon is associated with death, while the bright silvery moon is about rebirth.

Was that what I'd just witnessed? The lake had given me power?

The men rushed to me, checking me over, asking me if I was okay.

"You're not even burnt," Hendrix pointed out, rubbing the tips of his fingers across my collarbone where I'd been struck by the witch's fire.

Appearing just as lost as I felt, I remembered the voice in my head under the water.

"You will always sense the truth in someone's heart," I murmured. "That's what I heard while I was trapped underwater. And the thing on my arm." I lifted it, though there were no markings. I stared at my men, slightly confused.

"The water gave you power," Hendrix said the words I couldn't get out. "Just like it did to the three of us." He gingerly took my arm and ran a thumb across my forearm, his touch soft and warm. There was no reaction as it had done so with the witch.

"What you just did to the witch," he twisted his head to frown at the horrifying mess on the ground and back at me, "is a miracle."

I blinked at him, wanting to cry that he'd call such a terrifying ability a miracle. "We all gained our power to make ourselves stronger in a world that wanted us dead. And you, my gorgeous little wolf, are no different from us. You've fought your entire life, and now you've been blessed with some kind of power that might assess the truth in someone's heart and protect you no matter what."

"It also seems to then inflict punishment if it doesn't like what it sees," I answered, unsure how I felt about wielding such a power. Not to mention, I was also unclear on how to even activate it. Evidently, having my life threatened was one trigger. But would it appear if I touched the guys too much?

"You're badass, gorgeous," Caspian added, moving in close to me, his grin dangerously sexy.

River ran a hand through my hair, and said, "I find it extremely hot."

I nodded with a small smile, and then burst into tears. Apparently, thinking I'd lost my loves, defeating a horrible witch, being bestowed with a crazy strong ability, and saving my unborn child in one day was too much for me. I almost laughed at myself because when I worded it like that, I wanted to cry even more.

"We're getting off this goddamn island," Hendrix finally commanded, and there was no argument from any of us. We all rushed to collect anything we'd left behind and made a mad dash back through the jungle towards the beach.

Hendrix swept me into his arms, insisting I wasn't to run. I looped my arms around his neck as we moved with speed. I'd never get sick of being this loved, and when I glanced down at my inner forearm a sense of power filled me.

Gone was the fear.

Gone was the loneliness.

All that remained was pure love and a desire for a future I'd never felt before. I held onto Hendrix tighter, smiling to myself that maybe this time I'd finally been lucky enough to have found my very own happily ever after.

"That bitch betrayed us, just as the voice in the cave had warned me," Hendrix muttered as he laid a kiss on my brow, sitting so close that our bodies were almost joined at the hip in the back of the boat.

Caspian, on the other side, added, "The thing said the same to me. To be honest, I wasn't paying attention as I was too busy freaking out about my other leg missing." His lips pinched to the side with a lopsided grin, and I leaned in against him, kissing his cheek.

"Love you," I whispered, to which he smiled. The thing was, each one of us was broken in our own way, but together, we became whole.

"And me," called out River from the railing as we zipped across the ocean's calm surface. "But why the hell just tease us? Why not come out and say, hey, that witch you trusted is trying to kill you. This is what I don't get about the mystical world. It speaks in riddles."

He kept on ranting, and I smirked at how passionate he was. Me, I was just glad to not be facing constant death for a

"Well, at least it tried to warn you, which is better than nothing, right?" I pointed out.

"Is it?" River questioned. "We didn't predict the witch turning up to attack Syn."

"Who the fuck cares now? Anyway, Syn can take care of herself," piped up Caspian who had his hand on my thigh, lightly teasing me with the way he gently stroked my leg.

"The witch finally got what she deserved in the end." Hendrix pushed a loose strand behind my ear, staring at me, like he'd been doing since we got onto the boat to head back home. "It's taught me a lesson on who to trust outside our family. She said she'd been watching us for years, and it pisses me off that we never once suspected. I mean, we invited her into our home."

He tensed against me, and I held onto his hand.

"It's over now," I reassured him.

His brow furrowed. "I know. But it doesn't ease the sting that we missed the clues."

"The witch is dead, that's all I care about," River barked as he came and sat down, reclining with one arm behind his head. "I never want to think of her again. Fuck, she gives me the creeps."

Caspian groaned in agreement. I sat back on the couch between my two men, the cool air rushing through my hair, making it messier.

River turned to look at us once more, gorgeous eyes narrowed. "Okay, that's enough. Time's up," he finally announced. "Out of that seat, Hendrix. My turn to be next to Syn."

I laughed because the guy was serious. They'd been swapping seats every ten minutes, each needing to be pressed up against me, their hands all over me, kissing me, licking me. And I loved every second of it.

"It's only been a few minutes," snapped Hendrix.

"Ain't happening." River walked over to us, causing the boat to slightly rock from side to side from his movement, and he joined us on the outdoor seating at the back of the boat. This vessel wasn't small in the slightest. I was talking about luxury that was built for more extreme speed and entertainment. And a lot of comfort.

River sat down on the short table right in front of me, his hands on my knees, his legs spread, while wearing only his jeans and nothing else. I got hot at the way his gaze dipped up and down my body, and then he smirked to himself as if approving what he saw.

"Maybe we all need a small break," he suggested. "The sky has cleared up, the water is clear as crystal, and we're completely alone out here."

I scanned the area to confirm we were indeed completely alone with only water surrounding us. "It's so beautiful now. So tranquil."

"See, she agrees," River added. The guys exchanged a strange glance.

"Agree to what?" I asked.

It was Hendrix who finally twisted around to completely face me. "We're going to be a family soon, and to do that, we should officially bond our wolves with yours."

My body tensed at the implication. "Like marking me?"

"Yes," he answered, while Caspian's fingers danced over my bare shoulder and over my bra strap. River's hands slid up my thigh.

A moan caught in my throat—something primal and animalistic because I knew what they were implying. The lust in their gazes as they watched me screamed their intentions.

Their suggestive touches sent a buzz right between my thighs in such a way that I couldn't think of anything else.

"Here?" I gasped. "Like this? You're all injured." Of

course, I'd bandaged them once we arrived on the boat with the first aid kit, but they didn't seem to notice their injuries.

"What better place than here?" River suggested.

My skin prickled with excitement, while I clenched my thighs together. I had never lusted for anyone as much as I did these three brothers, even when they wanted sex out in the middle of the ocean.

I reclined in the seat, rather enjoying the way they stared at me like starved wolves. "There is only one issue," I countered.

"And that is?" They seemed to ask almost in unison.

"The doctor had said I needed to take it easy when it comes to group sex."

Hendrix blinked at me because he knew this too. They were all there. "We can't cause any stress to you and the baby," he admitted. "So, we can do this without pushing you too far." He licked his lips, holding onto me tighter. "For us to bond with you, we need to be with you at the same time, but we'll take it slow. Nothing strenuous. No one said you can't have an amazing time without us being too rough."

Of course, there was disappointment in his voice because I also loved when he fucked me hard, when all three of them did.

River's fingers kept crawling up my thighs, while Caspian slowly pulled the strap of my bra off my shoulder.

Hendrix slid a hand across my jawline, making me look at him. He was gorgeous—god-like with a square jawline and black hair that brought out the blue in his eyes. My hands fell to round biceps that flexed under my touch, and the thrill of knowing these men were all mine was exhilarating.

"Trust me, Syn. I would only do what keeps you safe and happy." He moved in and kissed me, while my heart roared in my chest. It didn't take long for my body to tingle with that thumping pulse between my thighs.

"How can I possibly say no when I'm burning up from a

single touch?" I whispered against his lips. "I don't think you three realize that maybe I want you more than you desire me."

River barked a laugh so loud, it slightly startled me. "Trust me, angel. You couldn't come close to my obsession with how many times a day I think about your pussy and boobs. At least forty times, no, make it fifty."

I laughed. "Yeah right. That means you're thinking of nothing else during the day."

"Yep," he confirmed immediately.

Caspian's nodding. "He's not wrong."

Hendrix smirked.

"I'm slightly alarmed," I teased. "So whenever you are supposedly thinking or keeping quiet—"

"We're most likely thinking about fucking you," Caspian finished my sentence.

"Well, then we have to do something about it, right?"I pushed myself to stand up and started to remove my bra. I didn't need to ask for help because six hands were suddenly on me, stripping me. And once I was left in nothing but my panties, Hendrix did the honors of curling his fingers into my underwear and slipping them down my legs. I stepped out of them just as River's hand reached over and cupped my pussy, his finger gently running over my slit.

I instantly responded with a moan, my body lurching in his direction.

There was no waiting, just the pulse at my core. I gasped as he kept playing with me, spreading my lips and finding my clit, while Hendrix held me by my hips, and Caspian kissed my lower back, cupping my ass.

"You are a goddess," Hendrix purred.

"Our fantasy girl," Caspian purred between kisses.

"Fuck, angel, I'm addicted to your pussy. I love the way it sucks down on my fingers." River glanced up at me, winking so beautifully, but I was floating already on the arousal curling in the pit of my stomach with the way he kept pushing a finger into me and back out. "Hear that wet sound? It's all honey."

The groans rumbled by all the guys sent a delicious shiver down my spine with excitement.

I turned to Hendrix, placing my hands against his hard chest, our mouths crashing. I burned up with desire, and while River fingered me, lifting one leg up and resting my foot on his lap to give him better access, I kissed Hendrix with the passion of a starved girl. Lust coiled in my chest as he pressed his tongue into my mouth, all while Caspian's exploring fingers teased down the crack between my ass cheeks.

I had to be the luckiest girl in the world to have three men devour me at the same time, to know they craved me. Their teasing burned me up, and my skin tingled.

Hendrix's cock pressed against my hip through his pants, and he was rock hard, grinding into me. I whimpered, needing all of him.

Suddenly, Hendrix broke from me, his eyes darkening to that of his beast. "How do you want us?" he asked like that was a normal conversation.

I swallowed hard, slightly distracted with the way Caspian ran his palm across the curve of my ass, squeezing.

"I'm not sure how this works, to be honest," I admitted.

"Well, there are three of us, and you have three holes," River stated with his usual directness, then proceeded to lick his fingers, his eyes fluttering in response like he'd just eaten the world's greatest chocolate cake.

"I have an idea," Caspian said. He proceeded to wrap his arms around my waist, then twisted me around to face the back of the boat with my back to the guys. Gently, he dipped a hand between my legs. "Spread open for me, gorgeous."

I followed his instructions because I was soaking wet, the slick already dripping down the insides of my thighs.

"Now bend forward for me," he urged me by running his large palm up my back, gently pushing me forward.

I gripped hold of the back of the outdoor lounge I bent over, my ass in the air, the cool breeze tickling my exposed pussy. This was definitely a vulnerable position but also ridiculously sexy.

When nothing happened for a few moments, I glanced over my shoulder to find the three of them standing there with the world's largest hard-ons, staring at my rear as if they were at an art museum admiring the Mona Lisa.

I might have blushed, but when I started to shift, River groaned. "Don't you dare."

"What are you all doing then?" I asked.

"Admiring," Caspian answered. "You have no idea how perfect the view is from back here."

"We're brainstorming on the perfect way to coordinate this, so we need inspiration." The smile in Hendrix's eyes gave me butterflies.

If they were wanting a show, then I'd give them one. While I called the guys' excuse to stare at me a lie, I caressed my hand down my body and between my legs, until I found my drenched core. I slide two fingers over the silky folds down to my entrance.

The explosive growl behind me told me they noticed. Good. I wriggled my ass a bit, then I slipped two fingers around the rim of my entrance. The horny wolves breathed louder now, and I let them take a good look before I pushed those fingers into me. I moaned at the sensation, at how my pussy did indeed suck down for more. She was a greedy thing.

Heat blazed through me the more I put on a show for them, but it wasn't long before I felt a thick erection pulsing against my ass.

"Close your eyes," Caspian ordered.

"And you have to guess which one of us is going to fuck your ass," River continued.

"We'll be gentle," Hendrix added. "But leave your fingers inside."

I quivered at their proposal, and quickly complied. "Okay," I answered.

The tip of the cock rubbed up and down my crack. I wouldn't lie, but I was so turned on right then, I was convinced I'd explode the moment he pushed into me.

Nothing right away, just the rubbing, which I guessed was to get me ready. Suddenly, the tip pushed into me. I paused, arching, anticipating being stretched. What I worked out immediately was that it wasn't Caspian. He was the biggest, and if it was him in my ass, I'd be gasping for breath.

Fire blazed across my insides as they pressed deeper, and it felt amazing. Taking in a shaky breath, I held on to the couch with one hand, my other still fingering myself, the delicious arousal intensifying.

"Oh, fuck me," Caspian snarled.

Heavy breaths danced behind me, and only once they grasped my hips, pumping in and out of me in slow motion, did I work out who was fucking me.

The steel grip of my hips, fingers digging into me, gave River away. He always held me powerfully.

"River," I moaned. "I know it's you."

Hendrix and Caspian broke out in cheers and clapped.

"Of course you'd work it out," River growled. "You know what it's like to be fucked by a god."

I chuckled, then moaned, my hips rocking for more. I removed my fingers, and I felt the slick dripping more now. River never pulled out either.

"She needs to be fucked. Look at how wet she is," Caspian growled.

Hendrix was at my side in moments, completely naked,

taking my arms and lifting me to stand slowly, while River drew out of me. I missed him immediately.

"Hello, little wolf," Hendrix purred, his hands falling to the back of my thighs, lifting me off my feet with ease. I curled my body around his, every inch of his skin like fire against mine.

"You smell so delicious," I murmured, taking in another inhale of his musky, wolf scent with a hint of freshly cut grass.

"I can't smell anything but you, beautiful. And my cock is hurting with how hard it is, my balls are almost blue because watching your ass get fucked is up there as one of the hottest things I've ever seen. But now, it's my turn."

"Yes, please. Please!"

Heat blazed between my legs the moment his cock found my entrance. Filthy, naughty needs filled me, and I held onto my alpha, moaning for him to take me.

He took a seat and I straddled his lap, just as he pushed in. Hendrix stared me in the eyes, his hands on my hips, guiding me lower on his huge cock. I tensed as he pushed deeper, wider.

"That's it. Be a good girl for me. I've been dreaming of you riding me."

I whimpered, panting the deeper he went, and that was when River stepped up behind me. He climbed on the seat, seeming to also straddle Hendrix's legs. But I couldn't even think of the logistics when he pushed back into my ass.

Suddenly, I was breathing heavily, biting on my lower lip as he got settled in. His hands curled around my body, cupping my breasts, squeezing them. With a bit of maneuvering, we found our rhythym, both men filling me completely, their cocks throbbing inside me.

"You look so gorgeous when you're being fucked. I want you to drain every last drop of cum from us," Hendrix murmured, then crushed his lips against mine, kissing me.

River tugged on my nipples, his mouth on my ear. "I've been thinking of being inside you since I rutted you up on the roof. Your smell has been in my nostrils, driving me crazy." His fingers slid over my hard nipples while Hendrix licked my mouth.

My pussy and ass clenched the more they worked in and out of me, moaning louder.

When a shadow fell over us, Hendrix pulled back and I glanced up at Caspian. He grunted as his hand palmed his hard cock. "Are you ready for me?" he asked.

"Always. Come to me, big boy," I gritted out.

He got up on the couch near us and sat on the back of it. With a bit of shifting on all our parts and me leaning toward his lap, I reached his cock. He was huge and already dripping.

I moaned as I slipped my lips over his shaft, taking him deeper.

Caspian growled, and we fell into a back and forth motion, and as unusual as it seemed, having three dicks inside me came close to undoing me. I clenched my mouth around Caspian, driving him wild as he groaned, while the other two thrust into me, never going too deep, I noticed. It didn't take away from how turned on I was right then, how my whole body thrummed.

Here I was feeling like a boss with three cocks in me at the same time. A fantasy that would stay with me forever.

The men weren't stopping, but they weren't being brutal either.

All three thrust into me, playing with me, pushing me, and I didn't know how much more I could take.

"She's close," Hendrix suddenly broke through my thoughts, then the guys completely took over.

Caspian pulled his erection out of my mouth and lifted me up between the other two, while cradling in closer, his mouth on the groove of my neck. "You're everything to me."

I could only respond in delicious cries.

Hendrix had his mouth on my breast, while River licked the other side of my neck. Neither stopped fucking me. But Caspian's hand dipped to my clit, rubbing me, tapping it. I grabbed his cock, my fingers curling around his hardness, and I worked him up and down.

"Oh, goddess," I cried out.

"That's it, come for us, squeeze our cocks," Hendrix purred, then flicked my nipples.

"You're so tight," River roared behind me.

I whimpered just as the wave of lust crashed over me. My screams filled the sunny day while I burst, convulsing.

In that perfect moment of climax, all three men bit down into me, sinking sharp teeth deep, breaking skin.

My thrashing and moans came from that perfect moment of pain and pleasure, from my wolf awakening.

I glanced down, seeing blood spill from the bite marks, and that was when Caspian growled, his wolf peeking through as he offered me his neck. "Bite me," he gritted out.

Without hesitation, I leaned in close to the warmth of his neck, my mouth parting. With my wolf already there, I sensed my teeth getting sharper. She was ready, knowing exactly what we had to do.

I bit down, sliding my teeth into his neck, tasting blood immediately. And with it, my wolf howled inside me, the sound in my ears, and I sensed Caspian's wolf too, like the fresh brush of fur against my skin. He growled and just then pulsed in my hand, coming hard. I held onto him and released his neck, licking the blood from my lips.

Hendrix was there, his hands on my face. "We need to finish this, and we need your bite." Just like Caspian, he craned his neck to the side and offered it to me. Planting my hand against his chest, I leaned in and lay my lips on his neck.

Teeth pierced his skin and I drove them deep enough that he hollered.

I loved the way he suddenly pulsed within me, flooding me with his cum while my wolf stirred. The electric connection danced up my arms because I knew this was so much more than just our animal's greeting. This was the bond Hendrix mentioned, the heartfelt thumping in my chest that I would die without these men.

Breaking free from Hendrix, River still rode my ass, and when he curled his wrist, he whispered in my ears, "Make it hurt, angel."

I smiled as I pressed his wrist to my mouth, teeth extending. I bit down, blood instantly flooding my mouth. It was barely a few seconds before River flew into his orgasm, pumping into me. The metallic taste of blood coated the back of my throat, and my wolf was ecstatic, pressing for release, whining at her connection to our three wolves.

What was different now was that I sensed their wolves as I would someone standing behind me before I saw them. The love pulsing from our connection was the most beautiful thing I'd ever experienced.

By the time we all calmed down and caught our breaths, we were a heaped mess of tangled arms, legs, cocks, and a lot of cum. I was talking the kind that needed a hosing down of the boat with a lot of it seeping down my inner legs.

"Good thing we're surrounded by water," Caspian joked, as it was obvious he made the biggest mess.

"That was so amazing," I murmured, collapsing against Hendrix's chest, exhaustion flaring over me. "I think I might sleep for a week now. And I may not be able to walk for a few days." I laughed. "But I wouldn't change a thing."

"You were incredible," he murmured in my ear. I nestled against his chest and actually felt his wolf stirring just behind his rib cage, sending me playful barking yaps at odds with the monster I knew it to be.

"I can hear and feel your wolf." I jerked upright to look at Hendrix, Caspian, and River.

They just smiled.

"You're so perfect, Syn. I knew that before...but feeling it like this. Fuck, I love you," Hendrix purred.

He kissed me, as did the other two, all over my face and neck. Was there such a thing as being loved too much? Highly unlikely because a girl could get used to this kind of attention.

"I'm yours, don't ever forget that. Now, who's going to carry me into the sea and help me wash?"

Suddenly, all three were bustling to get me up and into the water. At this frantic, competitive rate, I wouldn't be surprised if they dumped me into the ocean accidentally. I broke out laughing, knowing this would be a day I'd never forget.

A day when my family became mine for real. When I knew they'd protect me, cherish me, and most of all, loved the idea of raising children as much as me.

I couldn't wait...

Chapter 18

SYN

I walked into the dining area, or should I say, I "waddled" in, to eat. River had started calling me "little duck" as I'd lost the ability to walk normally with how large I'd gotten during pregnancy.

I wasn't sure how my legs were carrying my enormous stomach anymore. But it was almost time. He or she would be out any day now.

A wave of anxiety crashed over me at the thought, and I pushed it away. There were four of us, *I wouldn't fuck it up.* I had help.

That had been a theme the last couple of months. We'd had peace, everything had been dream-like, but this worry inside me had grown and grown that I was going to mess all of this up. That I wouldn't be a good mother.

"Everything all right, sweetheart?" Caspian asked as he helped me into my chair.

I smiled at him, putting on a happy face, which wasn't

hard. I had a lot to be happy about nowadays. "Just can't believe it's almost time."

"I can't wait," he said with a wink as he lifted the lids off five silver platters.

This was a tradition that we'd decided on once I realized I was ready to eat at all hours of the day.

Caspian and I had started to have a big meal in between lunch and dinner because I couldn't last.

It had become my favorite part of the day.

"What's on the menu today?" I asked.

"Chicken cordon bleu, broccoli cheese rice, and sourdough rolls, it looks like. And for dessert, we've got peanut butter brownies and fruit."

I was practically drooling already. I went to grab some of the chicken when a wave of strong freaking pain crashed through my insides.

Fuck. I'd just had a contraction.

"What is it? Is the baby coming? What just happened?" rushed Caspian in a panic.

I took a deep breath, waiting for it to pass.

"Just Braxton Hicks, I'm sure," I murmured, finally getting the chicken to my plate. The baby wasn't coming today. I was not ready. Maybe tomorrow, but not today.

"Okay, what's your guess today?" The pain was gone. Everything was good, and this food was so freaking good...as usual.

This was also a game we played, guessing the gender. My mind changed daily, and so did the guys'.

"Today I'm thinking a girl," announced Caspian, taking a big bite of his buttered roll.

"And why is that?" I asked with a laugh.

"You were snoring for most of the night."

I sighed, shaking my head, knowing he wasn't lying.

I had never snored in my entire life...until the last three

months. Now I whistled and snorted all night long. River had to wear earplugs to get any sleep. It was...not my favorite—

"Ugh," I cried out as my muscles tightened again.

"That was only five minutes. I'm getting the doctor." Caspian leaped out of his chair but I grabbed onto his arm with gritted teeth.

"Nope. I'm totally good. The doctor said I had to be less than three minutes in between and over a minute long with each one. I'm not even close to that."

Caspian eyed me doubtfully before sitting back down. I lifted some rice to my lips and then rolled my eyes in annoyance when he still just stared.

"I'm fine. Really. I'll know when it's time."

And it was not time. Not today. I still had a couple more days until my due date. Panic was trembling in my veins, so I put a big bite of bread in my mouth. Because carbs could cure anything...right?

A minute later, my fork clattered to my plate as it happened again.

"That's it! Hendrix! River!" Caspian yelled, his face paling, and sweat breaking out on his forehead.

"You don't need to call them!" I snapped, right as Hendrix and River came rushing in.

They let us have our "linner" together every day, but they were always nearby, waiting for the moment we were finished and they could be with me.

"What is it?" Hendrix rumbled.

"She's having contractions. Close together. That last one was only three minutes apart."

"Stop timing me," I growled, throwing him a dirty look. "I'm fine. I'm just hungry—" Right as I tried to take a bite, I shrieked with pain.

"Fuck! Okay. I've got this. Calling the doctor now," River

rumbled in a rattled voice as he pulled his cell phone out of his pocket.

I clamped down on his hand. "We're not calling the doctor!"

All three of them stared at me stunned. There were drops of sweat falling down my face from the intensity of the contractions.

Hendrix squatted in front of me, softly grabbing my chin. "Little wolf...what's going on?"

I burst into tears. All three of them crowded around me in alarm.

"I—I can't do this!" I cried.

"Can't do what, baby?" River asked cautiously.

"Have our baby! What if I'm a terrible mom? What if I mess it all up! What if I yell or I don't know...forget to feed it or something. Our gummy deserves a better mom!" I wasn't sure if they could even understand what I was saying with how hysterical my voice was, but it felt really good just to get it all out.

There was a long silence and then Hendrix pulled me into his arms, a tough task due to the beach ball I was packing.

"Little wolf. I have no doubt in my mind that you will be the best mother. Our child is so fucking lucky to have you. The luckiest, in fact."

"We can't say fucking when it gets here," I sniffed.

Caspian snorted. "That might be the baby's first word living in this house."

That only caused a fresh wave of tears.

"Okay, okay. No swear words," Caspian assured me in a panic.

"Syn. Sweetheart. You can do this. You've taken care of us and changed our lives since the moment you stepped into it. You've already shown how much you love our gummy. And you'll have us. Every step of the way. We won't ever forget to feed our baby."

"You promise?" I sobbed as another wave of pain crashed over me.

Caspian was grimacing when it ended as I'd been squeezing his hand hard enough to break it.

"We promise," they all swore, almost in unison.

"Can we have our baby now?" asked Hendrix, looking a second away from dragging me out of the room and doing what he wanted anyway.

"Okay," I squeaked.

The moment the word came out of my mouth, I was indeed in Hendrix's arms and he was racing towards the birthing room we'd set up with all the latest equipment and technology. With their status, it wasn't wise for us to go to a regular hospital where we could be caught unaware, so we'd basically made a hospital suite in our house.

The doctor was already waiting inside.

Caspian shrugged his shoulders sheepishly when I turned to him. "I may have texted her..."

I blew him a kiss and changeed into my hospital gown.

It was time.

River

James Khan, named in honor of Syn's lost brother, was born screaming at 5:22 p.m., seven pounds, eight ounces, with black hair and brilliant green eyes that were just like his mother's.

Alana Khan was born five minutes later...much to everyone's shock. Five pounds, four ounces with blue eyes and a patch of fuzzy, dark red hair. Evidently, she'd been hiding behind James the whole pregnancy. And it made sense why she'd never been seen. She was quiet from the moment she arrived, just staring at the world around her. The calm and quiet to her brother's chaos.

Hendrix almost passed out when the doctor announced there was another baby...but the second Syn delivered Alana, it was like the last missing puzzle of our little pack clicked into place.

I hadn't imagined that I could be any more in love with Syn, but watching her push out our babies...my heart nearly exploded.

All those times I thought I'd never be happy. All those times I thought the world might be better off without me.

Holding my babies in my arms, it was like they'd never existed.

I'd never known life could be so sweet.

///

One month later...

Caspian

James had just thrown up on me for the thousandth time that day, and somehow I was still smiling. I laid him down and began whistling, something he loved.

I'd read the baby books that River and the doctor had recommended...but I still hadn't been able to comprehend how much bodily fluids came with a baby. Drool, spit-up, pee...and fuck, don't get me started on all the poop.

James had literally spit up into my mouth the other day. Don't ask me how that happened, but it had. And I'd gagged and thrown up right afterwards.

Poor Syn had walked into the room to James and I both falling apart. Thank goodness she was already the best mom in the world and had quickly and efficiently figured it out.

All her fears had been unfounded; she'd taken to motherhood like she'd been born for it. There was a peace about her that had never been there before. Like she'd been waiting for something all her life and now it was here.

Right now she was swaying Alana back and forth in her rocking chair, softly humming a lullaby with a sweet smile on her face.

She must have felt my stare because her gorgeous green eyes lifted to mine.

"I love you," I murmured to her, any other words lost in the all-consuming emotions blasting in my chest.

"I love you too," she murmured...right as James took that moment to pee all over me.

Hendrix

I'd snuck into the babies' room again. I'd heard Alana hiccup on the monitor, and I just wanted to make sure she was okay—

"Babe." Syn's voice floated from behind me, amused as usual when she caught me. "I know they weren't crying."

"Well, Alana made a sound. I just wanted to make sure everything was alright."

She rolled her eyes at me, affectionately.

Truth be told, I'd been just as freaked out as Syn had been about having a child. I'd had nightmares leading up to the birth about my father, my face transplanted on his for parts.

Not fun.

But something had happened the second I'd first held them in my arms, something that pushed away the fear and replaced it with peace. I still worried every day that I was messing things up. Every time they cried, I rushed to their side, ready to do anything I could.

"You know...I saw the doctor this morning."

I frowned. "Are you okay?" I stepped away from Alana's crib. Watching Syn give birth had been beautiful, but also terrifying. Seeing her in pain like that, without being able to do anything, almost made me go feral.

"I was cleared," she said with a wink.

It took me a moment to realize what she was talking about. And as soon as I did...I was hard.

"You mean—?"

"Yep." She gave me a sexy wink and stripped off her shirt as she walked backwards into the hall. "Think I can lure you away from the babies long enough to have your way with me?"

I followed her without another thought. My mate was the sexiest creature alive, and I'd been dying to have her over these last weeks.

As her bra hit me in the face as I hurried after her, all I could think was I was the luckiest bastard alive.

Syn

The room was pitch black when he woke up, sitting up from the bed and searching the room. His hand reached to turn on the light...but I'd unplugged it.

I'd also handcuffed him to the bed frame with cuffs made of the strongest metal on the market. Unless he "monster'd" out, he wasn't going anywhere.

"What the fuck?" he snarled, trying to pull on the cuffs.

I stepped out of the shadows and he immediately stopped struggling.

"What's this, little wolf?"

"Mmmh. I just thought we could role play," I murmured, as I crawled up the bed towards him. "You like the sound of that, don't you, Alpha?"

Hendrix chuckled darkly, recalling immediately when he'd said something similar to me...all those months ago.

I straddled his dick and gave a quick tug to his already hard shaft. "Want me to offer you the world, baby?" I purred.

He groaned as I slid my soaking wet folds across his dick. "I can't believe I actually said that."

I broke character and giggled.

"Well, at least you lived up to your word." I took his dick and slowly lowered myself down on it.

His answer was lost in a moan as I fucked myself on his huge cock, my moans soon joining his.

We both couldn't have imagined what that fateful night would have led to.

But as Hendrix and I moved together, him fucking me with dirty scenes in my head, and in real life, I knew we both had gotten everything we could have ever wanted.

A happily ever after.

The End

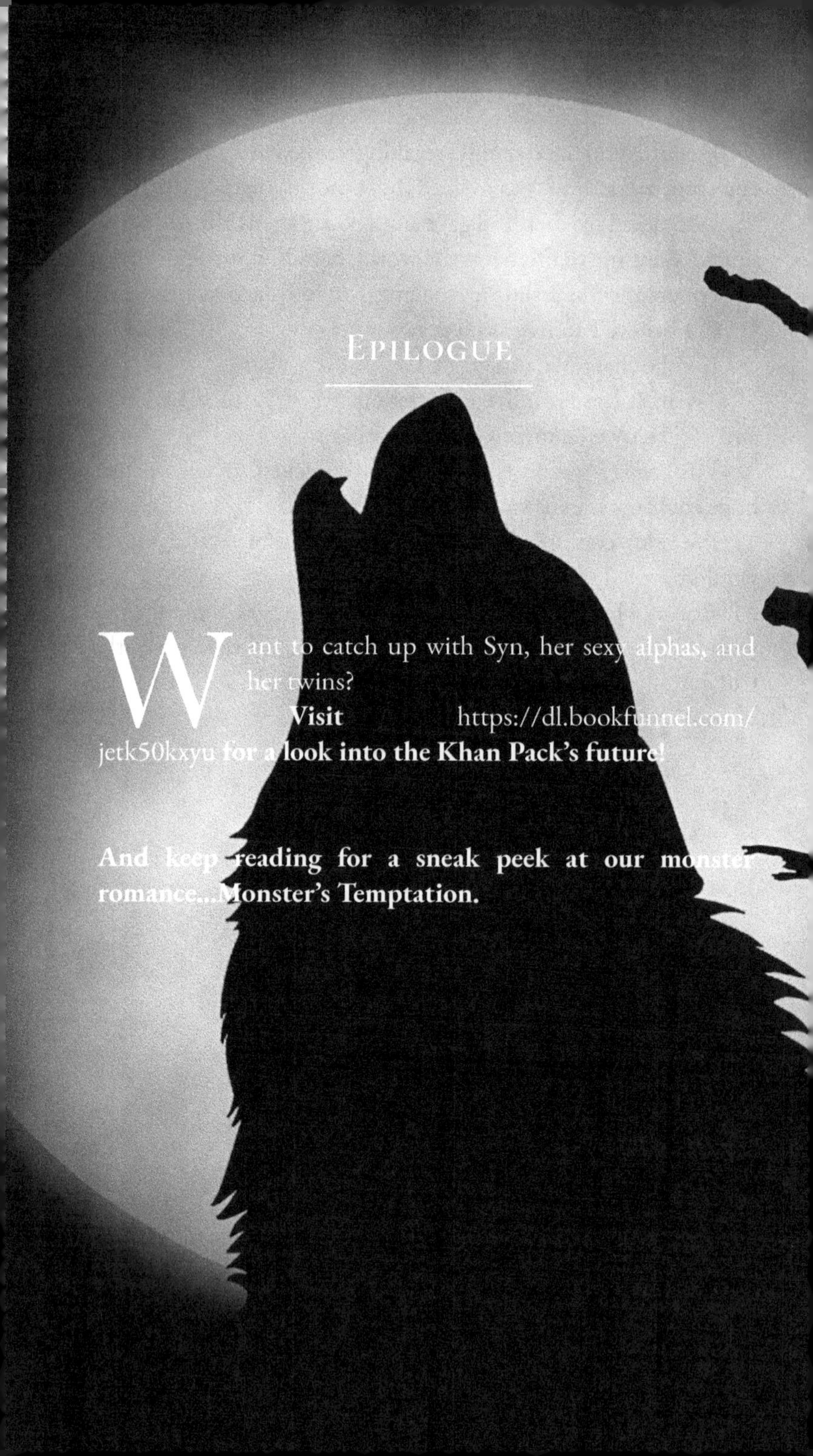

Epilogue

Want to catch up with Syn, her sexy alphas, and her twins?

Visit https://dl.bookfunnel.com/jetk50kxyu **for a look into the Khan Pack's future!**

And keep reading for a sneak peek at our monster romance...Monster's Temptation.

Monster's Temptation
Book 1

The Monster King wants to play...

It's been 1097 days and 14 hours since I've been locked in this place.

And they've come to me every night.

The monsters in my dreams worship my body.

And when I wake up, I'm desperate for more...

But they're never there to finish me off.

Dr. Adams says I can leave the asylum if I start to take my meds, but I've always hated how they made me feel...and I'm not sure that I agree with them that I'm actually crazy.

Because dreams don't make you crazy, right?

I've got to start living someday though...so I finally take the plunge and obey so I can get out.

My dreams stop, and the monsters disappear. I'm finally starting a new life.

And that's when he comes...the monster king.

Evidently my little dreams, weren't just dreams. And he and his demon horde were feeding off my lust.

Their glowing eyes, sharp teeth, and big...

They're all real.

The Monster King wants me back. I'm their favorite plaything after all.

And I just might want to play.

Get your copy of Monster's Temptation today!

Chapter 1

3 Years Later

BLAKE

"Don't you dare cover up, Pet," he growled as he pulled on my dress. My breath was coming out in gasps as my eyes moved across his muscled chest. He was wearing tight, black pants, and I watched as he slowly slid them down his sculpted thighs, revealing a huge red dick with two heads that were designed to give me as much pleasure as possible. As I watched, his clawed hand circled his thick base, and he bit his bottom lip with a half-lidded gaze, his sharp fangs peeking out over his full lips. He was mostly human looking with the exception of a few key parts... And I'd never seen anything hotter.

"Slide those panties down so I can make you come."

I had no choice but to obey. As usual, he had me soaked and ready even though he hadn't so much as touched my skin yet. I slid down my panties obediently, and he grabbed me, pulling me into his lap and rubbing my soaking wet core over his hard length.

"Fuck, you're sexy." He yanked me forward, and my hands

automatically moved to his broad shoulders for balance as he moved me into place—my legs spread wide straddling him, my breasts flush with his chest, his huge cock flexing under me.

Despite the fact that he towered over me, in this position we were eye to eye. He was beautiful, my monster. His glowing red eyes flecked with gold sparks, his chiseled nose, his sculpted mouth that would've made Michelangelo weep. I loved the hunger in his gaze. After an entire life of never being wanted, I couldn't get enough of him...and his friends.

His lips crashed against mine in a deep kiss, and I instinctively opened my mouth, allowing his forked tongue to slide in and tangle with mine. He devoured me. His licks were aggressive and filthy, and I could feel it all the way to my core.

There was an ache inside of me that I knew only he could fill. I moaned as I returned his kiss eagerly. My hands moved from his shoulders, up his face, until I was fisting his two long black horns. I held onto them as I moved, trying to get friction on my aching clit. I was mindless with desire.

But my king wasn't in a hurry, and instead of giving me what I wanted, he simply deepened the kiss, sliding his fingers through my hair so he could hold me in place as he continued his hot, wet licks in my mouth. His other hand softly stroked my lower back, the sharp tips of his claws teasing my skin.

Tension was building inside of me, and I knew from experience that I could come just from this. His hands on my back slid down, and he squeezed my ass before grabbing his dick and positioning it right where I wanted.

"You gonna give me what I want?" he growled, and all I could do was whimper in response as he pulled me down and pushed into me. I gasped at the tight stretch. He was so big, the two heads of his crown massaging different places inside of me.

"Fuck," he groaned, a guttural growl laced in his words. "Relax, Pet. You're going to be my good girl, aren't you?" he purred.

A soft scream slipped out of me as my thighs moved flush against his and he slid all the way in. My breath came out in gasps as I tried to get a hold of myself. I was so full, it was hard to think outside of the sensations.

"Good fucking girl," he rumbled as he moved both hands to my hips and lifted me up slightly before thrusting up hard.

I whimpered again, and his grip tightened at the sound. He started fucking me desperately, his movements rough and powerful, and all I could do was go along for the ride.

His cut abdomen bunched as he moved his hips, and his gaze was hungry and determined as he watched me closely.

One of his hands moved off my hip, and he sliced down the center of my dress with his claws, showcasing my straining breasts.

He began to suckle on one of my nipples, and I gasped as my body arched backwards.

"Yes," I breathed, caught in the sensation of his mouth torturing my nipple and his long, thick cock spearing in and out of me. I continued to hold onto his long horns as we moved desperately together. His sharp fangs pricked against my skin, setting me off in an agonizingly good orgasm that threatened to destroy me.

Something slid softly against my ass, and I gasped as I peeked backwards only to see nothing visible there. But something *was sliding in between my cheeks and caressing my rosebud softly.*

"Tightest fucking pussy I've ever felt," he growled as he moved to my other nipple, his hips thrusting desperately against mine.

"Going to keep you forever, Pet. My good girl," he breathed as he stretched me.

And then...

I woke with a gasp, sweaty, and with my core aching as my

breath left me in gasps. My whole body was a live wire, and I was on the edge of orgasm; one touch and I'd go off.

Just like every morning, I had to center myself and force my brain to start working again after a night of...dreams.

Not nightmares. Obviously. They made me feel way too good for it to be that.

Although it was always a monster ravishing my body.

I peeked up at the camera situated in the wall in front of me, the red light signaling that someone on the other end was watching me. Always watching me.

I'm sure they were getting off to the sight of me panting in my sleep, my nipples peeking out from my thin pajamas. At least I hadn't woken up with my hands rubbing furiously at my core. That happened quite a bit.

Although, at least those times my body had cum before I'd woken up. Now that I was awake, it was going to be hours before my body would settle down and I wouldn't be desperate for...a dick.

I fell back into my pillow, wanting to scream. It was this place. It was what was making me go crazy.

It had started slowly. A few dreams here and there of sexy scenes with...well, the psychiatrist here actually, but then one night it had morphed.

And *they* had begun to fill my dreams.

Every night, no matter what I tried, or how much I tried to stay awake, I was sucked into an erotic dreamscape. A dreamscape where...monsters ravaged my body over and over again.

It was the same four monsters. At this point, they really did feel like my lovers because I could tell you about every one of their features. I also could describe in detail all of their weird dicks. And all the ways they liked to play.

Considering I was definitely still a virgin, these dreams were quite alarming—and uncomfortable, and they'd only ratcheted up in intensity as the months and years had gone by. Last night's dream was relatively tame; I'd been gang banged the night before. A monster in my ass and pussy as I gave blow jobs back and forth to the other two.

I shifted uncomfortably in my bed as my core clenched again, begging to have some fucking relief.

If it weren't for the cameras, I would have. But with someone always watching...

My father had convinced everyone that I was crazy, and the sex dreams, the ones where my moans and screams of desire were so loud they rattled down the entire hallway...they were what cemented it.

There was no hiding what I dreamed about every night.

I'd tried the sleeping pills the doctors had given me, but those only trapped me in the dreams longer...much to the delight of Bright Meadows' other residents. Who needed porn when you had a soundtrack starring me, right?

So I didn't use the sleeping pills anymore.

The other medicine they tried to give me zombified me. The one time I'd taken them, a whole day had passed and I'd been mauled by another of the patients here, unable to do anything. I'd come to life in my room, the moon peeking through the tiny window above my head, terrified when I couldn't recall anything.

I'd refused to take the pills after that. No way was I going to be comatose at a place like Bright Meadows, where anything could happen to you.

And at least my screams weren't the scary kind. Not like all the other screams you heard in this place at night.

The screams from the other residents were always worse at night. Before I inevitably was dragged into my dreams, I would lay on my tiny cot that I was pretty sure was made of cardboard, staring up at the ceiling, and then the screams would start. It was much quieter during the day, but at night it was a cruel symphony. Maybe all the patients here found it impossible to sit with their thoughts at night too.

It's not like we were tired from the day's activities. Mealtimes, medicine time, group therapy, and art therapy—they weren't exactly activities that required a lot of energy. Maybe for some people, it would've been exhausting to share their feelings, but I'd stopped sharing any of my real emotions the first week.

Since my father had threatened to kill me if I ever opened my mouth, there wasn't much that I could say except that I wasn't crazy. And apparently, that sort of thing was frowned upon in this institution. Who would've thought?

Unlike the asylums you saw in movies, the rooms in this place weren't perfectly white; instead, they were black, which felt suffocating when you could walk across the room in two steps, and your window was only as big as your head. Mornings began with a bell that sounded more like a shrill siren. It woke us up at the same time every morning at seven a.m. Evidently, they were big believers in that adage, 'rise early and go to sleep early', because I now had the sleeping hours of an 80-year-old woman.

The bell rang just then, and I sighed as I dragged myself out of bed and went to change. You were expected to switch from your dishwater gray sleeping uniform to your dishwater gray day uniform in the minutes after the bell rang. There were no mirrors in the room, and the brushes they gave you were soft and completely ineffective so you didn't try and off yourself with them, thus everyone looked like a mess all day, every day.

If you weren't out of your room within ten minutes, one of the staff would barge in and force you out. I'd had that happen once, and I'd never let it happen again. Andrew, one of the resident assholes of the institution, had made sure to do a boob and an ass grab as he yanked me out of the room, so I'd learned quickly.

After dressing, I made my way out of the living room, along with most of the others that had rooms around me. We all walked slowly to the dining area filled with circle tables to facilitate a sense of "community", where we would be served a sugar-free, gluten-free, dairy-free breakfast that basically tasted like sawdust and paint thinner, but was apparently good for our brains.

There was one prisoner—I mean patient, who sat across from me every day, and today was no different. He must have felt the same way about the breakfast as I did, because every day he would use his fingers to smear it across his entire face. It didn't matter what they gave him. Seeing him try and slather himself with vegan bacon had been a particularly interesting experience.

Props to him for livening up the place. Even if he did it with drool dripping down from his mouth.

After breakfast, we were shuffled to the nurse's station, where they forced pills down our throats and stuck their fingers in our mouths to make sure the pills were gone. Luckily I was just on a mood stabilizer after I'd refused the other pill—not that I had anything against taking medicine for mental health. But considering I didn't have any of the disorders I'd been diagnosed with while under the influence of the drug I'd been injected with on that fateful day, taking anything stronger probably wouldn't have been great.

Evidently, my father was fearful of the effect that stronger meds could have on me and had ordered that I not be given any. He recognized that stronger drugs might have the detrimental effect of "loosening" my tongue, and he wouldn't want that.

Not that anyone was ever going to believe my story. It was so outlandish that I would sound crazy to anyone who heard it. That was the beauty of my father's plan. Have everyone on the outside doubt my sanity, and everyone on the inside doubt it as well. I would never have anyone believe me again.

We had an "A" schedule and a "B" schedule, just like school, and our routine was followed strictly. Except, instead of Calculus and English, we were learning how to paint our feelings, use recorders to "play our emotions out", and talk in small groups.

That was one of the hardest things about my new reality. Not only had I been thrown in here before the end of school, but I wasn't even allowed to take any tests to get my diploma, or even a GED, despite the fact that I'd been number two in my entire class. Stanford seemed like a fantasy that I'd made up in my mind at this point.

Most of the therapists were completely intolerable. They treated us more like toddlers than adults, and I cringed every time they spoke to me in their slow, sympathetic voices.

Since I knew I didn't have a chance to get out, and the therapists weren't interested in hearing about my innocence, I'd begun telling fairy tales during group therapy. But I'd make them so convoluted that it would take at least ten minutes for the therapist to figure out what story I was telling. It was a game I played, with only myself, of course, to see how long I could go before they caught on.

Anything to make the day go by quicker.

There was only one bright spot in Bright Meadows Asylum. Steele Adams.

Dr. Steele Adams, I should say.

Seeing him twice a week was most likely the only thing that kept me from falling off the deep end and becoming as crazy as my parents claimed I was.

Dr. Adams was the most beautiful man I'd ever seen. He looked like he'd just stepped off the catwalk, and he was completely out of place in the drab, gross atmosphere I existed in now. During our sessions, I honestly wasn't even sure what we talked about, because I would get lost just looking at him and listening to the cadence of his voice. It's like someone out there had scooped out any fantasies of male attractiveness I had lurking in my brain and created him just for me.

When I was in sixth grade, I'd been to Iceland and we'd visited the Blue Lagoon. That's what his eyes reminded me of —they were a glowing blue color I'd never seen on another human being. Combined with his raven-colored hair, the effect was stunning. It was no wonder I was having dreams about him.

It was a Thursday today, which meant that I would be seeing him after breakfast.

I was pushed out of my lustful daydream by a tray clattering to the floor nearby. I looked over and saw that Candace was brandishing her spoon at a girl I'd never seen before. The poor girl was covered in the sweet potatoes the kitchen staff was trying to pass off as breakfast, and there were big tears rolling down her cheeks.

Maybe in another life, I would've stepped up to defend her since I was pretty sure that Candace was one of the resident murderers in this place. But apathy...and self-preservation was about all I was capable of feeling right now. Plus, I had a scar on my leg where Candace had somehow whittled a spoon into a knife and stabbed me in the leg a year ago. I'd bled so much that I'd passed out.

So someone else could handle Candace.

Candace started cackling wildly as orderlies rushed in. As soon as they got to her, she began to flail her arms, hitting and scratching every person that she could. "I'll kill all of you mother truckers," she screeched, making the word 'trucker' much more menacing than you would think. For some reason, Candace had a thing against swearing. She didn't care about murdering and mutilating people, but swearing crossed the line of her moral compass. "Let go of me, you butt munchers!"

She managed to cut one of the nurse's cheeks with her spoon before someone plunged a needle into her neck.

Almost immediately, her eyes took on that glazed, faraway look I was used to seeing here, and she stopped struggling. Two of the orderlies led her out of the room and then we were all instructed to go back to eating like nothing had happened. Just a typical day in Bright Meadows.

I wished I could say that Candace was the worst resident in this place, but there were far scarier people than her. And a bunch of them at that. I did my best to try and stay away from them. But every couple of months I'd slip up, and I'd be caught somewhere where the staff wasn't present. Slammed against the wall, a piece of my hair hacked off, burned with a lighter they'd come across...they were always quite inventive.

The only time that I could let my guard down was about to happen. My session with Steele.

I put my tray down, keeping my head tucked just in case any of the psychos thought I was looking at them wrong, and then hustled out of the dining area towards his office.

Butterflies ricocheted through my veins the closer I got to his door.

My dreams might've been filled with him, but he'd never given me any notion he felt similarly.

But then again, why would he? Here I was, a 20-year-old locked away in an insane asylum, while he was an accomplished doctor, able to live his life out in the real world. I wondered if he had a girlfriend out there. I didn't think he had a wife. He didn't wear a ring; not that his lack of one really meant anything.

I knocked on the door of his office, and a minute later, he opened it, a warm smile on his beautiful, beautiful lips.

"Hi," I murmured, inwardly wincing as I realized how breathy my voice sounded.

"Blake," he said with a nod, a piece of his hair falling into his face. I bit my lip in an effort to prevent myself from being weird and reaching out and brushing the curl out of his face. I'm sure that would go over well.

He was dressed in his typical uniform—a perfectly pressed, buttoned-up white collared shirt and navy black dress pants—and looked like he was about to conquer a corporate boardroom instead of spending an hour asking me how I was feeling.

I passed by him with a nod and entered the room, and he followed me inside. In my daydreams—not my night dreams, since those were solely filled with creatures—he was checking out my ass as I walked right now. But our uniform pants were shapeless, so that probably wouldn't happen even if he was interested in me like that.

The room was cozy. He'd obviously done his best to make it feel welcoming. It had to have been him who decorated the place because there was no way that anyone else in Bright Meadows would care about something like comfort. There were tall shelves on every wall stuffed full of books. Most of them were boring psychology books, but there were some classics scattered in there as well. He had his patients sit on a comfortable leather couch that had an assortment of squishy pillows and throw blankets he encouraged me to use every time. There was a red and black oriental rug on the floor, potted plants here and there, and a massive fireplace on the far wall that he had lit most days. Which was heaven since Bright Meadows believed that its residents should feel like human popsicles judging by the freezing temperatures we were kept in.

I settled into the couch, immediately grabbing a fuzzy blanket and wrapping it around me. Dr. Adams walked over to the fireplace and threw another log in before opening his small fridge that sat next to it and pulling out a can of my favorite orange soda.

My mouth started watering just looking at it, and it was honestly all I could do to not jump up and grab it out of his hands like I was Gollum from Lord of the Rings. *My Precious*, my inner voice cooed.

That was creepy.

"You obviously were listening last week," I said with a blush as he handed me the drink.

He smiled at me, and the butterflies in my stomach started doing freaking cartwheels and flips like they'd made it to the Olympics.

"I always listen to you," he murmured as he settled into the warm armchair across from the couch. "It just took a minute to track it down. Evidently, they stopped making it last year."

While I was definitely twitter-pated…and interested in the fact that he'd tracked down the soda I'd mentioned was my favorite, I was also thinking that I'd been trapped in here long enough that they discontinued my favorite drink. I mean, I may have been the only person in the world who drank it, so that was probably why, but it still represented the stark passage of time and all that I'd lost.

"I made you upset," he commented, leaning forward in dismay. I threw him a tremulous smile and popped the tab on my drink before taking a large gulp of the drink, moaning a bit as the fizzy orange beverage hit my tastebuds.

"Finally, something that doesn't taste like old leather," I said as I glanced at him, almost spitting my drink out when I saw the expression on his face.

He looked—almost hungry. Starving, in fact.

For me.

Dr. Adams blinked and the look disappeared. His face was blank again, only the kind, caring psychiatrist to be found.

But I swore that I'd seen it.

Unless the dreams were driving me to see sexual desire everywhere.

I didn't think that was happening. I hadn't thought Mr. Drools-a-lot was into me at lunch.

Focus, I chastised myself as I took another sip of my drink.

"So, have you thought at all about what we talked about last session?" he asked, his bright blue eyes boring into me.

I shifted in my seat. "I've told you that it won't make a difference."

He'd been bringing up the medication he wanted me to try for weeks now. One of the main focuses of our sessions was my...intense dreams. He knew in general that they were sexual —the staff had told him that. But he'd never pressed me on specific details—thank god. Dr. Adams seemed to be under the impression I wasn't going to be trapped in this place for the rest of my life if I could get my dreams under control.

He seemed to think that was the main concern and not the fact that I was being held hostage here because of my father.

Dr. Adams leaned forward. "If you could just stay on it for a while, enough to convince them you're ready to be released—"

I squeezed my can so hard that orange soda went everywhere.

"Shit," I gasped, attempting to use my shirt to blot at the soda now all over the leather couch. Frustrated tears built in my eyes as I wiped. I knew what would happen—I would go on those pills but would still be trapped here, of course, and I'd lose even more when I began to walk around in a daze.

Suddenly, his hand was on mine, and I looked to see that he was crouched in front of me. This close to him, it was almost unbearable. He was so fucking beautiful.

"Blake," he murmured, his gaze searching my face. "I'm sorry. You can tell me if there's something else going on."

My lip trembled, and I was very much aware that his fingers were softly caressing my hand. I wanted to tell him about my father, and how I'd ended up here. I wanted to so fucking bad.

I opened my mouth, the story on the tip of my tongue, but then I remembered my father's warning the day I'd been dropped off. I remembered the way the staff had reacted when I'd even dared to say that I wasn't crazy.

Dr. Adams was my only safe space here. I didn't want to ruin that on a pipe dream.

"I'm fine, Dr. Adams. I'm so sorry I've made such a mess," I finally said stiffly, watching as disappointment leached into his features.

"Steele," he said as he pulled his hand away and stood up.

"Steele?" I asked, confused, and hating that I missed his touch.

"You should call me Steele." I watched as he went and grabbed some paper towels from a shelf in the back corner of the room and then walked back over and methodically cleaned up the rest of my spilled drink.

"Oh. Okay." I had to have cracked. That was the only way to explain what was happening. I mean, maybe to a normal girl it wouldn't have seemed like much—the special drink, the hand touch, the first name. But for me, it was a lot. A hell of a lot.

After throwing away the towels, he sat back down in his chair, and he asked his normal questions.

I responded with my usual answers, but everything felt different. I could feel it in the air. I could see it in his eyes. Something had changed.

And as his hand brushed the small of my back as he

opened the door at the end of our session, I wondered what I'd done to make the universe hate me so much.

Because in this life, I could never have Steele or anything else that I wanted. Even if he wanted me.

I walked down the hall away from him, feeling the heat of his stare caressing my back, but I didn't look his way.

The only comfort I was ever going to get in this forsaken place was in my dreams.

With my monsters.

I had to live with that.

Chapter 2

Blake

Three brutal years at Bright Meadows Asylum. And not one visitor.

Until today...

I tried to shake off the weird, ominous feeling that had stretched across my skin ever since one of the staff had come to take me to Dr. Adams' office, where apparently my guests were waiting.

Although Andrew, the asshole, wouldn't tell me who the visitor was, I knew it had to be my parents...which was terrifying. I didn't have anyone else in my life who would have shown up besides them.

I paused in front of Dr. Adams' office door, finding it difficult to make myself knock. I bit my lip as I tried to prepare myself. Was I ready to face them?

You've got this, Blake. Deep breath. And if it is your parents, try not to throw any sharp objects at their heads.

The thought made me smile. If they wanted crazy, I could show them how looney I could get. I'd had a lot of time to perfect that here.

I shook my head and sighed, knowing that would only end

with me in the isolation rooms where the real crazies were kept. Rooms with actual padded walls.

I'd been locked up in one on my arrival...and it had messed with my head for weeks afterward.

Drawing in a trembling breath, I knocked on the door, trying not to let myself get my hopes up that maybe they were here to finally let me out. I could move away, far away, and they'd never have to see or worry about what I'd do again.

"Enter," Dr. Adams answered in that deep voice that captivated me.

I pushed open the door, instantly catching Mother's harsh voice at the doctor before she twisted to look at me with a forced smile. But it vanished as quickly as it came. Her lips pinched with that look of disappointment she'd mastered.

She hadn't seen me for three years, and she could barely hold a smile. I shouldn't have expected anything less.

Ignoring the small pang in my chest, I shut the door and made my way to the empty chair beside her.

"Hi, Mother," I said with a strong tone, refusing to let her see me cower. I wouldn't give her that satisfaction.

"My darling daughter," she responded in a sickly sweet voice that made me want to puke. I saw no evidence of her affection to match her words.

She was a chameleon and knew how to perfectly work a room, to say the right things, even if they were lies. "Blake, you are looking pale." She eyed my gray t-shirt and matching tie-string pants. "And gray isn't your color, dear."

"I'd rather think it brings out my blue eyes," I answered and took my seat, catching the small grin tugging at the corner of Steele's mouth.

He sat across the desk from us in his white button-up shirt done up to his throat today, his bent arms resting on the table, studying us. He was the kind of man that you could get lost for hours just staring at and admiring his features. The kind of hotness that was really good at distracting you from your troubles. The doctor exuded confidence and an aura which had always calmed me. His presence alone made this visitation bearable. He was the one thing that had kept me sane in this insane institute.

On the bright side, there was no sign of Father, which made breathing easier. Perhaps I was about to learn that they'd split up, and somehow in her cold-hearted soul, she'd found enough empathy to help me.

She sat stiffly on the chair, legs crossed. She was wearing her rose-colored wrap-around blazer dress and matching heels, looking completely out of place in the warmly decorated room. Pins kept her hair fixed around her face, dark locks cascading over her shoulders. As always, she looked immaculate. Nothing was ever out of place with her.

Directing her attention to Steele, she asked, "I was promised she would be taken care of. Is she eating enough and getting sufficient sun? The girl looks deathly."

I blinked at her. She talked about me as though she was leaving her pet poodle at the doggie daycare. My hands curled into balls by my side, and I remembered my therapy lessons on anger management about breathing deeply and letting go of emotions.

They weren't doing much to help right then in Mother's company.

I eyed the stapler on the desk and mulled over how good it would feel to throw it at her. I'd picked up a penchant for throwing things since moving in here, which was really my only release and mostly came in the form of destroying my pillow. I was on my fourth one. Steele encouraged me to get my anger out that way, saying it was better done in my room when no one saw.

He obviously didn't know about the camera in there that was always watching me.

"Ma'am, I assure you, Blake receives the utmost care at Bright Meadows Asylum. Now, following procedures, I will remain in the room during your visitation. Normally, we hold these in the main visitors' room, but seeing this is a unique situation, I'll make an exception."

"What situation?" I asked, trepidation sliding up my spine.

Mother sighed, and I watched the transformation of her worried face morphing into something sorrowful, shadows flaring behind her eyes, darkening now. She would have made an amazing actress, able to change her emotions in the blink of an eye. But I suppose the skill worked well for her as a politician's wife.

"Your father has died," she murmured with no difficulty, no tears shed. "I know this will be hard for you, Blake, to lose your dad. Maybe it gives you solace to know that he truly cared for you, wanting only the best care for you by placing you in here."

My chest constricted, and it had nothing to do with my father dying. I didn't give two fucks about that, and I'd often wished that he'd died long ago. But for her to spread blatant lies in front of Steele infuriated me. It burned across my chest, coming at me in waves so hard that a sharp ache rose in my stomach.

Three years of her silence, and now this.

I couldn't hold it back, and my words streamed out. "He never cared for me, Mother. So, let's not pretend by spreading lies."

When you lived in a house of deception and hatred, there was no spark of grief for those who made your life hell. Only relief.

"Don't be so insensitive," she griped. "Your father is barely cold in his grave and you'd dare to speak so harshly of him."

"Wait, you've already buried him? Did you have a funeral?" I hated that I even cared, but it would have given me a chance to get out of here. For at least a little bit.

Mother huffed. "I didn't think it would be good for your mental state to attend, dear."

I reared back in my seat, and instantly, I lost all ability to remember any of my lessons on remaining calm.

"Are you kidding me? The only reason I'm in here is because I caught Father fucking Ryan, Dale, and Stacey...at the same time. There's nothing wrong with me, but if he's dead, he deserves it. And you should know the truth."

Everything came blurting out, words I'd held safely in my head for the past few years but had been dying to say. My father had threatened me from talking about what I witnessed, but with him dead, I wasn't going to hold back anymore.

And I desperately wanted Steele to know the truth.

Mother paused, the color draining from her face, and she eyed me like she'd morphed into the grim reaper coming to collect my soul. "Blake, you are sick, and only a crazy person would make up such horrible stories."

"Ma'am, we don't call anyone sick or crazy here," Steele interjected, sounding calm despite my outburst.

She turned to him with hatred in her eyes. "I do apologize you have to hear the filthy lies she tells. The strain she has put on our family is unbearable."

"Strain?" I stated, balancing on the edge of my chair, interjecting before Steele could say anything.

"Blake," he warned in the darker tone he used to remind me to take a deep breath. To reel my anger back in.

My words rushed out regardless as anger swallowed me. "I've been locked in here for over three fucking years because of his lies."

Without a word, Mother stood, straightened her dress, and collected the rose jacket hanging on the back of her seat. She held her head high, her cheeks flushed from the embarrassment I'd caused her. It was hard to tell if she knew about Father's deceit or if this was a real shock for her.

"You are ill, Blake, and this is the best place to make you better. You may not know it now, but one day, you'll thank your father and me." She glanced at the doctor as she talked, because everything she did was for show.

I bit my tongue until it hurt, until I tasted blood in my mouth and no longer felt the thundering ache tearing across my chest. For so long I'd played the quiet daughter, and I'd let them walk all over me.

"Please do not make a scene," Mother continued. "I've come to let you know the tragic news of your father. Let's leave it at that." She looked ready to leave, and I jolted to my feet, which had Steele doing the same.

"Please, wait."

She turned to me with fury pulling her manicured eyebrows together. Which was a feat considering how much botox I knew she got every couple of months.

"With Father gone, you can dissolve the conservatorship and get me out of here. I've spent long enough here. Please." Freedom teetered on the edge of my mind, so close I could almost taste it, while I internally cursed myself for lashing out at her. My mother was a vengeful person.

I sensed Steele moving in beside me. "Blake, your mother and I had been discussing this earlier."

"And?" I stared from him to her, and her grin was fierce. My mind raced with wild scenarios and excuses they'd give me to steal away my freedom, until I grew breathless.

"I'm moving out of the state, dear, and I just signed the papers today to dissolve my conservatorship over you. So you are free." She smirked. "But unfortunately, you're apparently still suffering from episodes, so your release from the asylum will be determined by the board of doctors once you've healed."

I gaped at her, my head spinning. I couldn't move, but stared at her, drawing in her every word.

Silence hung between us, and tears were running down my cheeks. I had zero control over my life, and I fucking hated it.

"You can't do this," my words choked out, my body trembling uncontrollably. "I don't belong here!"

Steele crossed the room and opened the door to his office for my mother to leave, while I wanted the world to crack open and swallow me. This couldn't be happening.

Panic clawed at my heart, and before I could think straight, I reached for my mother, grabbing her arm, my fingernails digging into her arm out of pure desperation on my part.

She barked a yelp, her eyes widening while she ripped her hand free from me.

"Mom, please!" I looked at her for sympathy, for something other than just her icy stare. I stepped closer to her, and she flinched back. That small reaction stung right through my heart.

Steele was suddenly beside me, his arm looping around mine with his warm touch, holding me tightly against him. "Blake, I need you to calm down for me."

Fury drummed through me as the world tilted around me, swirling too fast.

Mother checked her wrist where I drew blood and wiped it away with the pad of her thumb. Lifting her gaze, she scowled. Glancing at the doctor, she barked, "She needs discipline, and maybe you're not the right person. She just attacked me. I hope you intend to punish her for such a crime or I will take this higher."

I gasped aloud and my gut clenched. I stared at her incredulously, wanting to lash out for all the horrible things she and Father did to me.

"This is an emotional situation, a grieving moment," he explained. "I will ensure this is dealt with."

I glared at my mother, so angry, so desperate that I wanted to throttle her, to force her to treat me as her daughter for a change. But I guessed that was too much to ask for.

She flicked her gaze in my direction. "We all have to live with our own demons, dear. Enjoy yours." Then she strolled out of my life. And I knew that would be the last time I'd ever see her.

That bitch.

I fought against Steele's grip, lunging to go after her, but he tightened his hold on my arm and slammed the door to his room, closing us in there alone. Then he spun me around by my shoulders to face him.

"Let me go," my voice crackled with the first tear rolling down my cheek.

"Blake, you can't attack people here. I can only do so much to protect you," he explained in a low, soothing voice that seemed to almost lull me into a false state of calm. "I don't want them to force me to sedate you while you're handling your grief."

"This is not grief for my monster of a father." I fisted my hands, and I wanted to scream. "This is from years of them mentally and emotionally abusing me. From being thrown in here so I was silenced, and now I'm told I have to stay here because I have stress dreams? How the fuck is that fair?" Tears pooled in my eyes, and they blurred the doctor's face while cold rushed through me with the reality of my fucked up circumstance.

"Nothing's changed," Steele tried to explain. "You're progressing nicely, and we focus on that."

Except he was wrong. "I. Don't. Belong. Here," I cried, shaking. "My mother could have taken me out because she knows why I'm really here. I'm innocent."

Steele reached out for me, but I backed away from him because no one would help. No one cared. At this stage, I was crying hysterically, hugging myself, and suddenly the room spun with me, tilting at an angle, while darkness feathered at the edges of my eyes.

And the last words I heard from Steele were, "I just need you to take your pills to stop the nightmares, and I'll do everything I can to set you free."

"You should take it. You'll feel better," the nurse in her white dress persisted as she handed me a small plastic cup with a blue pill inside over the dispensing counter. "It should help calm you down."

The familiar sense of helplessness filled me as it had done before. They'd never offered me this kind of pill before, mostly under Father's instructions, but Nurse Rose was new here and had been monitoring my sleep. She was sweet, and I saw the pity on her face that morning.

"Will it help me sleep?" I whispered over the counter.

She nodded. "It should."

My fingers tightened around this tiny cup with a shaky hand, staring at this crazy little pill. The temptation to take it sat on the edge of my mind, along with the trepidation of what it would do to me.

What if she was right and I could finally have a good night's sleep?

"Are you done already?" a girl lining up behind me snarled and drove a sharp shoulder into mine, causing me to stumble and almost lose my cup. By some miracle, I managed to fumble it but not drop it.

I turned, furious, only to come face to face with Madison— the girl who liked to cut herself and others if given the chance. She creeped me out, because when you looked into her eyes, there was nothing there. Did she even have a soul?

Somehow, all the crazies in this place were drawn to me.

I stumbled out of her way quickly before she became too interested in me.

I glanced up to the orderly watching me. "I need to see you take the pill before you leave, or I'll administer it myself," he stated harshly, his gaze flickering to the line of girls waiting for their morning doses.

A debilitating panic slithered through me that I'd be trapped in this asylum forever, and maybe the nurse was right about the blue pill taking away the dreams.

Without another thought, I popped it into my mouth and swallowed it with no water.

"Open your mouth," the orderly stated, and I did just that, sticking my tongue out. With his approval, I made my way to the TV room.

I don't remember how long I sat on the couch, and I didn't know what I watched–I slouched in my seat lifelessly. It was a strange thing to not feel your body while your mind floated. Escaping my memories was almost liberating though, and I just hoped this sensation helped me sleep peacefully tonight.

Maybe being completely numb wasn't so bad...

A spark of something sharp stuck into my arm. Something I didn't understand right away. I craned my head down to my arm where the girl who'd shoved me out of the line earlier was gripping my arm, her fingernails in my skin, pushing down.

"Ouch," I managed, moments after it happened because my mouth didn't want to move. I had been partially aware of the pain, while thoughts flickered in and out of my mind. But moving to get away from her seemed an impossible thing to do.

"Don't ever push in front of me again, bitch. Next time, I'll cut you until you bleed to death," she snarled in my ear, raking her nails down my arms, breaking the skin.

I cried out that time, and she jolted out of the seat before rushing away. I sat there a second later, staring at the droplets of blood rolling down my arm. And a tinge of worry crawled through me at how vulnerable I felt right now. How I seemed to have forgotten how to even get up from this couch.

I shut my eyes and cradled my cut arm against my middle in my drug-filled haze. And I kept feeling like there was something important I should be doing...

Get your copy of Monster's Temptation today!

Acknowledgments

We are truly blessed to have such a strong support system. We could not have done this book without some amazing people.

Leah, thanks for taking my hand and literally staying up for hours every night to write with me. Every single night. There is no way I could have written this book without you... and your Taylor Swift Gifs. You're the best friend a girl could ask for. 10/10 I recommend.

Caitlin, you're my ride or die. You're always there for me. Thanks for coming into my life from Day 1 and being who you are. BFFs forever.

Jasmine, our editor-seriously couldn't do it without you being okay with our crazy deadlines. You put so much love into our books, and we're so grateful to you.

And last but not least..to you. Our readers. Isn't it nice when we give you a book without a cliffy (although not nearly as fun). Thanks for coming along on this wild ride. We love you all so much for making our dreams come true.

XOXO,

C.R. & Mila

Books by C.R. Jane

www.crjanebooks.com

The Sounds of Us Contemporary Series (complete series)

Remember Us This Way

Remember You This Way

Remember Me This Way

Broken Hearts Academy Series: A Bully Romance (complete duet)

Heartbreak Prince

Heartbreak Lover

Ruining Dahlia (Contemporary Mafia Standalone)

Ruining Dahlia

Pretty Madness (Omegaverse Standalone)

Pretty Madness

The Fated Wings Series (Paranormal series)

First Impressions

Forgotten Specters

The Fallen One (a Fated Wings Novella)

Forbidden Queens

Frightful Beginnings (a Fated Wings Short Story)

Faded Realms

Faithless Dreams

Fabled Kingdoms

Fated Wings 8

The Rock God (a Fated Wings Novella)

The Darkest Curse Series

Forget Me

Lost Passions

Hades Redemption Series

The Darkest Lover

The Darkest Kingdom

Monster & Me Duet Co-write with Mila Young

Monster's Temptation

Monster's Obsession

Academy of Souls Co-write with Mila Young (complete series)

School of Broken Souls

School of Broken Hearts

School of Broken Dreams

School of Broken Wings

Fallen World Series Co-write with Mila Young (complete series)

Bound

Broken

Betrayed

Belong

<u>Thief of Hearts Co-write with Mila Young (complete series)</u>

Darkest Destiny

Stolen Destiny

Broken Destiny

Sweet Destiny

<u>Kingdom of Wolves Co-write with Mila Young</u>

Wild Moon

Wild Heart

Wild Girl

Wild Love

Wild Soul

Wild Kiss

<u>Stupid Boys Series Co-write with Rebecca Royce</u>

Stupid Boys

Dumb Girl

Crazy Love

<u>Breathe Me Duet Co-write with Ivy Fox (complete)</u>

Breathe Me

Breathe You

Breathe Me Duet

<u>Rich Demons of Darkwood Series Co-write with May Dawson</u>

Make Me Lie

Make Me Beg

Make Me Wild

Make Me Burn

Books By Mila Young

www.milayoungbooks.com

Savage

Lost Wolf

Broken Wolf

Fated Wolf

Shadowlands

Shadowlands Sector, One

Shadowlands Sector, Two

Shadowlands Sector, Three

Shadows & Wolves Complete Collection

Chosen Vampire Slayer

Night Kissed

Moon Kissed

Blood Kissed

Monster & Me Duet Co-write with C.R. Jane

Monster's Temptation

Monster's Obsession

The Alpha-Hole Duet

Real Alphas Bite

Kingdom of Wolves

Wild Moon

Wild Heart

Wild Girl

Wild Love

Wild Soul

Winter's Thorn

To Seduce A Fae

To Tame A Fae

To Claim A Fae

Shadow Hunters Series

Boxed Set 1

Sin Demons

Playing With Hellfire

Hell In A Handbasket

All Shot To Hell

To Hell And Back

When Hell Freezes Over

Hell On Earth

Snowball's Chance In Hell

Kings of Eden

At the Mercy of Monsters

Kings of Eden

Stolen Paradise

Ruthless Lies

Wicked Heat Series

Wicked Heat #1

Wicked Heat #2

Wicked Heat #3

Elemental Series

Taking Breath #1

Taking Breath #2

Gods and Monsters

Apollo Is Mine

Poseidon Is Mine

Ares Is Mine

Hades Is Mine

Sin Demons Co-write with Harper A. Brooks

Playing With Hellfire

Hell In A Handbasket

All Shot To Hell

To Hell And Back

When Hell Freezes Over

Hell On Earth

Haven Realm Series

Hunted (Little Red Riding Hood Retelling)

Cursed (Beauty and the Beast Retelling)

Entangled (Rapunzel Retelling)

Princess of Frost (Snow Queen)

Thief of Hearts Series Co-write with C.R. Jane

Siren Condemned

Siren Sacrificed

Siren Awakened

Broken Souls Series Co-write with C.R. Jane

School of Broken Souls

School of Broken Hearts

School of Broken Dreams

School of Broken Wings

Fallen World Series Co-write with C.R. Jane

Bound

Broken

Betrayed

Belong

Beautiful Beasts Academy

Manicures and Mayhem

Diamonds and Demons

Hexes and Hounds

Secrets and Shadows

Passions and Protectors

Ancients and Anarchy

Subscribe to Mila Young's Newsletter to receive exclusive content, latest updates, and giveaways. Join here.

About C.R. Jane

A Texas girl living in Utah now, I'm a wife, mother, lawyer, and now author. My stories have been floating around in my head for years, and it has been a relief to finally get them down on paper. I'm a huge Dallas Cowboys fan and I primarily listen to Beyonce and Taylor Swift...don't lie and say you don't too.

My love of reading started probably when I was three and with a faster than normal ability to read, I've devoured hundreds of thousands of books in my life. It only made sense that I would start to create my own worlds since I was always getting lost in others'.

I like heroines who have to grow in order to become badasses, happy endings, and swoon-worthy, devoted, (and hot) male characters. If this sounds like you, I'm pretty sure we'll be friends.

I'm so glad to have you on my team...check out the links below for ways to hang out with me and more of my books you can read!

Visit my Website www.crjanebooks.com

Sign up for my newsletter to stay updated on new releases, find out random facts about me, and get access to different points of view from my characters.

About Mila Young

**Find all Mila young books at
www.milayoungbooks.com**

Best-selling author, Mila Young tackles everything with the zeal and bravado of the fairytale heroes she grew up reading about. She slays monsters, real and imaginary, like there's no tomorrow. By day she rocks a keyboard as a marketing extraordinaire. At night she battles with her mighty pen-sword, creating fairytale retellings, and sexy ever after tales. In her spare time, she loves pretending she's a mighty warrior, walks on the beach with her dogs, cuddling up with her cats, and devouring every fantasy tale she can get her pinkies on.

Ready to read more and more from Mila Young?
www.subscribepage.com/milayoung

Join Mila's **Wicked Readers group** for exclusive content, latest news, and giveaway.
www.facebook.com/groups/milayoungwickedreaders

For more information...
milayoungauthor@gmail.com